THE VISCOUNT'S SINFUL BARGAIN

The Dukes' Pact Series

Book One – Cassandra

By Kate Archer

Text by Kate Archer
Cover by Wicked Smart Designs

Dragonblade Publishing, Inc. is an imprint of Kathryn Le Veque Novels, Inc.
P.O. Box 7968
La Verne CA 91750
ceo@dragonbladepublishing.com

Produced in the United States of America

First Edition May 2020
Print Edition

ARE YOU SIGNED UP FOR DRAGONBLADE'S BLOG?

You'll get the latest news and information on exclusive giveaways, exclusive excerpts, coming releases, sales, free books, cover reveals and more.

Check out our complete list of authors, too!

No spam, no junk. That's a promise!

Sign Up Here

www.dragonbladepublishing.com

Dearest Reader;

Thank you for your support of a small press. At Dragonblade Publishing, we strive to bring you the highest quality Historical Romance from the some of the best authors in the business. Without your support, there is no 'us', so we sincerely hope you adore these stories and find some new favorite authors along the way.

Happy Reading!

CEO, Dragonblade Publishing

Additional Dragonblade books by Author Kate Archer

The Dukes' Pact Series

The Viscount's Sinful Bargain (Book 1)

PROLOGUE

White's, London 1816

THE SIX DUKES gravely sipped their port. Or, in the case of the Duke of Wentworth, gulped it. That particular duke stared glumly at his bandaged foot, which was just now elevated on a stool. He was eternally gouty and though his physician blamed it on port, the duke was equally certain port was the only thing that soothed that blasted appendage.

The six gentlemen had entered the realms of late middle age, that time period when a reliable body begins to betray in surprising and unwelcome ways. Youth had fled and they had resigned themselves to it. At their time of life, they looked forward to doting on grandchildren. Specifically, a male grandchild born of their eldest son, and a spare for good measure. A man could not be satisfied to consider departing the world until his line was secure for generations to come.

Though they looked forward to that blessed state of finding grandsons all round, it seemed always to be far ahead of them. Not a one of their rogue sons had managed to marry. In truth, every damn one of them had studiously avoided the state.

"Gentlemen," the Duke of Gravesley said, "while we are grateful beyond measure that we still *have* sons to carry on for us, the war is over. A new war, a more personal war, is set to begin."

"Hear, hear," the gentlemen murmured.

"If we do not force these scoundrels to marry," His Grace continued, "we are in danger of never setting eyes on a grandchild."

"Dash it!" the Duke of Dembly exclaimed, as if the idea had just occurred to him. This drew various looks from the others, as the matter had been the subject of their discussions for some months.

"We did our duty in producing these scoundrels," the Duke of Carlisle said, "and now it is time for them to do *their* duty."

At the mention of duty, which was an idea that greatly stirred the dukes' hearts, there was a gentle stamping of feet in approbation. Even the Duke of Wentworth stamped his good foot.

"The time has come, my friends, to take steps," the Duke of Gravesley said. "Dire steps."

One by one, the men nodded. They had debated for weeks on the correct course, now it was time to act.

"We are agreed," His Grace said. "We enter into a formal pact and swear that none of us will fold under misplaced affection."

And so, the six dukes took dire steps to secure their respective lines for generations to come.

Very dire steps.

CHAPTER ONE

"ALL HAIL THE pact. Absolutely everybody was talking of it," Lady Marksworth said, buttering her toast with relish.

The breakfast room, filled with sunshine that morning, had also been filled with Lady Marksworth's various comments. It might have been Greek for all Cassandra understood it.

Cassandra Knightsbridge, only daughter of the Viscount Trebly, had been sent out of the quiet environs of Surrey to live with Lady Marksworth for her first season—her father was certain Cass would do far better under her aunt's guidance and tutelage. After all, if anybody knew how to avoid a misstep in London, it was Lady Marksworth and if anybody needed to know the same, it was Cassandra Knightsbridge.

Cassandra's life in Surrey had not been typical or usual or regular or whatever society would term the proper mode of going on. Growing up in a house with no mother, and dominated by a practical, no-nonsense father, had given her a latitude that most young ladies could not dream of.

Despite her governess complaining endlessly, Cassandra rode to the hunt on a sidesaddle specially modified for jumping, it would not be unusual to find her in the stables at midnight, assisting in bringing a foal into the world, and rather than carrying around a precious lap dog, she was the owner of a great beast of a mastiff named Mayhem. Perhaps most surprising, her father had gone so far as to allow her to shoot pheasant and she had not shied away from the opportunity.

Cassandra was not entirely unaware that some of the particulars of her upbringing would shock those in a London drawing room. She understood her little corner of Surrey, but navigation through the opportunities and pitfalls of a season was needed, and Lady Marksworth would expertly steer the ship. Her aunt had already got her through her curtsy to the queen, an experience Cass likened to finding herself a pheasant flying by the throne and hoping not to be bagged.

"Has anything more divine ever occurred to launch a season?" Lady Marksworth said. "An actual pact."

"I am sorry, Aunt," Cassandra said, "what is the pact?"

"*The* pact," Lady Marksworth said. "Little else was spoken of last evening."

"Nobody said anything to me about a pact," Cassandra said.

Lady Marksworth's forehead wrinkled, as it was wont to do when she considered her niece. Then it quite suddenly cleared. "Ah! I see, of course nobody would have discussed it with you. I sometimes forget—while to me you are wise beyond your years, to others you must appear a very innocent young lady."

"I hope I may be considered innocent," Cassandra said, in some alarm that anybody should think otherwise.

"Yes, yes," Lady Marksworth said, waving her hands. "In any case, I suppose Lady Blanding's guests would have avoided the topic with you and Sybil, as it may have caused you both some embarrassment."

"I, embarrassed? How?" Cassandra said.

"It is just this—six dukes have conspired together to cut their eldest sons' funds off if they do not marry. They've got two seasons to do it, and no more. I heard the gentlemen were all informed by letter, and the letters were nearly identical. Apparently, there were threats of living forever to encourage those sons to consider how many years of poverty they might face if they do not comply. As well, it was suggested the young men might tour Cheapside to have a look at their future accommodations if they defy their fathers."

"Goodness," Cassandra said.

"Not *goodness*," Lady Marksworth said, "*good* is the term better suited."

"How so?" Cassandra asked. "Do you have an argument with any of those gentlemen, that you should wish to see them so harried by their fathers?"

Lady Marksworth's forehead wrinkled to such a degree that Cassandra was certain she'd gone wrong somewhere.

"Cassandra," Lady Marksworth said, sounding very much like she talked to a small child. "Six gentlemen destined to become dukes must marry in all haste. Here you are for your first season. You see?"

Cassandra suddenly did see, though the idea was preposterous. Her aunt would have her set her cap on one, or all, of the gentlemen before she'd even set eyes on them. It was perfectly ridiculous, and in any case, she had no great wish to find herself a duchess. She was certain the role was one of tedium. She'd much rather marry some middling sort of gentleman—not too poor, but not so elevated that they did not have the freedom to live as they pleased. If one went too high in society, the many eyes upon oneself made life constrained and far too regulated. She had seen for herself how it was every time she'd visited Lady Melby—the marchioness' house was a tomb of discretion and reserve. She could barely breathe until she'd got out of it.

For a moment, Cassandra thought she might apprise her aunt of these well-considered opinions, until she noted the eagerness with which Lady Marksworth awaited her reply. She supposed she ought to keep her thoughts to herself, but she could not allow her aunt to go on deluded into thinking she would throw herself at the nearest would-be duke.

"I suspect," Cassandra said boldly, "that the gentlemen named in the pact have all fled to the countryside to hide from the circling wolves."

"If, by circling wolves, you mean mamas across London," Lady Marksworth said, "you can be assured that claws are being sharpened in every drawing room. Those young gentlemen may wish to flee the specter of determined mothers, but they cannot. I have it on good authority that the letters they received outline very strictly how they are to conduct themselves, and one of the stipulations is that they accept every worthy engagement that arrives at their door. I had hardly dared hope to land so many single gentlemen of excellent prospects for our own ball, but I think we have a very good chance of it."

Though her aunt was enthusiastic in considering this pact, Cassandra saw nothing but trouble ahead. The circling wolves, and that *was* just what they were as far as she could divine it, would make the season almost perilous. She'd gone to her first ball, which had been an experience so far removed from a local Surrey assembly as to be almost unrecognizable. Gone were the casual proceedings of Guildford, and in were the formal rules of town. She'd kept her eyes wide open and took in everything. One of the most alarming sights was of various mamas' hawk eyes scanning the ballroom and none too subtly sizing girls up, as if they were all some sort of impediment to their own daughter's happy future.

If there had been some undercurrent of desperation among ladies whose daughters were out, that undercurrent would transform itself into a North Sea storm when six gentlemen destined to be dukes were dangled as bait. She wondered to what lengths some of those mamas might go to land a large fish at the banks of their daughter's hopes. For that matter, she was rather afraid of what her aunt might do.

"I am only glad," Lady Marksworth said, "that I had the foresight to order all of your dresses early. Every decent dressmaker in town will be hired before noon today."

"Certainly," Cassandra said, "it will not suddenly occur to anybody that they need more dresses on account of this pact."

"It most certainly will. Wardrobes will be declared woefully inadequate. It is the fathers, you see, my dear. A once firm amount to be spent on clothes will have tripled when they consider the chance their daughters may have. Depend upon it."

Cassandra did not know if she should depend upon it or not. She could not quite envision her own father opening the purse strings to secure a duke for his daughter. On the other hand, her father generally did not open purse strings for anything that did not support his estate—it had been her aunt who'd supplied most of her clothes. She'd come with one trunk and Lady Markswoth had examined the contents of it. After much head shaking and sighs, she'd called in her favorite dressmaker.

Her father would stagger at the array of dresses she now called her own. The Viscount was perfectly well off and her dowry was respectable, but he did not go in for frippery. As much as she adored her new wardrobe, she suspected her father to hold a sensible opinion on such matters—nobody in the history of England had ever married a dress.

EDWIN WESTON, VISCOUNT Hampton and eldest son of the Duke of Carlisle, brushed his dark hair from his eyes and stared morosely into the fire. His coat was off, his shirt sleeves rolled up, and his long legs were propped on the desk in front of him. He'd sat in his library in Carlisle House, sometimes with brandy and sometimes without, for the better part of two days. His mastiff, Havoc, lazed at his feet, delighted to have his master to himself.

The confounded letter that had caused him to closet himself away lay on the desk in front of him. He'd read it a dozen times, each time hoping it would say something other than what it did.

His blasted father! Now was to be a time of freedom. The war had ended, he'd served well, and he should be rewarded, not punished with a wife.

He blamed the Duke of Gravesley for this. The man was always an agitator on the subject. Still, those old men might think they'd outfoxed him, but he was certain some solution would present itself. As he knew from fighting the war, there was a slim way out of every lost cause. He must just find it.

Edwin snatched up the letter and read it once more.

Hampton,

It is with a heavy heart that I must force you to do your duty. Take this letter as a directive from me, outlining various steps to be taken and various consequences if you refuse.

You will have two seasons to wed a lady of suitable background. The timeframe I give you is most generous as you could easily get the thing done in a month if you wished.

I will grant much latitude on the subject of the lady's dowry, so that it may not present a hindrance to you. (I think of Lady Isabella, fine background but dashed little money.)

Should you fail, the consequences to your way of life will be considerable and swift. At the end of this season, if there is no engagement, your funds are cut by half. At the end of next season, if there is no engagement, it is cut to nothing and you will be forced to vacate Carlisle House. If you intend on ignoring this directive, you might consider putting money aside now for payment later to your future landlord in Cheapside. Otherwise, you will need to find employment for your daily bread, perhaps as a valet to a gentleman with more sense?

Should you be so obtuse as to run through the two seasons with nothing to show, you will be cut off for a period of one year, and then you may begin again, under the same terms. Do not hope to be released by my early demise, I am in splendid health. Do not bother to importune your mother, I have given her my decision and she will abide by it. If you were to be so foolhardy as to go to your grandmother, I'll cut you off this instant. The Dowager Duchess is long in years and I will not have her aggravated.

Though I have returned to the country, I have a far reach, my boy. If you are not attending balls and routs and other likely places to meet your intended, I will know it. Gird your loins and do your duty.

By the by, jolly clever of you to make it through the war unscathed. Your mother is pleased as punch over it.

Carlisle

Edwin could see the old man had put a lot of thought into how he might box his son in, though some of it seemed thin. Painting the Dowager Duchess as a poor old thing who should not be bothered bordered on the ludicrous. His grandmother was more energetic, and more opinionated, than either of his parents.

Still, it might not be wise to appeal to the Dowager. For one thing, a gentleman ought not go running off to a grandmother in the face of a difficulty. For another, one never knew precisely what the Dowager would do about any little matter coming to her attention. Should she fall on his father's side of things, he would have a far fiercer opponent than he currently had.

Edwin's butler, Dreyfus, softly knocked and opened the door. "Lord Lockwood to see you, my lord," he said in the low voice he used when he was not certain what sort of mood his master was in.

Edwin waved, which Dreyfus knew to be a signal to show Lord Lockwood into his lord's presence.

Lockwood, never one to wait to be shown in, strode past the butler and into the library. He was not as tall and lean as Edwin and his hair was a deal lighter, but he was powerfully built. The men of his regiment called him *the pile of bricks.*

Lockwood threw himself into a chair and pulled a letter from his pocket. "I suppose you got one, too? Blasted business."

"*I* suppose I can thank your father for this," Edwin said drily. "He's been whipping the old boys into a frenzy for months."

Lockwood had the good manners to flush, as he knew perfectly well that His Grace had been the instigator.

"Why could not some other unlucky gentleman have been swept up in this madness?" Edwin said. "But then I suppose it does not pay to be too well-acquainted with you."

Lockwood peered at him. "I see you have not heard. We've *all* been swept up in the thing, with the exception of Burke. His father belongs to Brook's and was well away from those conniving old schemers."

"All?" Edwin asked.

"All. You, me, Ashworth, Dalton, Cabot and Grayson. You must have been living in a dressing room these past days to not have heard. Somebody in Grayson's household copied his letter and it's being sold all over town. Worse, word got out on who the letters were sent to, most likely by some curious ears at White's. We are the talk of every drawing room, my friend."

"Lord help us."

Lord Lockwood had poured himself a brandy and now propped his feet on Edwin's desk. "You might appeal to the Lord, though I am not expecting any particular help from our heavenly father. No more than I would get from my own not-so-heavenly father."

"What are we to do?" Edwin asked, not that he thought Lockwood would have some brilliant plan. His friend's style was more "fight one's way through" than anything with finesse.

"Dashed if I know," Lockwood said. "We're all right for now, so I say we enjoy ourselves to the hilt and pay the price later. Let's take ourselves off to some interesting hell and throw dice like madmen. We'll live as if we head for the gallows in the morning."

The idea was tempting, but Edwin thought it would not advance their cause. "For one thing," he said, "we cannot afford to throw away vast sums just now, which you invariably do. We may need the funds to pay for a garret in Cheapside if it comes to it. For another, we must appear to play the game, lull the old fellows into a sense of complaisance."

"Calm them down until we think of a way out," Lockwood said. "It sounds dead dreary, but I suspect you are right."

"I am right. Especially now, when they will be watching what we do like hawks circling a field mouse. In truth, all of London will be watching. The Bergrams' ball is tonight and if we do not appear, it will be widely noted."

"By God, I cannot countenance those people," Lockwood said. "He's a stuffy old thing and she's a nervous slip of a creature. I always think he's about to transform into a statue and she's about to fly off like a bird."

"Nevertheless," Edwin said, "we'd better go. Best to stare down the gossipers now and get it out of the way, rather than allow the rumors to expand and take flight. If we arrive and appear as if nothing at all is the matter, we will take some air out of the talker's lungs."

CASSANDRA REGARDED LADY Sybil standing with hands on hips in her bedchamber. Sybil was petite and her cascades of dark hair charmingly framed her pert features. She was like a little doll, though a spirited one.

The evening before had renewed their acquaintance. Lady Marksworth's dear friend, Lady Blanding, had hosted a small dinner. Lady Blanding's house was the next door down from Marksworth House, and along with the lady and her lord in residence had come their only daughter, Lady Sybil. Cassandra and Sybil had met with each other here and there over the years, but their friendship had blossomed once they had confided in one another their trepidation of what was to come over the course of the season. They had become comrades-in-arms and vowed to go into battle together.

Lady Sybil examined the two gowns Cassandra had selected. Or rather, the two gowns that Cassandra's maid Peggy had selected. Cass was certain she'd asked for the gowns with the pale pink and cream overlays, but what laid on the bed were the sky blue and pale yellow. Peggy was a confounded creature and had just decided for herself which dresses would be best. Cassandra had yet to work out how to manage her.

The Bergrams' ball was that evening and Cassandra's aunt had claimed that absolutely everybody would be there. Lady Marksworth would not be surprised to see six recalcitrant gentlemen who would more often be found gambling in some low place, but who had recently received stern letters from their fathers.

"The blue gauze is divine for your coloring, I think," Lady Sybil said, "though they are both charming. You will conquer in either of them."

"I am not certain I wish to conquer," Cassandra said. "Sybil, have you heard of this pact everybody is talking of?"

"I could not hope to avoid it; it has been a regular topic in my house," Sybil said laughing.

"Does it not give you pause?" Cassandra asked. "Does it not make you uneasy?"

Lady Sybil sat on one of the upholstered chairs and said, "At first, yes. But then, Cass, I thought about it and I believe it may be to our benefit. Neither of us wish to marry a man who is forced to do so by their father and this way we know who to avoid."

Cassandra had not considered that aspect of things. "That is true. All that has gone on might have proceeded in secrecy and we would have no way of knowing. Should one of *them* have pursued one of *us*, we might have remained unaware that it was to be a loveless transaction. Unaware, that is, until it was too late."

"Precisely," Lady Sybil said. "Now that we do know, we shall not be caught. Let some silly girl who thinks of a lofty title with no care for anything else trade her life for a position."

"Agreed," Cassandra said, feeling lighter than she had all day. "We will find love, while some foolish girl discovers herself an unloved duchess left behind at some country estate, and lonely and bored all her life."

Cassandra counted herself fortunate that she had the liberty to hope for love, as not every girl did. It was not that her father had said she might marry for love, the Viscount was not of a very romantic turn of mind. However, he had made known his opinion that females were not idiots and were therefore capable of choosing their own destiny. He had also made it known that if she were to make an idiotic choice, she must live as an idiot forevermore. None of that came as a surprise to Cassandra—the Viscount felt commonsense to be the bedrock of every well-formed opinion and expected his daughter to carry on accordingly.

Cassandra paused in her mental wanderings, an idea suddenly occurring to her. "How shall we know which gentlemen to avoid? I have not even heard their names."

Lady Sybil laughed and said, "I have. My mama and Lady Jemima spent an hour this morning working their way down the list and examining every candidate while I pretended to sew." She counted off on her fingers, "The lords Hampton, Lockwood, Ashworth, Dalton, Cabot and Grayson."

Cassandra silently repeated the names. *This* was a list of names she had no intention of forgetting.

Chapter Two

Lady Bergram and Sir John were the sort of people that nobody could claim to particularly like or dislike, with the exception of Lord Lockwood, who had strong opinions about everybody. For most, they were neither here nor there, though one might not guess it upon viewing the enormous amount of invitations that arrived at their door or the enormous amount of people who came to their annual ball.

Neither Sir John nor Lady Bergram were engaging, one a bore and the other looking as if she might go up in a puff of smoke at the slightest provocation. However, as was always the way in London, once a family had been established as being worthy of notice, they were forevermore worthy unless they did something shocking. The Bergrams were less likely than a vicar on a Sunday to do something shocking, neither of them having any ideas in that direction. Or many ideas at all, really.

What the Bergrams *did* have was a large house with a cavernous ballroom and the funds to entertain lavishly. Their house on Grosvenor Square was just now lit up like noon sunshine with torches on the drive and hundreds of candles burning indoors.

Cassandra had got in her carriage in Berkeley Square just as Sybil entered her own next door, and so she had taken some comfort that her friend followed behind and they would not be parted long. She might wish the trip had taken longer than it did, as she felt a sense of nerves that she had not felt upon attending her first ball at the Tremanes'. She'd had mild flutters over that one, but this was more of a foreboding and wishing to turn the carriage round and go home.

She supposed it was the size of the ball, or perhaps the pact and the idea that everybody would be talking of it and looking for those gentlemen while she, herself, would attempt to avoid them. It all seemed too fraught. Though she had looked forward to her first season, there were moments when she wished herself back in Surrey, quietly reading by the fire and petting Mayhem while the dog chewed up something valuable. This was one such moment.

Now, as their carriage waited in the line leading to the front doors, Lady Marksworth said, "You are very quiet, Cassandra."

Cassandra smiled. "Am I? I did not mean to be. I suppose the size of this ball makes me rather feel as if I might get lost and never be found again."

"Heavens," Lady Marksworth said, laughing, "though I do enjoy a card table, you do not suppose I would leave you on your own in such a place? The Tremanes' ball was a different matter; it was small and everybody there was well-known to me. But here, though I assuredly know many of the people and have at least heard of most, I will stay nearby."

Cassandra was both relieved and yet slightly worried. She would wish her aunt to forgo disappearing into a card room. However, Lady Marksworth had made no mystery of her favorable opinion of the pact and the gentlemen involved in it. While Cassandra would seek to avoid them, her aunt would be pleased to see just the opposite.

"The Bergrams," her aunt went on, "though they are generally dull, are clever in some respects. Their ballroom is so large that there are tables set round the dancing area. I and Lady Blanding shall occupy one of them."

Her aunt would have her in view all evening. It would not be so easy to refuse one of these pact gentlemen, were she asked for a dance.

Cassandra paused. How exactly had she planned to refuse anyway? She and Sybil had determined that they would, but how was it to be done, precisely? If one of those gentlemen approached and asked for her card, was she to stare boldly at the man and say no? Then she must sit out, and in any case, others would have seen what occurred, including her aunt.

It had all seemed easy while being discussed with Sybil in the safety of her bedchamber, but rather more difficult to achieve now that she'd nearly arrived. Particularly more difficult as her aunt and Lady Blanding would be happily watching from some nearby table.

"Do cheer yourself, Cass," her aunt said kindly, "you are absolutely stunning. You will not find yourself sitting out. In any case, if I remember correctly from last year, there will be so many gentlemen about that Lady Bergram will even have a master of ceremonies or two wending their way round to smooth over introductions. Who knows who you shall meet?"

Though her aunt pretended at ignorance over who Cassandra might meet, she had an uncomfortable feeling that Lady Marksworth harbored hopes that at least six of those newly met gentlemen would be destined for a dukedom.

The carriage jerked forward and they moved ever closer to the entrance. Two men on horseback reined in their spooked horses, those animals startled by the sudden movement of the line of coaches.

Cassandra heard one of them curse as he wrangled with a large bay. He sat tall in the saddle and worked his horse as one with vast experience, most likely from the war. She'd seen for herself the difference when their neighbor Sir George had returned from the continent—there was a confidence and skill that could not come from daily rides through the countryside or the occasional fox hunt.

The man on horseback turned his head and Cassandra noted his dark hair and strong jaw, his shadow illuminated by the torches lining the drive. His coat and cravat were elegantly simple—the coat cut well, and the cravat tied in a neat but unassuming fashion. He was what her father termed "a man's man." The Viscount could not abide a gentleman who appeared to have taken inordinate amounts of time to dress and thought Mr. Brummel should pitch himself off a bridge. That Mr. Brummel was rumored to have fled England to escape gambling debts only confirmed to him that dandies were useless.

Lady Marksworth peered out the window and then sat back, smiling. "Well, well," she said, "Hampton and Lockwood. Did I not say they would all turn up?"

Cassandra's heart sank. She did not know if all six gentlemen of the pact would arrive, but at least two of them already had.

EDWIN HAD JUST experienced his first irritation of the night. Mercury, though well used to the sounds of war, was apparently less used to the sound of a line of expensive carriages all lurching forward together.

It had been an embarrassment to struggle with his mount in such a fashion. One of the many embarrassments to come, no doubt.

Of course, it had not gone unnoticed, he'd seen a curtain pull back and a pretty face staring at him. Damn pretty, in fact. He'd always had a weakness for a heart-shaped face.

He reminded himself that the ball would be full of pretty faces, like so many jewels scattered across a velvet-lined box. That was precisely why his father would force him to attend such occasions—every English rose in the country had descended upon London for the season. His father was well aware that he'd not recently spent any time in places where a proper English rose could be found.

After Waterloo and their narrow victory, Edwin had returned home and sought to forget what he'd seen that day, and all the days he'd followed Wellington. He'd been in the habit of haunting places proper ladies had never heard of, or if they had heard of them, would never own it. The women he encountered in those low places had helped him through many an hour, blotting out the uncomfortable pictures of war that still lingered in his memory. Where those women were all laughter and amusement and only demanding a few pounds payment, the ladies at this ball would be all discreet smiles cloaking steely determination to get their hands on *all* of his pounds, permanently.

Edwin felt as if he prepared to cross the enemy's line. He must be on his guard. He could not be distracted by a pretty face. He would accomplish the incursion—turn up, dance with a suitable number of ladies, encourage none of them, and slip away unscathed.

He would buy time to develop a real plan of escape.

LADY MARKSWORTH AND Lady Blanding had escorted their charges through the chaos of being introduced to the Bergrams, depositing their cloaks in the cloak room, and collecting dance cards. The ladies had then settled themselves at a table and left Cassandra and Sybil to stand at the edges of the ballroom floor.

As far as Cassandra was concerned, it was the most uncomfortable moment of any ball. The ladies must stand there, like so many apples in a grocer's bin, and wait to be selected. This was even worse than the Tremanes' ball, where she'd been swiftly introduced to nearly every gentleman by her aunt. Here, there was not one, but several, masters of ceremonies, who walked with every willing gentleman to provide introductions before a dance was claimed.

No lady could begin to relax until the first had been taken. One might carry on with certain holes in one's card, as long as it was not the first or before supper. No lady willingly sat out the first set and it would be clear to anybody who viewed such a thing that the lady had not been asked. To be unescorted into supper… well, she supposed if that ever happened to her, she would hide in the retiring room and hope her absence had not been noted.

To Sybil, she said softly, "At such a moment, one lives in terror of being overlooked, and of *not* being overlooked."

Sybil laughed behind her fan. "You are in little danger of being overlooked, Cass."

Cassandra did not know if that were quite true. Though she had felt she had measured up well at the Tremanes', she now realized that there had been far fewer ladies there and so they'd *all* measured up well. This ballroom was rapidly becoming a sea of beautiful faces. While she had no illusions about her looks, and judged them pretty in the usual way, they did not compare to some of these ladies. Where did they all come from?

She spotted a master of ceremonies very determinedly heading in their direction, followed by the two men who'd made such a show on horseback.

Softly, she said, "Oh no, it is two of them."

"What?" Sybil whispered hurriedly, "which two?"

Before Cassandra could answer, the three gentlemen were before her. The master's sonorous voice intoned, "Miss Knightsbridge, daughter of Viscount Trebly, Lady Sybil Hayworth, daughter of the Earl of Blanding, may I introduce Lord Hampton, son of the Duke of Carlisle, and Lord Lockwood, son of the Duke of Gravesley."

Cassandra curtsied, the gentlemen bowed, and the master walked off to search out new victims.

As Cassandra rose, she could not but help admit to herself that Lord Hampton was the most handsome man she'd yet seen in London. His height, his broad shoulders, his dark hair and dark eyes, his tanned skin, as if he spent a deal of time out of doors. If only he were not to be a duke or involved in that ridiculous pact. How might she view him if he were only to live as a Viscount or Baron in some pleasant spot in England with a father not so much in a hurry to marry him off?

She dismissed those thoughts, as they were fantasy and she must face the reality of this man. A reality she meant to keep herself well clear of.

"May I?" Lord Hampton said, holding his hand out for her card. She handed it over and noted Sybil doing the very same to Lord Lockwood. She and her friend were a pair—they'd so boldly talked of avoiding the gentlemen of the pact, and here they were meekly handing over their cards. Still, she did not see what else they could do.

Lord Hampton filled in his name for the first, bowed and walked off. Cassandra supposed she should be relieved that the first was claimed, regardless of who had claimed it. She could also be grateful that the lord had not lingered. She noted him tap another master and approach another lady. And then another. He was moving through the operation in a military fashion and it relieved her to know that she was not at all marked as singular. It was clear enough that Lord Hampton sought to do his duty and be done with it.

After Lord Lockwood had moved on, and he had not taken himself off with the incredible speed of Lord Hampton, Cassandra said, "Our well-laid plans have crumbled to dust."

"I rather think," Lady Sybil said, "they were not particularly well-laid to begin. I cannot imagine how we did not foresee that refusing a man a dance would be difficult. I suppose I had some vague idea of dashing from place to place so that none of them could catch up to me."

"Ah well," Cassandra said, "perhaps we might comfort ourselves in the idea that it is only a dance. Neither of us will have to go into supper with them."

Cassandra watched both lords put their names on various cards and wondered who that lady would be that would find herself escorted into supper by a gentleman of the pact. She noticed that the ladies who were approached by the two gentlemen appeared rather delighted, but then she could not know their real feelings. They might only wear a mask of politeness, just as she did herself.

As she glanced at the tables, she saw that her aunt and Lady Blanding wore no such masks. They *were* delighted, that could not be mistaken.

Her attention was taken from her aunt by the stream of gentlemen approaching her. Some she had met at the Tremanes', some were introduced by one of the masters. Lord Burke, who she'd danced with at the Tremanes' and found very pleasant, took the dance before supper. He was to be a duke, which must go against him. However, he was not included in the list of names associated with the pact and that must be in his favor.

The ballroom had grown crowded and Cassandra could not imagine that many more people were to be crammed into it. The musicians had been tuning for some minutes and so it could not be long before the first dance would begin. She would hurry it, as the faster it arrived, the faster it departed. She would dance with Lord Hampton with all good grace and then begin to really enjoy her evening.

Lord Hampton came to collect her, and she shot Sybil a glance before her friend was led away, too.

The musicians took their cue and began to play. The ball was to begin with a quadrille. Cassandra had been vastly relieved when she'd examined her card that there was no mention of an endless minuet. She had only danced the Quadrille for the first time at the Tremanes', but she'd practiced with a dancing master endless times in Surrey. Her dear father might hold the purse strings tight when it came to frippery, but he would view it an abomination to send his daughter to a ball uninformed of how to execute the various steps.

The lead couple, along with Lord Burke and his partner, the strikingly pretty Miss Daisy Danworth, began the dance. Cassandra stood next to Lord Hampton as a side couple, waiting for their turn.

It would be customary, while one waited, to strike up some sort of common conversation. It would be customary for the gentleman to initiate such conversation. Yet, Lord Hampton stood stone-faced and said not a word.

Cassandra was both gratified and irritated. It was well he did not wish to speak. On the other hand, was she deemed so uninteresting that he could not bother himself to make some comment on the size of the ballroom or the skill of the musicians?

Le Pantalon having been completed by the first two couples, Lord Hampton led her expertly. Whatever his dour temperament, he'd certainly had the benefit of a dancing master.

Cassandra was careful in her steps, and relieved to get through creditably. She found herself once again standing next to the silent man.

Her irritation grew as she watched the other couples take advantage of those moments for conversation. A gentleman said something amusing, a lady laughed and replied. Just as it should be.

Finally, to avoid looking a complete fool, and she would with so many eyes trained on Lord Hampton, she said, "The weather is particularly fine just now."

Rather than reply to this innocuous salvo, the lord only nodded.

Irritation coursed through her. Now she was to appear an even bigger fool. She had initiated a conversation and been firmly rebuffed. It would be impossible to believe it had not been noted, and it would be discussed. If Cassandra had gained any slight understanding of London, it was that balls were minutely dissected in drawing rooms across the town. Every move, every overheard conversation, every look, was to be analyzed down to the last detail.

"You might at least attempt some sort of civility, my lord," she said.

Lord Hampton appeared startled, though he quickly recovered. "I am sorry, miss?"

The way he said the words left no doubt to their meaning. His tone fairly dripped with condescension. To call her miss, rather than Miss Knightsbridge, as if she were an inconsequential person whose name was not worth the effort of recalling. She supposed the lofty lord felt he conferred some mighty favor on a country girl like herself.

She would not stand for it.

"Do not feign ignorance," she said. "And do not suppose that every lady you encounter is desperate to know you."

It was their turn to step into the square and so Lord Hampton did not reply. He *did* look fairly furious, however.

While Cassandra had gone some way to shocking herself with her boldness, she found she was not overly sorry for it. She had wished to avoid the gentlemen of the pact, and she was certain she would never be opportuned by Lord Hampton again. That left just five more to insult into silence.

The thought of it nearly made her giggle, but she suppressed the urge.

THE FIRST DANCE had come to a blessed end with no further words exchanged with Lord Hampton. After the urge to giggle had passed, Cassandra had begun to regret her daring. It was not that she thought he deserved any kinder treatment; it was only that she was well-aware that it would not be the done thing in London.

In Surrey, she had never felt constrained in her speech. If she thought something strongly, she would say it. She'd not soon forget the taking down of a certain Mr. Longmoore. He'd opportuned her in a shocking manner at a ball, grasping at her arm as she exited the lady's retiring room and suggesting she, as he termed it, "Take him on." She presumed this to be some sort of low marriage proposal, and quite ridiculous at that—Mr. Longmoore was a tradesman in the village who had the unfortunate reputation of drinking too much. The habit had been on unmistakable display on that particular evening.

After she'd pulled away from the drunken fool, he'd had the audacity to attempt to kiss her. She'd slapped him hard and informed him that she viewed him in no more favorable a light than a kitchen mouse, and if he were so ill-advised as to approach her again in such a manner, she'd chase him with a kitchen broom. The man was lucky she had not informed her father, who would have chosen a weapon a deal more deadly than a broom.

Mr. Longmoore had given her a wide berth after that.

Still, in London, where everybody and everything were so minutely scrutinized, where ladies were held to such strict standards, speaking one's mind did not appear to find much approval. She only hoped Lord Hampton was embarrassed enough over the encounter that he'd not mention it to anybody.

Now, Lord Burke escorted her into the supper room and Cassandra anticipated an amusing repast. The lord had somehow the skill of telling of war as if it had been one long joke—she remembered vividly his tale told at the Tremanes' of the horrors his cook would dream up, being saddled with so few ingredients that were edible, and the bright face that cook would put on them. One evening, the cook had grandly announced *vieux lapin dans une sauce pire.* If Lord Burke's French had been poor, he may never have realized he ate "old rabbit in a worse sauce." Still, the lord supposed it was better than the evening he'd dined on *racines que j'ai trouvé dans la forêt,* which had loosely translated to "roots I found in the forest."

"Miss Knightsbridge," Lord Burke said, leading her into the dining room, "how do you enjoy the evening now that I've had the pleasure of leading you about the floor? I managed to avoid knocking you over, which I always consider an accomplishment."

"I enjoy the evening very well, Lord Burke," she said. "I have come through entirely unscathed. Had you knocked me to the floor, I am confident we might have passed it off as the latest figure from Mr.

Wilson."

"You understand the *ton* all too well," Lord Burke said, laughing. "If Brummel says tie it this way, it is tied. If Wilson says step this way, it is stepped."

Cassandra smiled up at Lord Burke. She found she had a great appreciation for his wit. And, for all her consternation during her first dance with Lord Hampton, she could not deny that the ball had been pleasant since then. In truth, she felt positively lighthearted—her card had been filled and a few gentlemen turned away on account of it. She supposed she'd carried on quite creditably.

The dining table was already crowded. Lord Burke pointed to a few empty chairs and said, "Just there, and good luck too. There is my friend Hampton."

Chapter Three

WHILE CASSANDRA WOULD have gladly chosen any other chair than the one empty across from Lord Hampton, she had not been able to posit an excuse before Lord Burke had led her there.

Ever jolly Lord Burke did not seem to note the coolness with which both she and Lord Hampton confirmed that they had been introduced. Lord Hampton's dinner partner, the beautiful Miss Daisy Danworth, her blond curls charmingly escaping her lady's maid's best laid plans, *did* seem to note it. The lady looked amused.

"Dashed inconvenient thing, that pact, eh, Hampton?" Lord Burke said. "I've some kind of luck that my own father does not conspire so."

Cassandra was surprised to hear of the pact spoken of so openly to one who was affected by it. Lord Hampton appeared filled with consternation to hear it mentioned. He said, "Perhaps we should not discuss it in front of the ladies."

Lord Burke laughed. "Good Lord, there is no end of things that ought not be discussed in front of the ladies, it's a wonder they hear anything at all."

"Nevertheless," Lord Hampton said, beginning to look dark as thunder.

"My friend," Lord Burke said, "there is not a chimney sweep or fish wife in London who could not recite you a version of that letter backward and forward."

"I think it is very unfair to the ladies," Miss Danworth said. "The moment one of us shows the trifling amount of interest we shall be pegged as the most determined title-hunters."

"Though," Cassandra said, unwilling to resist the remark dangling before her, "I do not suppose it will be very difficult to remain *uninterested*, thereby nullifying the problem."

"Ah," Miss Danworth said, "Miss Knightsbridge speaks very decidedly. Have you met and dismissed all six gentlemen of the pact?"

Cassandra smiled. "I have not and have no need of it. I have no wish to be a duchess, I would find it rather boring."

"Boring?" Lord Burke said. "Now you must elaborate, Miss Knightsbridge, as I am very sure that is a unique opinion."

With a small smile, Lord Hampton said, "Yes, do enlighten us on the boredom of it all."

Cassandra had not meant to let slip her real views on such things, but she'd gone and done it, and there was no turning back now.

"I am sure it is only my own eccentricity," Cassandra said, "but it seems to me that the higher one goes in the strata of society, the more one is stared at. I'd prefer a bit more freedom than that. I'd prefer to gallop my horse over hill and dale, leaving my groom far behind, and have nobody comment upon it."

Lord Burke said, "Gad, I see what you say. My mother is forever telling my sisters what people will think about this or that. They barely make a move without her informing them of it. I do not suppose they've ever galloped in their lives."

"You are in the habit of wild rides, Miss Knightsbridge?" Miss Danworth asked.

Cassandra very much thought Miss Danworth sought to make her seem foolish. She had met such women before, and she thought she knew how to manage them.

"Miss Danworth," she said sweetly, "a horse who is never given its head is an unhappy creature. It is only a kindness to give them leave to see what they can do. I hope I have enough sense to keep my father's stables in contented good order."

"What I believe Miss Danworth means to point out," Lord Hampton said, "is that ladies galloping round the countryside, sans groom, is not exactly the done thing."

Cassandra felt herself flush. Who was this man to inform her of what she ought to do and what she ought not to do? Her own father did not dictate in such a manner.

"Apparently," she said, "it *is* the done thing by some, as I do so often."

"If that is so," Lord Hampton said, "one wonders what else might be on the list of done things in Surrey. I suppose you shoot pheasant and go round in trousers if you have a mind."

"If there was a practical reason for going round in trousers, I might very well do it," Cassandra said, anger rising in her chest, "and anybody might take a shot at a bird."

"Gosh," Lord Burke said, "I cannot quite imagine my own sisters taking up a shotgun—I'd be afraid of who would end up dead on the drive."

"Certainly, Lord Burke, any female might learn the skill," Cassandra said. "It is not an overly complicated operation."

Miss Danworth looked enormously pleased with the conversation. Cassandra was mortified. She'd not wished to reveal any of what she'd said. But then, that stupid, arrogant lord had purposefully baited her into it!

She went on far quieter after that and was relieved that Lord Burke would entertain them with more stories of his cook in the war. The fellow had once picked mushrooms for a repast but turned out not to be skilled at selecting edible varieties. The lord had been sick for days. The man had since been installed in Grosvenor Square and was a deal more comfortable ordering from a grocer than he'd ever been wandering forlornly round foreign forests.

EDWIN AND LORD Lockwood rode their horses through the quiet streets, the Bergrams' ball blessedly over.

"A successful sally, I'll wager," Lockwood said. "Here we are, free at last and having given nobody reason to hope."

Hampton did not answer. His head was still too full of his encounters with Miss Knightsbridge. Of all the high-handed misses! First, she demanded he speak to her and then insulted him when his conversation was deemed unsatisfactory. What had she said? "Not everyone is desperate to know you." *That* was what she said.

Then Burke would bring her to his notice again! She would apprise him, pointedly, that she did not care a fig for the pact and the last thing she'd wish to do was become a duchess. Of course she did not, she was too busy galloping around and shooting birds.

Who ever heard of such a thing? What went on in Surrey, that a viscount's daughter was in the habit of shooting birds? The notion was absurd. The habit of muff pistols was ridiculous enough—a lady was fortunate not to shoot off her foot and if a lady really wished to be defended from highwaymen, that lady ought to bring enough well-armed men to do the job. It was a silly conceit to carry a toy pistol in a reticule and a worse conceit to claim skill with a shotgun.

He'd never heard of a lady successfully fending off an attack with her delicate little pistol and was certain he never would. He supposed Miss Knightsbridge would be better prepared, as she'd have a fowling piece by her side.

"Close one on Lady Sybil, though," Lockwood said. "Manning was supposed to take her into supper and was called away on some emergency. Dash it—I stepped in before I could even think. I'd not claimed the dance before supper and had thought to take myself off to some balcony or other to avoid a protracted conversation with a lady. Then, there I was, arm out and leading her in. She's a charmer, I won't lie."

Hampton had not particularly attended his friend's speech. He looked over and said, "What?"

"Never mind," Lockwood said in exasperation. "You will attend on the morrow, I suppose?"

Hampton knew perfectly well what Lockwood referred to. The gentlemen named in the pact were all to meet at Dalton's house. Dalton was already an earl and had a large residence in Berkeley Square.

"I will attend," Hampton said. He did not know what would be discussed, except to assume they were all to come up with some idea of how to put their fathers off without having to move to Cheapside.

Hampton could not say how they would do it, but they must do it. As for the other side of the coin, the danger of falling for the charms of some lady or other, he was in no danger whatsoever. The ladies he'd danced with that evening were all of a kind—eager to display their beauty and wit. Except, of course, Miss Knightsbridge. She was only eager to flout her confoundedness, horsemanship and skill with a gun.

"How did you get on with Miss Knightsbridge?" Lockwood asked. "I know you have a weakness for her sort of looks and I saw you conversing with her at dinner. Did she attempt to cast a net?"

"Miss Knightsbridge is too busy galloping her horse and firing off a fowling piece at passing birds to cast any nets," Lord Hampton said drily.

LADY SYBIL WAS shown into the drawing room and hurried to Cassandra's side. Lady Markswort greeted her civilly and rose. "I shall leave you two alone," she said. "I remember all too well the day after a ball in my own youth and am certain there is no end of things to discuss without the eavesdropping of an old woman."

"You are not old at all!" Cassandra said, and she meant it. Lady Marksworth was a distinguished looking lady of early middle age.

"I am not old to myself, anyway," Lady Marksworth said goodhumoredly. "I will have tea sent in. Now, talk away."

Lady Marksworth swept out of the room and Cassandra thought her aunt understood her better than she had initially given the lady credit for. She and Sybil *would* have much to talk of.

They settled themselves on the velvet cushions of the window seat that overlooked the lady's charming front garden, fronted by an ironwork gate. The sun shone down, the clip-clop of the occasional carriage sounded softly through the glass as it passed them by, and the distant sound of neighboring front doors opening and closing spoke of a street filled with people coming and going.

Cassandra preferred this little perch above all others in her aunt's house, as it so differed from Trebly Hall and its isolation in the countryside. Its excellent view of the street had provided no end of entertainment, including what she suspected was a budding romance between a governess and a butler. That lady was in the habit of pushing her charge's pram down the street at precisely the time the butler came out for air. As well, there was a gentleman living across the road who bore a long scar on his cheek and appeared always to be serious—she imagined him as having been one of Wellington's right-hand men.

"You begin," Cassandra said, holding her friend's hands in her own.

"Very well," Sybil said. "Ever so much happened, but I will start by telling you of a near disaster."

"A disaster!" Cassandra said, very much surprised.

"Nearly so," Sybil said. "Mr. Manning was meant to take me into supper, but as we walked toward the dining room, a messenger delivered him a letter. An old aunt in Kent did poorly and her neighbor had written about it. He is ever so kind, as it turns out. He said his aunt would never bother him, not even if she were on her deathbed, and so he was most grateful the neighbor had been bold enough to write. His butler saw at once that it was from his aunt's neighborhood and sent the message straight to the Bergrams' knowing his master would not wish to be delayed. He set off for Kent that very instant, not even returning home to pack a case. And so you see, though he apologized profusely, there I was standing alone while everybody else was led in."

"Did you make haste to the retiring room?" Cassandra asked. "I have thought of what I should do if I were to be without a partner for supper, and it is the only thing I can think of."

"It was very strange," Sybil said. "I was perplexed about what I ought to do and thought of going to my mama, but then Lord Lockwood appeared by my side and offered to take me in."

"How lucky!" Cassandra said.

"Yes, I suppose it was lucky," Sybil said thoughtfully. "Though I cannot account for why he did so. He barely said a word throughout. You know how awkward that can be, having to hold up a conversation alone. I cannot imagine what more I could have said about the weather."

"At least you were not holed up in the retiring room, praying that no lady would come upon you and stare at you with a pitying gaze."

"Very true," Sybil said. "And perhaps Lord Lockwood was only momentarily tongue-tied, the pact may have weighed heavily on his mind. They must all know it is the topic of the town."

Before Cassandra could comment, Racine came in with the tea. The old butler had been known to her as long as she could remember. He'd always been exceedingly kind—delivering her no end of biscuits when nobody was looking. She'd been in the habit, as a young girl, of creeping down to the butler's closet and pouring out her heart to him whenever she experienced some little upset. He'd always taken her side of things, even when she could see now that he ought not have.

The butler set down a tea tray with a plate of the cook's marvelous fairy cakes.

"You spoil us, Racine," Cassandra said.

Racine was a formal sort of fellow when he was not comforting a heartbroken young girl in the butler's closet. Cassandra still remembered fondly his commiseration with her when the viscount had denied her idea of acquiring another five mastiffs to make a proper pack. Racine had told her it seemed a fine idea and the viscount might change his mind someday.

Now, he said, "It is a butler's purview, I think, to show those little considerations that might indicate favor."

"Goodness," Sybil said. "I can hardly convince Merrydon to deliver a bit of dry bread so soon after breakfast."

Racine clearly looked askance at that way of going on. He raised an eyebrow in the most delightful disapproving manner and left the room. Cassandra had no doubt he was moments away from informing the housekeeper of Merrydon's unsatisfactory habits.

"Now," Sybil said, "you must tell me of your evening. I know you were to go into supper with Lord Burke, he is an amiable fellow, is he not?"

"Very amiable," Cassandra said. "A deal more amiable than was Lord Hampton, both during the opening of the ball *and* across the table at supper."

"Lord Hampton? He did not offend?" Sybil asked.

"He very much offended me actually," Cassandra said. "He was all but wordless on the ballroom floor. I thought it rude and told him so."

"You did no such thing!" Sybil said.

"Oh, I most certainly did," Cassandra said resolutely. She did not see a reason for pretense. Lord Hampton had been rude, and she had informed him of it. "I think," she went on, "that the lord flatters himself over this pact. He wished to make it known that he was not on the auction block. I made it equally known that I was not bidding."

"Goodness," Sybil said. "But then, you spoke to him at supper too? Was that not uncomfortable?"

"Terribly," Cassandra said. And, if she were truthful with herself, that part of the evening she'd prefer to forget. There had been no cause to inform anybody that she liked a wild ride on a horse or, worse, that she'd ever raised a shotgun.

"Well," Sybil said, "at least you have no worries over Lord Hampton approaching you again."

Cassandra smiled. "I have not the slightest worry over that, my dear Sybil. That gentleman will view me as no more alluring than the plague."

Sybil squinted her eyes, appearing to look out the window over Cassandra's shoulder. "There is Lord Lockwood, going into Lord Dalton's house."

"Lord Dalton's house?" Cassandra asked. She'd had no idea that the gentleman with the scar was one of the gentlemen named in the pact.

"Oh! And there is Lord Hampton, himself, just rode up on a horse!"

Cassandra had no wish to look and could not quite understand why her eyes insisted on doing so. Nevertheless, her eyes would force her head to turn.

Lord Hampton leapt off his horse and handed it over to a groom. He took the steps two at a time and disappeared into the house with Lord Lockwood. Three more gentlemen arrived in quick succession, all bounding into the house.

Whatever Lord Hampton's temperament might be, Cassandra could not deny that he cut a dashing figure.

"It would not be too difficult to guess who the unknown gentlemen are," Sybil said. "Dalton, Lockwood and Hampton are all to do with the pact, those other three must be Ashworth, Cabot and Grayson."

"I suppose they conspire to thwart their fathers," Cassandra said. "They must feel they are hunted stags in the forest, with mamas circling round and ready to fire."

"You do not think mamas behave so," Sybil said.

"I do," Cassandra said. "Though I do not have the benefit of my own, I have been careful to observe. What does your own mother say to it?"

Sybil's expression took on a slight aspect of worry. "She's delighted with the pact and has discussed the gentlemen in some detail. I have been clinging to the hope that two of them are already struck from the list—Lockwood and Ashworth. My mama told me last night that my father has recently reminded her that he does not like either of those gentlemen's fathers. Something to do with a long-ago card game. I am hopeful my father recalls he does not like the rest of their fathers over some other ancient insults."

"My aunt approves of the pact very much, and does not seem to dislike *anybody's* father," Cassandra said. "She's also told me that my own father has had a long connection with Lord Hampton's grandmother, the dowager, though my aunt does not know if the lady still lives. She hopes I may mention it in conversation."

Cassandra felt her cheeks tinge pink. "I failed to mention that it would be unlikely that Lord Hampton and I have any future conversations, much less about any family connections."

"Do you recall your father ever speaking of the dowager?"

"I do not," Cassandra said, "but my father keeps up a vast correspondence and never talks much about it. He once told me I could read all his letters after he died, and I would find much amusement in them. Though I have begun to wonder if the lady is not the same person that my father has sometimes spoken of—I do not know the details but there was some gentlewoman who helped him out of what he's termed 'a scrape' in his youth. I have always been under the impression that the lady had been a deal older than he at the time."

"Goodness, and now you are pressured to pose the connection to Lord Hampton. I see what you say about a mama's enthusiasm. That is just the sort of maneuvering I worry over," Sybil said. "When I came to town, I had my heart set on a fellow who would sweep me off my feet, not one who was under contract to secure himself a wife."

"We must stay strong and united, Sybil," Cassandra said. "That is our only way through this muddle."

HAMPTON GAZED AROUND Dalton's library. He'd not been in the house for ages and it was just as disheveled as he remembered it. Opened books lay on every surface, as if Dalton could never decide what he would read, and the dust surrounding them spoke to a lax household.

Lord Dalton himself, an earl and someday to be Duke of Wentworth, was a tall and muscular man with only a long scar running down his left cheek marring his appearance. He'd got it at the battle of Quatre Bras, a Frenchman coming within range and delivering the blow. His mother claimed it gave him a dangerous and dashing look. Dalton thought that idea was hopeful nonsense—ladies did not flock to damaged gentlemen. On the other hand, that they did not flock to him was a benefit at this particular moment in time.

Dalton's butler shuffled in with a tray of glasses and poured out brandy, though it was far too early for it. Considering the servant's advanced age, Hampton was only thankful he'd managed to set the glasses down without falling over.

Dalton motioned toward a table with six chairs round it. "To the war room, gentlemen."

As they settled themselves, Hampton mused that, as much as he'd thought on it, he still had not devised a plan to counterattack his father's directive without finding himself on the street.

Dalton said, "My own opinion is the whole thing hangs on Lockwood. It's *his* father that's got them all riled."

"If I could manage His Grace," Lockwood said, "I'd have already done it. I've argued backwards and forwards and he's resolute on the thing. I think he even wishes me to fail—he said living without funds for a year would cure me of my fondness for gambling."

"Why did we even go through this damnable war, if it was not to return home and do what we like?" Ashworth asked.

"We all know the injustice of it," Cabot said, "the point of this gathering is to discover what we can do about it."

"We are the talk of the town," Hampton said. "Burke spoke of it at supper last evening as if it were the most usual topic in the world."

"Lucky Burke," Grayson muttered. "I wish my own father belonged to Brook's. There is no such lunatic talk at that club, it is only at White's that such bizarre schemes are hatched."

"Perhaps we burn White's to the ground," Lockwood said hopefully. "Take away their meeting spot."

Hampton smiled. Lockwood's mind always went to the most drastic action possible. "They've all gone home to the country," he said, "and I suppose we cannot stop them communicating by letter without burning down the Royal Mail."

"We will not be forced to take rooms in Cheapside, at least," Dalton said. "I inherited this house from an uncle and my father cannot touch it. If it comes to it, you can all stay here. Though don't expect good dinners, not much money came with the house."

Ashworth looked around and said, "You can sell off some of these books you never finish. That'll keep us in beef and brandy."

This idea cheered the gentlemen no end. They toasted Dalton and drained the brandy already in their hands. Hampton was among those cheered: he had all but resigned himself to living in a garret somewhere. Here, there was a very good wine cellar that would take years to get through.

"What we need, in the meantime," Grayson said, "is some bit of new gossip that will knock us out of people's mouths. The talkers are always eager for the next thing, and to be the first to know it, and then the first to tell it to another."

They sat in silence for some moments. Then Lockwood said, "Hampton, were you in jest last evening about Miss Knightsbridge? About her shooting birds?"

Hampton shook his head. "I was not. She said as much, as well as a penchant for galloping over hill and dale without a groom, in front of both Burke and Miss Danworth. God only knows what else goes on in Surrey."

"Well, well," Dalton said. "That is certainly enough to begin. I'll send a man to Surrey to find out just that—what else *does* go on in Surrey in the environs of Miss Knightsbridge? With any luck, we'll discover some little thing that, combined with shooting birds and riding off without a groom, should set tongues wagging."

The rest of the gentlemen at table began to look hopeful. That they would clutch desperately at any idea, Hampton did not doubt. He *had* begun to doubt the rightness of exploiting Miss Knightsbridge's ill-advised words. He did not like gossip in general and had never been the means of spreading it.

Though, after all, without knowing him the lady had informed him she did not *wish* to know him. In fact, she claimed there might be no end of people who did not wish to know him. Further, nobody had forced her to own that she wielded a shotgun.

He supposed she could be left to her own devices.

Chapter Four

Lord and Lady Sedway's dinner was to be a cozy evening for only thirty guests. Of all the invitations that had piled up on her aunt's silver tray in the hall, Cassandra felt most comfortable considering this one. All of her childhood, she'd known Lady Sedway as Anne Hamilton. Though Anne was five years older than herself, the lady being a close neighbor meant that the Hamiltons had been often at Trebly Hall.

When she had been younger, Cassandra had gloried in Anne coming into her bedchamber and advising her on her hair or showing her the latest fashion. Cassandra might not have understood half of what Anne said or cared much for the parts she did understand, but she was very admiring of Anne's confidence. Anne had been like an elder sister and, though so unlike herself, dearly loved for it.

Anne was all hairstyles and clothes and whispers about balls and the gentlemen who could be found at them. Cassandra, being raised in a male-dominated house, rather looked upon her older friend as some exotic creature who was mystifyingly privy to the secrets of an unknown world.

Now, Anne Hamilton was Lady Sedway, having married an earl. She still wrote her old friend and had been delighted to hear that Cassandra would come for her first season. Cassandra had been promised a dinner and Lady Sedway was as good as her word.

Cassandra supposed her old friend would be surprised to see her appearance after four years' absence. Back then, it would be unlikely that she'd manage an entire day without soiling her dress from climbing over a fence or ripping her riding habit on a loose nail in the stables. Now, she was to arrive a proper-looking young lady.

They entered the house and Lady Sedway rushed to greet them. "Dear Cass!" she said, "goodness, look at you. I do not know what I expected, perhaps that you would turn up with mud on your cheek as I was so used to seeing you, but you are positively grown! And Lady Marksworth, how good of you to come. I do not believe I have seen you since that last Christmas at the Viscount's house the year before I married."

Lady Marksworth graciously nodded.

"Lady Sedway," Cassandra said, "you cannot imagine how cheered I am to see you."

"You must still call me Anne, just as you do in your letters," Lady Sedway said, laughing. "I cannot be addressed so formally by the girl I used to experiment on with curl papers."

As Lady Sedway led them into the drawing room, Cassandra thought her friend had not changed much, only become even more elegant than she had always been.

The lady's butler announced them and they went in.

The drawing room was already peopled with various guests. Cassandra was introduced to Lord Sedway, who she found a friendly sort and surprisingly knowledgeable of her long-standing friendship with his wife.

She was cheered to see Lord Burke on the other side of the room, talking to Miss Penny Darlington, a pleasant lady she'd met on a call to Mrs. Darlington some weeks ago.

Cassandra was further cheered to see that none of the gentlemen of the pact were in the room. Now that she'd seen them all go into Lord Dalton's house, she was certain she could recognize them.

Behind her, she heard the butler say, "Lord Hampton and Lord Ashworth."

Cassandra's heart sank. Why? Why must two of the pact attend? And worse, why must one of them be Lord Hampton? She dearly wished Sybil to be at her side, but her friend attended a dinner elsewhere. Lady Marksworth *did* stand next to her, but she suddenly felt very alone.

Lady Sedway guided the two gentlemen to Cassandra and her aunt. "I do not know if you have been introduced—Lord Hampton, Lord Ashworth, may I present Miss Knightsbridge and Lady Marksworth."

The gentlemen bowed. Lord Hampton said, "We met at the Bergrams' ball, I believe."

Cassandra knew that to be the snub it was intended to be. To say he *"believed"* they had met was to say she had not made much of an impression. She supposed she was meant to be insulted by it, but she was far from it. She would be very grateful to be forgettable, including all she had said, in the lord's mind.

Lord Ashworth said, "Miss Knightsbridge."

Cassandra thought he said it almost as a question. He had such a quizzical look that she began to wonder if Lord Hampton had seen fit, after all, to repeat her unique views expressed over supper.

Lady Sedway led the gentlemen away to introduce them to Miss Darlington.

"Well," Lady Marksworth said softly, "I see the pact gentlemen have taken their fathers seriously. They *will* attend everywhere they are invited. I imagine a small dinner such as this would not generally attract their notice."

Cassandra did not answer and Lady Marksworth went on.

"Of course, I believe Lord Hampton is a cousin to Lord Sedway somehow or other so that might account for it. In any case, the circumstances are fortuitous for our hostess; it is often hard to balance a table for a dinner."

Cassandra did not particularly concern herself over whether the table was balanced. She only concerned herself with the wish that Lord Hampton be seated far away from her at that table.

Lady Sedway had left Lord Hampton and Lord Ashworth speaking to Miss Darlington. She glided by Cassandra and whispered in her ear. "I will have Hampton take you in, you may thank me later."

Cassandra felt the blood drain from her cheeks and had a great urge to run after her friend and somehow convince her to have things changed. It would be far more convenient to have Lord Hampton take in Miss Darlington.

She did not do so. She could not do so. Nobody would dare trifle with a lady's dinner arrangements. Worse, she was all but certain that dear Anne had put careful thought into the matter and viewed herself as doing a great favor for her friend. Lady Sedway could not know that Cassandra and Lord Hampton had got off on the wrong foot. No, that was an understatement. They had got off on the wrong two legs.

"Did she say Hampton?" Lady Marksworth said softly. "Well done, Lady Sedway."

BY THE TIME dinner was announced, Cassandra had steeled herself to be taken in by Lord Hampton. Further, she'd decided that it was not very sensible to make an enemy of him, despite her personal opinions. It appeared she was to be encountering him everywhere and so it would be more comfortable to smooth things over in some manner.

He had taken her in silently, gravely even, and now they sat next to each other. It was becoming apparent that the lord would not initiate a conversation so, just as she had been forced to do at the Bergrams' ball, she would need to say something.

"How do you know Lord and Lady Sedway, my lord?" she said.

Nothing could be more commonplace and guaranteed not to offend.

"My father is second cousin to Lord Sedway's father," Lord Hampton said. "And you?"

At least he had followed his answer with a question, which was a deal more than he'd done when they'd danced at the ball. "I have known Lady Sedway since I was a child," Cassandra said. "Her father's estate is very nearby my own father's in Surrey."

Lord Hampton nodded, but did not reply. Cassandra supposed that was to be the end of any light conversation between them.

She said, "My lord, I really must apologize for my remarks at the Bergrams', both in the ballroom and at supper. They were ill-conceived, to say the least."

There. She'd said it. Now, if he were any sort of gentleman at all, he would accept the apology and they would go on as if nothing had ever occurred between them.

"Ill-conceived? Do you say, then," Lord Hampton asked, "that you do *not* ride without a groom or shoot birds?"

Truly? He would wish to go on with it? Why did he not simply nod in acknowledgement of her regret? She had no wish to expound on anything she'd said, nor would she outright lie by denying any of it.

"I say, my lord," Cassandra said cautiously, "that I regret what I said. Perhaps that may be deemed sufficient?"

Lord Hampton did finally then nod his assent, though it perturbed Cassandra that he should still be wondering what she did on her own estate. She supposed the idea of shooting off a shotgun was particularly surprising. Other ladies had been known to ride at a gallop through Hyde Park, their grooms falling somewhat behind. They were perhaps looked at askance, but it did not rise to the level of shock. The shooting birds, though. Even her father had said she ought not mention it and her father did not bow to convention very often.

Much to her relief, Lord Burke on her other side had turned to her, and Miss Penny Darlington had turned to Lord Hampton.

The dinner went on in such a manner. On her one side, voluble Lord Burke and his war stories, not the least of which was a horrifying tale of his cook refusing to even name a dish, and then when forced, calling it *Un cheval que vous avez peut-être vu récemment*, otherwise understood to be 'a horse you may have seen recently.' It had completely put her off her beef.

On her other side, a stilted conversation with Lord Hampton. She had tried asking him of the war, but he was not as eager to speak of it as Lord Burke. She had asked him about his county, but it appeared that Derbyshire was an uninteresting sort of place with little to mention. Finally, at a complete loss, she had asked him if he were fond of dogs. That topic, of all others, seemed at least mildly interesting to the lord.

"I am fond in the usual way," he said. "My father's master of the hounds and I have just designed new kennels in the modern style."

"My own father's hounds live better than some people, I think," Cassandra said. "He's been very careful to put drains low, keep their beds off the floor and ensure they are warm in winter. He takes great care matching their food to the season."

"I am not surprised by it," Lord Hampton said, "anybody wishing their hounds in good form must do all of those things."

"I suppose so, and while I admire the whole operation exceedingly, I must admit having a particular affection for my own mastiff. He does nothing useful and ought to be in the stables, but I prefer to keep him in the house. I am certain he rather prefers it as well."

In an instant, Lord Hampton looked truly interested. "I, too, own a mastiff. His name is Havoc and he spends the majority of his time in my library, gnawing on my books."

Cassandra laughed, and it was not a forced laugh. "My own is named Mayhem, May for short. She will happily chew up anything she suspects has any amount of value."

"I had been under the impression that most ladies preferred a lap dog," Lord Hampton said. "My mother has some kind of little dust ball—a Pomeranian, I think."

"I find larger breeds have a better temperament," Cassandra said. "Perhaps because they do not spend all their time worrying about being stepped on. May, when she is not destroying something, is generally ranged out in front of the fire and fast asleep, as comfortable as if she were the master of the house."

Lord Hampton nodded. "I do believe the larger breeds are more content with their lot. My mother's dog is forever yapping at the air."

"Yes," Cassandra said. "I suppose their bark is meant to make up for their lack of size."

Suddenly, both seemed to note that they'd had a civil exchange for once and both looked away in embarrassment. Cassandra could not say why in particular she should be embarrassed over it, except for perhaps the meaningful glance coming from Lady Marksworth from the other end of the table.

They had one further interesting conversation before the dinner ended. Cassandra had mentioned her father's interest in safety measures for his farm workers. Lord Hampton had commented that his own father routinely ordered sick hands to stay abed, as it had been his observation that one sick hand would lead to all sick hands unless the first to come down with the sickness was separated from the rest. That had led to a conversation on safety practices in general, and Cassandra had noted that nothing could be more prone to accident than the sidesaddle and she'd added a second girth to her own to mitigate the risk of sliding.

After she'd said it, she worried that she'd wandered dangerously close to the subject of riding without a groom, but the lord did not allude to it. Instead, he had appeared to view it as good sense and had even hinted he might pass the idea on to his sister.

It occurred to Cassandra that while their conversations were commonplace, his words somehow managed to make Lord Hampton even more attractive than she had originally thought him. When he was engaged in a subject, his features were more lively and his strong jaw softened. When he looked at her with interest, she felt a soft shiver run down her back.

It was a ludicrous thing to feel a shiver while a man talked of dogs. And it was also a shame he was to be a duke and involved in that ridiculous pact.

In any case, it appeared the rift between them was mended and for that she was grateful.

LORD HAMPTON LEFT the Sedways' dinner in some internal consternation. That consternation had evolved quite significantly over the course of the evening. At first, he had been confounded to find Miss Knightsbridge in attendance, and then further aggravated that he was to take her into dinner. Despite her looks, and they could slay any man with eyes in his head, he had no wish to hear of anymore of her bizarre habits. He already carried a touch of guilt over Dalton's plan to dig up gossip, even though he tamped it down by convincing himself she'd earned it.

But then, she had apologized for her remarks at the Bergrams'. She'd not rescinded them, which he'd thought odd, but she regretted them. He had begun to feel sorry that he'd allowed Dalton to take what the lady had said and attempt to make something of it. It began to feel shabby to cause a lady trouble, no matter how little, in an effort to move the attention away from the gentlemen subjected to the pact.

That regret only grew the more they spoke. When they'd talked of dogs, there had been a real ease to it, very unlike his usual conversations with a lady. She'd even understood the importance of drains in a kennel, a subject he'd spent months discussing with his father's master of the hounds.

And who would have guessed a gentlewoman would prefer a mastiff over a puff of fur meant to be carried round the house like a bad-tempered reticule?

Then, of course, she'd modified her sidesaddle to make it safer. He would only see the good sense in that and was determined to write his sister about the idea.

All that, and there was that pretty face to contend with as well.

Though Lockwood knew he had a weakness for a heart-shaped face, his friend did not know the beginnings of the inclination. When Hampton had been eight years old, he'd fallen hopelessly in love with Jenny, one of the dairy maids on his father's estate. He'd even thought of how he would convince his father that they ought to marry. He'd hung around the barn when she milked the cows and one day finally worked up the nerve to tell her of his undying love.

He blushed to think of it now. The girl had laughed as if it were the greatest joke in the world, called him a goose, and told him she planned to marry a young farmer down the road.

It had taken him months to recover from being thrown over for a farmer, and he never did recover from his attraction to a heart-shaped face. He supposed now that his preference had been there all along and Jenny had only been the first female with such a face who'd crossed his path.

Hampton reined in his horse, leapt down and handed it over to a groom.

Here was another such heart-shaped face to cross his path, and far more complicated than Jenny had ever been. Miss Knightsbridge *was* unusual, that could not be denied. He still could not resign himself to approving of a lady wielding a shotgun. But then, he'd felt far more favorably about a lady knowing something about a well-built kennel. And, of course, she was a lady and not a dairymaid.

Was that all, though? There was something about her that drew him in despite having no inclination to be drawn in. Each time he had turned to talk to Miss Darlington, half his attention had stayed directed toward Miss Knightsbridge and her conversations with Burke.

His opinion of her felt in flux. What was not in flux was his determination to see Dalton and call off the scheme to use Miss Knightsbridge as a decoy for the convenience of him and his friends. *That*, he was now decidedly against.

MR. TUTTLE HAD found no difficulty at all in making his way round Guildford and its environs, gathering information for Lord Dalton on a certain Miss Knightsbridge. He'd been managing such clandestine forays for high and mighty gentlemen for two decades and Surrey was very like every other county in England—express interest in its doings and there was no end of folk who wanted to talk about it. Particularly, those on the low end of the stick delighted in talking about those on the high end of the stick.

It was true that this particular business was not like his usual jobs. He'd been in the habit of tracking down a fellow's wife, invariably that lady found with some ridiculous paramour or other. Or sometimes, locating a gentleman who'd run out on a debt. He'd even collared a clergyman who'd skipped off with the parsonage's silver and brought him back to face his accusers. This was different. It had taken him quite some time to understand Lord Dalton's meaning, but it seemed this lady did not cuckold a husband nor owe anybody a vast sum of money. She was to have broken more delicate rules, like riding her horse without a groom and shooting pheasant.

He wondered what England was coming to, now that the high and mighty spent their time on such inane matters. Nevertheless, Lord Dalton had said he had reason to believe there was something more seriously amiss about the miss, and Tuttle was to discover it.

Through his many conversations in various taverns, and the hours of useless information he'd gathered, there had finally been a diamond in the ashes. A man down on his luck, having been fired as the master of ceremonies at the Guildford Assembly Hall, had told him a remarkable story. He'd seen with his own eyes a certain Mr. Longmoore in heated conversation with Miss Knightsbridge. From what the man could overhear, the conversation had been of a personal nature. The old sot had even winked and said, "Very personal, if you understand. The lady hit him right in the face."

Tuttle did not understand precisely the meaning of what the unemployed master of ceremonies had witnessed, he'd not enough facts to go on, but he'd managed to find Mr. Longmoore and watch the man's movements carefully. Finally, the gentleman in question had taken himself into the Beef and Boar, and Tuttle had followed him in.

It was never any great trouble, when one insisted on buying one's quarry a considerable amount of ale, to become fast friends within an hour. Within two hours, Tuttle had guided the man to the event in question and hinted at a large payment if the information was sufficiently interesting. Eyeing Mr. Longmoore's rather frayed cuffs, Tuttle guessed any sort of unexpected funds would be most welcome.

"I only say," Longmoore said, "well, blasted, you know."

Of course, Mr. Tuttle did not know, and was becoming irritated with the gentleman. He'd run into his sort before—a man in the habit of saying a lot of words while saying nothing.

"Mr. Longmoore," Tuttle said smoothly, "my patron is very highly placed and has particular reasons for knowing what there is, if anything, against Miss Knightsbridge. He is prepared to pay handsomely for such information. Now, had you any sort of encounter with the lady that might prove interesting?"

Mr. Longmoore drained his ale and Tuttle signaled the barkeep to bring another. Mr. Longmoore said, "She's a dashed evil little miss, if you ask me."

"I *am* asking you," Mr. Tuttle said. "My patron requires specifics, if you please."

Mr. Longmoore took a long swig of the ale that had just been placed in front of him. "I have a lot to offer, you know. Steady business and all that. She would have been comfortable, is all I say."

"I see," Mr. Tuttle said, praying to the Gods that they were finally getting somewhere. "May I infer that you proposed to the lady and were declined?"

The word "declined" seemed to strike Mr. Longmoore as a glove whipped across his cheek.

"Declined? *Me*? Declined?" Mr. Longmoore said, pounding his fist on the table. "See here, good fellow, Ignatius Longmoore is never declined."

"No, of course not," Mr. Tuttle said. "May I ask, then, when is the happy day to take place?"

"Oh, uh, well, as to that…"

Mr. Tuttle sighed. They were back to saying words with no meaning.

"The day, Mr. Longmoore. If you please."

Tuttle watched with interest as Mr. Longmoore searched his mind for the day. The man finally seemed to find what he was looking for and said, "There will be no day, sir. As it happens, I broke it off. She was all too happy to accept, but *I* broke it off."

"You surprise me, Mr. Longmoore!" Mr. Tuttle said, fairly delighted with this development. "What reason could you have to call off the engagement? It must have been serious, indeed, if the viscount failed to kick up a fuss over the break."

Mr. Longmoore seemed rather perplexed by that question.

"Come now, Mr. Longmoore," Mr. Tuttle said. "It must have been terrible indeed. Of course, some things are well known, the lady's habit of riding in an unseemly manner—"

"She rides to the hunt on a specially-made saddle!" Mr. Longmoore cried. "Everybody knows about that!"

"And the lady has been known to handle a shotgun," Mr. Tuttle said.

"She shoots birds with it!" Mr. Longmoore exclaimed. "Everybody knows about that."

"Yes, yes," Mr. Tuttle said, motioning the barkeep to bring yet another glass of ale. "It seems everybody knows quite a few things about Miss Knightsbridge. What I wonder is, Mr. Longmoore, what is it about the lady that everybody does *not* know? What terrible thing was revealed that caused you to end the engagement?"

Mr. Longmoore was silent for some minutes and Tuttle had the idea he was thinking hard. "It was very terrible," he said, "naturally, I could not overlook it."

"Overlook what?"

Some further minutes passed, Mr. Longmoore gazing over Tuttle's head as if he admired a far-off vista. Very suddenly, he cried, "She had engaged herself to another! No, two times! There were two other promises made!"

"Good Lord, Mr. Longmoore," Tuttle said, working hard to display the right amount of shock, "how did you find it out?"

Mr. Longmoore stared hard into his glass of ale, as if he'd been told the bad news via that particular libation. He suddenly looked up. "We all arrived at the Viscount's estate at the same time. Yes, that is how it happened. We met on the drive leading to the house and when we discovered each other's business, well, you can imagine!"

"Indeed," Mr. Tuttle said. "And so, did the other two gentlemen break it off, too?"

"Oh, yes, they certainly did."

"And may I presume that you informed the lady that relations were at an end at a local assembly, thereby leading to the slap on the face?"

Mr. Longmoore looked as if he would challenge that idea, Tuttle held up his hands. "Dear Mr. Longmoore, there is no use denying that part of the tale—it is too well-known."

Seeing he would be forced to own the slap, Mr. Longmoore nodded sadly. "She was that put out about it, sir."

"Excellent, Mr. Longmoore. Now, if you will meet me here on the morrow at two o'clock and sign a sworn statement, that would be most convenient."

"A sworn statement? Well, I don't know..."

"I will bring fifty pounds in consideration, naturally."

"Fifty pounds?" Mr. Longmoore said in wonder. "Fifty?"

"Not a pence less," Tuttle said, smiling. He did not know if even half of what the blowhard had said was true, but a sworn statement would do for Lord Dalton. He would make his way to the Guildford Arms this very moment to relay the good news to his patron.

Mr. Tuttle rose and muttered, "Lord Dalton shall be *very* pleased."

Chapter Five

The following day, Lord Hampton sent a note to Dalton's house to call off the manufactured rumors against Miss Knightsbridge. He'd waited nearly all the afternoon to hear word back and, when he did not, he made his way to the house.

He was aware that Lady Marksworth's house was just across the street and glanced surreptitiously at it as he mounted the steps. The more he'd thought of Dalton's plan, the more he was bound to stop it.

They had all been so casual about casting an aspersion on a lady's reputation! He knew Dalton did not plan to paint her as scandalous. His friend hoped to dig up some other untoward habit of Miss Knightsbridge's—just enough, taken together with riding out ahead of a groom and a penchant for shotguns, to set tongues wagging. For all he knew, it would be an unnatural understanding of kennels or that she owned an unusually large dog for a lady. It was not the sort of gossip that would ruin her, and yet it was the type that would be endlessly repeated. It was even the type that might cause a few invitations to dry up. There were those formidable ladies in London who would not tolerate a whiff of boldness from a female just out.

He'd been the architect of it, having allowed his own pique to color his judgment. *He* had repeated Miss Knightsbridge's words. To the others, it must be some far-off idea happening to an unknown person. But he! *He* had encountered the lady twice now, and the second time had been a deal more pleasant than the first.

He thanked God the occupants of Lady Marksworth's house could have no way to divine the reason for his visit to Dalton.

As his thoughts ran this way and that, Dalton's butler answered the door. Bellamy was as stooped and decrepit as ever. He'd been the old duke's butler for twenty-five years, until he could no longer keep up with such a great estate. As he'd known Dalton since he had been a boy, it had seemed the most natural thing in the world to take him on for Dalton's London house.

Dalton said he and his butler had a very convenient arrangement—Dalton gave him twice the footmen he really needed so he might do next to nothing, and Bellamy did not comment on his master's activities, as he really could not care less about them. Bellamy wished for a comfortable bedchamber, a warm butler's closet, and a general ease of life. He had all that, and so Dalton might bring home a cadre of actresses of an evening and Bellamy would not look askance.

"Ah, Lord Hampton," Bellamy said, clutching the doorknob for support. "Lord Dalton is not at home. Do you wish to come in and refresh yourself?"

"That depends," Hampton said. "When is he expected back?"

"He said the day after tomorrow," Bellamy said, "but as he's gone to see his father, he may very well be delayed."

Gone to see his father? What for? He'd said nothing about going to Somerset.

"Do you know if he read my note sent yesterday before he left?"

"Oh, no, my lord," Bellamy said. "It is still right here in the hall. If it is vital, I can send it on, but it might very well cross paths."

Hampton was thoughtful for a moment. He had no idea why Dalton would have gone to his father so suddenly. Especially at this moment, with the pact hanging over their heads. Though, perhaps it was lucky. Dalton *had* planned to go to Surrey with the seedy Mr. Tuttle to find something further on Miss Knightsbridge. Apparently, the project had been postponed.

"Would you see that he is given my letter first thing when he returns?" he said.

Bellamy nodded and clutched the doorknob ever harder. Hampton thought he'd better not delay the man another minute lest he fall over. He nodded, turned, and jogged down the steps to the waiting groom.

Hampton thought it was a funny thing to have a butler who could barely stand at the door. It was his own opinion that Dalton really ought to pension the old fellow off rather than go on with such nonsense.

BELLAMY SHUT THE door behind him and smiled. There were some advantages to appearing as old as Methuselah. No matter how great a personage arrived at the door, they would state their business in all haste when they noted him clutching the doorknob. His footmen thought the whole thing a jolly bit of fun, and he did too.

And then to be questioned on the doorstep as to his master's location? He thought Lord Hampton rather naïve. Bellamy never gave away his master's whereabouts. If his master was in Surrey just now, gathering information on the unfortunate Miss Knightsbridge, that was his master's business.

Bellamy could not say he fully understood the ins and outs of the whole thing, but Miss Knightsbridge had something to do with that God-forsaken pact. Whatever efforts could be made to thwart the demands of those inconvenient fathers must be made. Bellamy had no wish to find himself faced with a *Lady* Dalton. He and his lord had a most comfortable set-up, they didn't even employ a housekeeper and had maids come in on a day basis. The house went on comfortably male—he, the cook, and the footmen had an endless amount of wine and little real work to accomplish. The grooms made certain the lord's horses were well taken care of, and then lounged at their leisure. There was no room for a lady that might get ideas and attempt to change their way of going on. Or, heaven forbid, a housekeeper. Those awful persons had the unfortunate habit of peering into every nook and cranny and glaring at any lazing staff.

CASSANDRA AND LADY Sybil sat cozy in the window seat at Marksworth House as Sybil described the courses at the Jennings' dinner. Cassandra was not sorry to have missed that particular engagement, it sounded like an overly formal and stultifying affair. The only particular thing of interest was that two gentlemen of the pact had been there.

"As there were sixty attending," Sybil said, "I thought my chances of avoiding them rather good."

"And did you?" Cassandra asked.

"I did," Lady Sybil said, "and lucky I was. Lord Cabot and Lord Grayson appeared very glum, as if they were both in a sulk. Mrs. Jenning seemed to notice, and not take it kindly. Poor Miss Danworth went into dinner with Lord Cabot and she looked as if she worked very hard to entertain, all to no avail."

"Well," Cassandra said, "if Miss Danworth cannot entertain with all those marvelous blond curls of hers, the lord must have been very determined to sulk."

"She shook her curls around very charmingly, yet he was entirely unmoved," Sybil said, laughing.

Before Cassandra could answer, Sybil pointed toward the window and said, "Ah, look, there is Lord Hampton, going to see Lord Dalton."

Cassandra turned more eagerly than she had the first time the lord had been spotted on Lord Dalton's steps. She would not say her conversation with the gentleman the evening before had been carefree, but it *had* got a deal more comfortable when they'd got on the subject of dogs. After that, they'd even discussed saddles and the modification she had made to her own to include a double girth. She had almost hesitated in mentioning it, but in fact the lord had seemed interested in the improved safety of it. His own sister had experienced a serious head injury in her youth from a slipping sidesaddle.

Now, Lord Hampton leapt off his horse, as handsome as ever. Cassandra had begun to think that part of his attractiveness stemmed from his seeming carelessness of his appearance. Of course, he could not be careless, nobody careless was dressed as he was. Yet, his mode of dress was not over-studied. She had now met her share of dandies, their neckcloths tied in fabulous configurations, and she did not care for it.

As the lord stood at the door, speaking to Lord Dalton's butler, Cassandra said, "I have not yet told you that I was taken into dinner at the Sedways' by Lord Hampton."

Sybil laid her hand on Cassandra's arm. "My poor darling, how did you manage through it?"

Cassandra reddened, seeing that she had painted such a grim picture of Lord Hampton that it must now be modified.

"It was not as you think," she said. "Remarkably, it was rather enjoyable. It began as awkwardly as you might guess, but somehow got a deal more pleasant when we got to talking of dogs."

"Dogs?" Sybil said, laughing.

"Indeed, dogs," Cassandra said. "As it happens, he owns a mastiff, too, and was quite voluble on the subject. And kennels. Oh, and then saddles. It turns out we are of the same mind on those subjects."

"Dear me, you almost seem as if you like him, Cass," Sybil said in wonder.

"Like him! No, I would not go so far as that," Cassandra said hurriedly. Though, as she said it, she was mortified that it did not sound completely true. "I would say that I do not dislike him as much as I did, which is a very long way from liking."

"Let us hope it is a very long way," Sybil said, "else you might find yourself an unhappy duchess someday."

Cassandra smiled at her friend, even as she felt the pink spread across her cheeks. "Now you are being ridiculous, Sybil." She meant the words, it was just entirely unfortunate that Lord Hampton was so agreeable to look at, and now he'd begun to make himself agreeable to speak with.

She watched the lord go back down Lord Dalton's steps without being admitted. He leapt on his horse and clattered down the street.

Ah well, it was true she had encountered the lord twice in short order, but London was a big place and the chances of encountering him so often in future were unlikely. Further, the rest of the dinners on her calendar would be a deal larger and so the odds were greatly diminished that she would be taken into supper by that gentleman.

She could not ascertain whether that was a welcome idea or not.

MR. TUTTLE HAD earned his scratch on his most recent assignment. Lord Dalton had been well-pleased with the sworn statement from Mr. Longmoore. Tuttle had thought that had been the end of it. Though the point of the job had baffled, he'd eventually come to the conclusion that the information against Miss Knightsbridge was to be presented to one of Lord Dalton's friends who thought of engaging himself to the lady. He'd managed other arrangements where a gentleman's friends had taken measures to separate him from an unsuitable match.

That had not been the end of it, though. It turned out Lord Dalton wished the information to be spread far and wide, and he did not wish to personally do it, as he did not want to be in any way connected to the scheme.

It was to be Tuttle's job to get the information spread throughout London.

Tuttle had balked at the idea. He was not so certain that Mr. Longmoore had been completely honest. He rather felt Longmoore was a blowhard who would invent no end of fictions to protect the delicate ego that every blowhard proudly owned. Further, he had never involved himself in a public campaign to impugn the reputation of a lady. At least, not on such flimsy evidence.

Still, Dalton had offered him such a sum that it could not be turned away. He could send that money to his widowed sister in Manchester and she might live comfortably with her two young boys, no longer taking in sewing or washing. If he were to weigh the fate of his long-suffering sister against a privileged miss from Surrey, he must always come down on the side of his sister.

Tuttle could all too easily guess why Lord Dalton had offered such a handsome payment. It must seem to the lord a difficult thing to plant a story all over town with nobody quite knowing from whence it had come.

Tuttle knew otherwise, of course. He did not have access to those places filled with the chattering women of the *ton,* nor did he need to. It was not in the elegant drawing rooms that the idea would put down roots. It was below stairs and in the attics. It was through a carefully curated labyrinth of connections.

It was through the lady's maids.

Tuttle had made it his business to cultivate relationships with all manner of staff and there was not a well-heeled house in town he could not slip into via the servants' entrance. Though he knew his share of housekeepers and butlers, it was lady's maids who had those confidential conversations with the mistress that allowed for the spread of gossip. In truth, the ladies of the *ton* expected their maids to deliver whatever interesting chatter they'd heard from other servants.

The lady's maids would, for a few pounds, repeat the story. It would be impossible to know from where it had first arisen. It was only necessary that the first group of maids be given a copy of the declaration from Mr. Longmoore and become apprised of Miss Knightsbridge's inclinations to ride without a groom and shoot like a man. They each would take bits and pieces to compose their own version until the story would swirl into the air like a whirlwind of veracity.

All the hints and innuendos taken together, it would not be a week before Miss Knightsbridge was known as bolder than any Mary Wollstonecraft.

CASSANDRA CURLED UP on her bed, just now in receipt of two letters from home. She had opened the one from her friend Lily Farnsworth first, and it was just what she had expected. Lily prattled on about ribbons and shopping for ribbons and thinking about what sort of ribbons she would design, had it been her business to do so. She asked that Cassandra write her in minute detail of any interesting ribbons she had seen in the London shops. After Lily had done examining the idea of ribbons, there was a lengthy paragraph on the decorating of a bonnet.

Cassandra might have thought the girl shallow to have written such a long letter on the subject of ribbons and bits and bobs, but she knew the Farnsworths to be a fine family financially strained. Poor Lily's father had inherited an estate badly managed and plagued with debt, and he'd made it his life to drag Farnsworth House out of that quagmire. He'd done a remarkable job, and put a respectable amount away for Lily's dowry, but there were not extra funds for much else. Lily was not in the habit of acquiring new dresses and bonnets, and so freshening up what she already owned consumed her imagination.

Cassandra was determined to bring home a basketful of interesting notions for Lilly so that she might refurbish to her heart's content.

The second letter was from Cassandra's father, and it contained all the usual news of the estate. The pigs did well on the new feed, the hunting dogs were in fine form, and her own dog, May, had shredded a volume of poetry, though the viscount did not suppose he would miss it. The viscount's views on poetry were scathing—he condemned those persons who puttered around all day attempting to pretty up the English language as a bunch of layabouts. The sun was the sun and if a gentleman were to agonize over whether or not he should call it a giant orb or some other nonsense, that gentleman ought to join Brummel on the continent. Mayhem, if she had done anything at all, had rid his sanctum of a book that should never have had the audacity to be there in the first place.

That idea was nothing less than what Cassandra would expect from her father. What was not expected was the news near the end of his letter.

You will hardly be surprised, I think, as you have made your opinion known on the gentleman, that Mr. Longmoore appears to have taken a bad turn. Some say it is his habit of too much drink, others say he must have been hit on the head. He's taken to talking to himself aloud on various street corners in town and they say his business does very badly as he is rarely there. Some of the lower elements of the neighborhood follow him into the Beef and Boar of an evening as he has got into the habit of buying ale all round. One wonders where he gets the money for such idiocy, as he does not tend to his business. Those that drink with him say he laments about a trickster's bad dealings with an innocent man and how our heavenly father will no doubt understand the innocent man's mistake. I am of the opinion that the fellow has lost his wits. I suppose we shall see how he gets on, though I expect things will only go downhill from here. (Once a rational mind is lost, it is not easily found again.)

They say too much drink can permanently addle the mind, and so for myself I stick to only six glasses of ale and three glasses of port a day to avoid the state.

Though Cassandra did hold a very low opinion of Mr. Longmoore, she was surprised at this turn of events. She had thought he would go on as he always had done—drinking to excess and importuning women. She had assumed at some point some woman would agree to his propositions, that lady likely to require the financial security of his situation and able to overlook absolutely everything else about Mr. Longmoore's person.

She supposed she ought to pity the man out of simple Christian charity. She was determined she ought to. Though, she understood it would take some work on her part to see her way clear to accomplishing such a thing—he was an oaf of a man.

Her father had ended his letter more cheerfully.

> *I do hope you get on with your aunt and do not cause her too much trouble, though I doubt you do, as you have never caused any trouble to me. Feel free to give those young bucks roaming London a good deal of trouble, as they have no doubt earned it somewhere in their lives.*

Cassandra smiled. She supposed she *had* given a young buck some trouble, though she'd not set out to do it. Of all people, her father would not be surprised at her interactions with Lord Hampton, though perhaps not wholly approving of her talking about her skill with a shotgun. Still, he would sympathize with how she had been provoked.

In any case, as gruff as her father could be, he was never harsh with his daughter. Her entire childhood had been one of racing up and down stairs and through rooms, breaking things as she went—the breaking of things only compounded when May came on the scene. Her father had watched the shattered porcelain and broken plates swept up in all good humor.

AS THE WORLD turned on its axis and the days and hours passed, whispers of a certain Miss Knightsbridge spread throughout London like a monstrous sea creature with endlessly growing tentacles. The whispers began below stairs and slithered their way up polished staircases and down carpeted passageways to the hushed sanctums of lady's bedchambers. From there, they hopped into carriages and skipped into drawing rooms, creating doppelgangers as they went, who then slipped into different carriages and made their way to new drawing rooms. One told one and two told four and four told eight and so on it went.

For those who knew each other well, the news was generally relayed forthrightly.

"Jemima, do come in. Have you heard the dreadful tale of Miss Knightsbridge?"

"Goodness, who has not? It appears she is the most determined flirt."

"Flirt? My dear, a mere flirt does not take the thing all the way to an engagement. At least three engagements, none sanctioned by her father, and she jilted in every one of them, all the while firing a shotgun at anything that moves."

"I did not realize it was as bad as that! I wonder she has the audacity to hold up her head."

"Appalling. There is no other word for it."

More distant acquaintances began the tale in a cautious manner. A lady might begin with something suitably vague such as, "Heavens, one hears such shocking things these days." Of course, the lady would be pressed to reveal the shocking thing, which she would invariably do, looking prettily shocked all the while.

Mamas everywhere were only too happy to hear of the ghastly story that was told in hushed whispers. After all, one less female out husband hunting was always to be celebrated. It was the general consensus that there *was* one less female out husband hunting, as who would take such a lady on?

Perhaps no end of gentlemen might have taken the lady on, but as with all rumors and innuendos, the story had grown in its scope and seriousness. There was even talk of Miss Knightsbridge having engaged herself to *five* different men at the same time, with her father none the wiser, and having shot at a farmer she did not like for her own amusement.

That the tentacles had wended their way through London was not surprising, nor was it surprising that the person named in the story and those closest to her remained unaware of it. After all, it would be bad form to repeat the story to the person it concerned, and everybody knew who was connected to who. The Blandings and the Sedways and certainly Lady Marksworth herself were to remain blissfully unaware that something was afoot. Miss Knightsbridge would be the very last to hear of it, as that was part of the grand tradition of unfounded gossip.

Nobody in Lady Marksworth's house had in the least noticed that invitations arriving at the door had begun to dwindle. Why would they, when so many invitations had already been received? A hostess did not wait until the last moment to secure her guests and so invitations to most of the season's events had been received and accepted long ago.

As it happened, no hostess had yet had the nerve to rescind an invitation already given to Lady Marksworth and Miss Knightsbridge. They would not know how to go about such a thing and, in any case, Lady Marksworth was not a figure to be trifled with. Most of the ladies simply hoped that the offending persons would leave London and not trouble them further.

That, of course, was impossible. The offending person and her close circle had not yet any idea they offended.

Chapter Six

Edwin had finally heard from Dalton in response to his note to put a halt to digging up gossip against Miss Knightsbridge. He could not say it was a satisfactory response, as it had only said, "You had best come and see me."

He supposed his friend would argue for going on with the scheme to cause talk about the lady, but Edwin was more determined than ever to put a stop to it.

Regardless of his opinions of Miss Knightsbridge, and those opinions had undergone a fairly radical transformation, it was not acceptable to toy with another's reputation in such a manner. He need only think of explaining the scheme to his grandmother to acknowledge the ungentlemanliness of it, the very lowness of it. The dowager had ever been his moral compass and while he could not always predict what she would say to a thing, he could very well predict it in this instance.

He had arrived at Dalton's house in all haste, in case the man was set on taking himself off to Surrey sometime soon. As he had dismounted his horse, he had surreptitiously glanced at Lady Marksworth's house across the street, looking for any flutter of curtains to say that his arrival had been noted. He saw nothing and forced himself not to ponder the notion that any in that house would ever understand what his current errand was about.

Bellamy admitted him and showed him into Dalton's library. One of the footmen came in with brandy, though it was well before noon. Edwin was beginning to think nobody in the house was acquainted with anything else. He could not remember ever being offered tea.

Hampton waved the fellow off just as Dalton entered the room.

"What now, Hampton," Dalton asked, "your feet turning cold?"

Edwin could only assume this was in reference to his request that they forgo the idea of damaging Miss Knightsbridge. "I should never have allowed the idea to go forward," he said. "In any case, it is fortunate that you decided to take yourself off to your father, rather than enact the scheme."

"My father?" Dalton asked. "Why would I visit that old rotter just now?"

"I do not claim to know… wait, you did not go to your father?"

"Not a bit of it," Dalton said, laughing.

"But Bellamy said—"

"Bellamy never says where I go. What sort of butler would he be?"

Edwin felt as if a block of lead was slowly settling in his stomach. "So then, you went to Surrey?"

"I did, and Tuttle has got a marvelous little document claiming Miss Knightsbridge was engaged to a local tradesman, but he broke it off. Can you guess why? It's too amusing, really. The tradesman, and two other fellows, all turned up to apply to the Viscount at the same time. They discovered one another and they all broke it off with Miss Knightsbridge."

Miss Knightsbridge involved in three engagements? One to a tradesman, no less? It could not be true. Aside from the unlikelihood of any lady engaging herself to three different gentlemen, the elements of the story itself were too convenient.

"Come now, Dalton," Edwin said. "You know that's a bit of fiction. Three gentlemen? Then they all conveniently turn up to see her father at the exact same moment? It's absurd. That sort of contrivance belongs on the stage."

"Possibly," Dalton said. "But the fellow swore an oath on it."

"Never mind what the fellow did," he said. "I am certain he was well paid for his story and it *is* a story. We must put an end to this nonsense at once."

"I am afraid it is too late for that," Dalton said. "It would be rather like closing the barn door after the horse has been out for hours. Tuttle was given his orders two days ago in Surrey."

"Good Lord, what have we done?" Edwin muttered.

Dalton clapped him on the arm. "All we've done is give the wags something to talk about. We don't do real damage to the lady. She will be known as having too many suitors, I suppose that is not any real crime."

"This is going to end badly," he said.

Dalton shrugged. "It was you, Grayson and Lockwood that came up with the idea. You know me well—once I am given a mission, I carry it out. If you did not want it accomplished so quickly, you should have asked Burke—he'd still be in his library making jokes and telling stories about his ridiculous cook."

"Come now, Dalton, you can recall Tuttle from his work, I am certain of it."

Lord Dalton picked up a sheet of paper from his desk. "I do not claim to understand Mr. Tuttle's methods, but he is all efficiency. Along with a shocking bill, he writes that the story has taken flight and no more need be done by him."

"Blast," Edwin said.

Dalton crossed his arms and surveyed his friend. "You seem to take an inordinate amount of interest in Miss Knightsbridge's reputation. A *suspicious* amount of interest."

"There is nothing suspicious in it, I assure you," Edwin said hurriedly. "I simply do not like that we act in a less than gentlemanly manner."

"Well if that's all it is," Lord Dalton said, "I would not worry your head over it. Nobody will know we had anything to do with it, Tuttle has seen to that."

⋙⋘

EDWIN HAD LEFT Dalton in a daze. He carried a deep sense of shame from the house and it was a feeling he was not accustomed to. He had done things in the past that he'd considered not quite right, but this! To be part of such a low scheme! And why? Because his pride had been stung. It had been childish and not worthy of a gentleman.

The only bright spot in the whole thing was that he was certain if he just had time to think of a solution, he would find a solution.

He'd sat all evening in his library, Havoc happily gnawing on his boot, as he thought of possible actions he might take. At least he'd *tried* to think of actions he might take. That none occurred to him had come as a shock—no matter how badly a thing unfolded, there was always something that might be attempted. His shock began to fade as he considered the nature of slander and gossip. It was an enemy that could not be caught. It wafted through the air invisible and all that could be seen of it were those who had been laid waste by it. It could not be subdued, nor struck down, nor chained. In that way, it was more deadly than any Napoleon.

Miss Knightsbridge was about to encounter a disaster she had not earned, and he was the author of it. It was unlikely anybody would ever discover he was behind the stories told of her, but what matter? He would know it, and it would sit on his shoulders like an uncomfortable friend.

But then, the story Dalton had related, an engagement to three gentlemen and one of them a tradesman to boot, was so outlandish. Might it not be taken as such and dismissed by all who heard it?

Edwin's mood was buoyed by the idea, though the feeling did not last. It was just as likely that various gossipers would glory in the tale and gleefully embellish it. Only last year, Prinny had been reported on his deathbed when in fact he'd been jolly at the theater and Lady Cattrail was reported to have left her husband when she'd only gone off to care for a sick niece.

As the moon hung full outside of his window, he was forced to conclude that Miss Knightsbridge would not come through unscathed.

The only question left was what he could do about it.

Lady Montague's ball was on the morrow, and if ever there was a condemning woman it was her. If Lady Marksworth and Miss Knightsbridge remained unaware of the tale that swirled around them, they might just attend and find it out there.

Edwin did not see how to stop it, but he was determined to go and do what he could.

CASSANDRA FINALLY HAD the determination to challenge Peggy on which dress she would wear. She had been decided on wearing a cream silk with lovely rose-colored flowers embroidered around the hem. Peggy had been equally determined on the white satin with a pale-yellow gauze overlay, going so far as to claim the cream dress had been mysteriously misplaced.

After a half hour of arguing that dresses do not fly off on their own and then finally hinting that if the dress had really disappeared, Peggy would be responsible for it, the cream-colored gown had been produced.

Peggy had not accepted defeat with any sort of grace and for the hundredth time Cassandra thought she was the most confounded girl alive. She was certain other people did not wrestle with their maids in such a fashion.

Nevertheless, she was in the cream with the pink rosettes and in the carriage, on her way to the Montagues' ball.

"Lord Montague is a friendly enough fellow," Lady Marksworth said, "though Lady Montague is a bit of a beast."

"A beast?" Cassandra asked.

"Do not be frightened by her," Lady Marksworth said. "I knew her as Miss Harriet Wellburne in our youth. She was forever putting herself forward as the arbiter of how one should go about things, a bit of a prig, actually. I remember her whispering all over town about poor Miss Jumble and that lady's lack of a wardrobe. It was Harriet's opinion that if one could not afford a suitable range of attire, one should not come for the season."

Cassandra felt very badly for Miss Jumble, as the lady reminded her very much of her friend Lily Farnsworth. Poor Lily thought a new ribbon would mask an old dress, but Cassandra supposed that was not to be when one entered the confines of London.

"Do not pity Miss Jumble, however," Lady Marksworth said. "She is the Duchess of Somerston now and can have as many dresses as she likes."

"The Duchess of Somerston?" Cassandra said, both glad and amused. "Is that not Lord Burke's mother?"

"Just so," Lady Marksworth said. "For all Harriet's complaining on the subject, Miss Jumble's very modest wardrobe did not show her to disadvantage. She was a darling girl and the duke could not have cared less about her dresses."

Cassandra was much cheered by the tale and would be sure to tell it to Lily Farnsworth. Though, she did feel a flutter of nerves to encounter a woman such as Lady Montague, despite Miss Jumble's success.

"As for Harriet and I, when I discovered she was impugning Miss Jumble's right to a season, I told her in no uncertain terms that she'd gone wrong. I am not so certain she has ever forgiven me for that. Though we both invite each other to large parties, I have never been asked to dine here, nor have I asked *her* to Marksworth House."

"Goodness," Cassandra said.

"Never mind," Lady Marksworth said. "It is the way of the world. One may not adore all of the *ton,* but they're what we've got and so we must make the best of it. What else are we to do? Sail to Massachusetts and have tea with some awful Americans?"

Cassandra did not know, but she wondered if awful Americans might be a deal less frightening than Lady Montague.

THE MONTAGUES' BALL was to be a large one, but unlike the other large events they had attended, Cassandra and Lady Marksworth did not sit overlong in their carriage. As far as Cassandra could tell, it was not because there were less carriages lined up, but because the footmen were many and moved with military precision. She supposed Lady Montague would not tolerate anything less than perfection.

They were helped down in good time and entered the house. Ahead of her, Cassandra could see the great Lady Montague herself. She was a regal-looking woman, wearing an intimidatingly high silk turban sprouting ostrich feathers. The headdress helped her appear seven feet tall; her expression was one of condescension, as if to say, "How fortunate you must feel to have been granted leave to enter my house."

Lady Marksworth handed over her invitation. The butler intoned, "Lady Marksworth and Miss Knightsbridge."

There was a sudden hush around Cassandra that she could not account for at all. Lady Montague looked down her rather long and thin nose. She curtly nodded and then turned away.

Cassandra heard her aunt say, "Goodness, Harriet, you might smile."

As they passed the lady into the hall, Cassandra noted that Lady

Montague pressed her lips into a hard, thin line upon hearing the comment. In fact, she appeared rather incensed. How extraordinary that the two ladies should maintain such a long-standing frostiness to do with poor Miss Jumble all those years ago.

CASSANDRA HAD GOT her card, and then been very happy to hand it over to Lord Burke for the first. Though he was such a genial gentleman, she got the impression that he might be somewhat under the weather. He looked more serious than was his usual mien.

Cassandra's dance card filled up quickly, though she could not help but notice the glances she received from some of the other ladies. Why did they stare so? She surreptitiously checked her dress to ensure there was no stain or tear, but it looked well. Could it be jealousy? She did not see why it should be so, she was by no means the beauty of the evening and there were certainly enough gentlemen to go round.

Though she had been surprised at the looks she received, she was even more surprised to see Lord Hampton make his way to her so determinedly, and then take the dance before supper. He had filled in his name quickly and then departed with all haste.

She might even say the lord had looked embarrassed to see her again. She supposed she felt the same—she had thought it lucky that they had hit on the welcome subject of dogs at the Sedways' dinner, but now she began to wonder what other topic might take its place. Certainly, they could not return to talking of dogs—she was rather afraid everything that could be said on the subject had been said.

On the other hand, she felt strangely pleased that he would take her into supper. Or, if not pleased, then something she could not exactly identify. Some hint of nerves, she supposed.

The opening of the ball had not passed as Cassandra expected. She had looked forward to Lord Burke's amusing tales of his cook, but he told none. She had initially suspected he was under the weather and now she was certain that was the case. He was very subdued and not joking at all. She thought it a recommendation of his character that, feeling as poorly as he must, he was so entirely solicitous of her. He inquired how she did, and then nodded gravely when she said she did quite well.

After the first, she was led round the ballroom floor by a variety of gentlemen she had not encountered before. She did not know if these new gentlemen were all friends, and therefore in the habit of landing on the same subjects, but down to a man they were all remarkably interested in Surrey. Was she indeed from that county? What sort of society did she keep there? How did Miss Knightsbridge spend her time there? Was she fond of horses? What did she think of the shooting in Surrey?

She had answered all of their questions, careful to leave out any penchant for riding Juno like the wind on an early morning ride or standing by her father while he taught her how to handle a fowling piece.

She had nearly lost her patience with Mr. Mumsford.

"I only wonder, Miss Knightsbridge, how you find the general company in Surrey?"

Good Lord. He had already asked if she had many acquaintances there and if the gentlemen to be found in that neighborhood were amusing.

"The company is pleasant," Cassandra said.

"I suppose the shooting is very good?"

And here they were back to shooting, a topic touched on twice already.

In the end, she felt all of the gentlemen had read the same book on making casual conversation at a ball, and it was not a very interesting book.

Her dance with Lord Hampton had felt as if they went back in time. He was just as grave and silent as he had been at the Bergrams' ball. This time, however, she did not press him to speak. She had been speaking all night and had not the least inclination to discuss Surrey one more time.

Lord Hampton led her into supper amongst looks all around. Cassandra supposed that was to be expected—all eyes were perennially trained on the gentlemen of the pact.

After a long silence, the lord said, "Forgive me, I have not even asked the most civil of questions. How do you do this evening, Miss Knightsbridge?"

"Very well, my lord," she said, relieved he had chosen to say anything at all. "I presume you have fared well since the Sedways' dinner?"

"Well enough," Hampton said. "I wonder, how do you find London these days?"

How did she find London? How *was* she to find London? It was as it ever was, she supposed.

"Town is of course different from home, though it is welcome in its own way," she said. It was a nonsensical answer to a rather nonsensical question.

"Home, yes, Surrey," Lord Hampton said quietly.

"Indeed, Surrey," she said, confounded by the near constant allusions to Surrey this night. Seeing that it would be she who must find a subject to engage, and having had time to think about it and not coming up with anything other than dogs, she said, "As we did speak of kennels at our last meeting, I wonder, my lord, if you have given any thought to this latest idea of using fountains for drinking water, rather than troughs?"

"Ah," Lord Hampton said, seeming to shake off his gloom, "Bedford's idea. He thinks the circulation of the water keeps it uncontaminated. I am inclined to agree."

"I, too," Cassandra said. She noted that the couples around her had gone silent, as if they listened to her conversation. She could not say that she wished all and sundry to hear her views on a dog's water fountain, but neither was she willing to allow the conversation to lapse into silence again.

She said, "I have spoken to my father about it and he agrees, though it will be a large project to endeavor."

Lord Hampton was silent for a moment and Cassandra noted that he stared hard at a gentleman across from him until that gentleman turned away. Finally, he said, "I have in my possession written plans on how it may be accomplished in a kennel already built. Lord Trebly is most welcome to them."

And so they went on, speaking of kennels and their design. She did not know if the lord had any other interests, but if he did, she did not know what they were.

There were moments when the lord seemed to forget himself. In those moments, Lord Hampton appeared at his ease. She supposed it was the way he looked at home, surrounded by his family, or sitting in front of a fire in his library.

It was a deal more attractive than his original stiff way of going on. In truth, it was *very* attractive. It would be all too easy to forget the pact, though she made a concerted effort to remember it. There had been something in imagining the lord at ease in his house that had caused that now familiar soft shiver to run down her spine, as if a light touch traced it.

EDWIN LEFT THE Montagues' in a fury. It was all too obvious what had occurred. Dalton's ridiculous story had made the rounds thoroughly.

He'd noted the various ladies staring at Miss Knightsbridge, like so many cobras ready to strike. Dressed in silk and pretty they might be, but poisonous all the same.

He'd noted the gentlemen who filled up Miss Knightsbridge's card. Those gentlemen were, with the exception of Burke, the type who would find amusement in going to their club the next day and describing their encounter with the Miss Knightsbridge everybody talked of. Burke, at least, he thought he could trust not to be so callow. In truth, Burke had seemed more serious that was his usual wont, and Edwin got the idea he'd heard the rumor and was displeased by it. For all Burke's levity, he was a practical and well-meaning gentleman and was unlikely to put much stock in the story. Edwin would be ashamed for Burke to discover how the rumor had begun.

He'd noted Lady Montague's glare at Lady Marksworth when the lady's back was turned and considered it lucky she and her charge were even let in the door. Lady Montague was an ill-tempered and opinionated creature, and if anybody would have had the temerity to refuse them entrance, it would have been her.

He'd taken the dance before supper to send a message—whatever talk went round, Miss Knightsbridge was not shunned by a gentleman who would someday be a duke. He'd never been in the habit of flaunting his standing, but in that instance, he felt it might serve well.

At dinner, he could hardly think what to say. His shame at the coming storm was too deep and cut him like a sharpened sword. The lady had gamely suggested fountains and he found it a subject he could speak on without much concentration. Though, he could not ignore the unnatural silence around him. Everybody wished to overhear what Miss Knightsbridge would say. How else would they have something to repeat in the morning?

My God, when would she discover what was being said? *How* would she discover it?

It was bound to be some sort of public humiliation.

He wondered if he should not write an anonymous note and send it to Lady Marksworth to give them warning.

But what then? Would the lady whisk her niece back to Surrey?

Was that wise? He could not be certain whether Miss Knightsbridge would be better served to disappear or stand firm in front of the thing. He did not know if she would be better served to know it or go on oblivious. To return home might be to validate all that had been said. To know it might cause her to do just that, or if not flee, then wear her feelings on her sleeve. Any sign of weakness would be as a deer to a wolf, and the *ton's* predatory instincts would lead them to go in for the kill. If she went on as she did now, might she weather it? Might there be another story about another person that would capture society's imagination?

How to unsay what was being said? Though he had thought long and hard and come up with nothing, he felt he must do something. They must all do something.

He resolved to call a meeting of the gentleman of the pact. Six heads were better than one, even if some of them were blockheads. They must do something for Miss Knightsbridge.

My God, they were to be dukes of the realm someday. They had responsibilities. They must show themselves to be above reproach, not the sort of base creatures who put their own comfort above all else. As the whole world had seen, a nobility forgetting those things was a nobility violently ended.

Edwin paused. Perhaps that was it. Perhaps that was the idea that would spur his friends to action—a reminiscence of what had happened in France.

As he thought of it, Edwin began to develop what might be a persuasive argument. At least, he hoped so. It was the only idea he'd had so far.

THE BREAKFAST ROOM was filled with sunlight. It was perhaps the cheeriest of Lady Marksworth's rooms—it had none of the formality of the public rooms nor any of the restraint of the carefully composed decorations of the bedchambers. It had the friendly feel of dark wood and worn cushions that reminded Cassandra of home.

"I am certain tongues will be wagging today," Lady Marksworth said.

"Are you, aunt?" Cassandra asked. "What will have captured the *ton's* imagination this time?"

"My dear," Lady Marksworth said, "did you not note the looks when Lord Hampton took you into dinner? People positively stared."

Cassandra began to feel uneasy. People *had* stared.

"I do not wonder at it," Lady Marksworth said. "Here is Lord Hampton taking Miss Knightsbridge into dinner for the second time."

Cassandra wrinkled her brow. "But surely nobody who was not in attendance would know that Lord Hampton took me in at the Sedways'."

"*Everybody* who was not in attendance would know it. Little remains unknown in this town, my dear."

"Well, if they did know it, they would certainly know that at a dinner it is the hostess who directs such things."

"I suspect that fact has been conveniently put aside," Lady Marksworth said. "The looks you received last evening were too marked to be ignored. In any case, it was entirely the lord's choice last night, and he chose *you*. Of course, it will be remarked on."

Cassandra *had* wondered why Lord Hampton had taken her in, but she had decided the lord wished to secure himself a dinner partner who was not in the least a danger in regard to the pact. Whatever the reason, she could not be comfortable in the idea that her name was mentioned in somebody's drawing room, and certainly not in any conversation to do with the pact.

"Do not look so grieved, Cassandra. Many a girl would welcome the idea that she has been noticed."

Many a girl might, but Cassandra Knightsbridge did not. Her

cheeks were pink just thinking of it.

Or, perhaps her cheeks were pink because she realized she had not been suitably unhappy to be escorted into dinner by Lord Hampton. He was inscrutable, and not the easiest gentleman to converse with, and they had far too many awkward moments. And yet, she had not been entirely unhappy.

She found it was becoming hard to resist gazing upon that handsome face when it did not condemn her. When he spoke at ease, he was interesting and interested. She very much would have wished to have such a brother.

Cassandra paused her runaway thoughts. It would not do to lie to herself. A gentle fib, perhaps, but not an outright lie. When she looked upon Lord Hampton, she did not see a brother. When she heard the timbre of his voice, she did not hear a brother. He did not, on occasion, stare into her eyes like a brother.

CHAPTER SEVEN

THE GENTLEMEN OF the pact had convened at Lord Dalton's house once more, by the urgent request of Lord Hampton. Aside from Dalton, the rest of the men looked uncomfortable. Sheepish, even.

Edwin had no trouble divining why—they all would have heard the circulating rumors by now, and how wildly those rumors had grown. Worse, he'd been sent a copy of a satirical print by his sister. She'd thought it amusing, but would like to know who it was about, as she remained in Derbyshire and was not privy to all the London talk.

The print depicted a young lady on a rearing horse, aiming a fowling piece at three gentlemen flying overhead.

Edwin laid the print on the table and said, "We have done this. It will not be a week before the lady's initials are in print too."

Cabot tented his fingers and said, "Nobody ever knows the meaning of the initials. At least, not usually."

"Ah, yes," Ashworth said. "That is true."

"There might be no end of ladies with the same initials," Grayson said.

Edwin had thought the men would attempt to rationalize their crime. It was the way of men and their deeds—an awful thing must be bargained down to manageable proportions. They had done it in the war, they had done it as children telling a lie to avoid trouble. He'd done it himself when first this blasted idea had been discussed. There was only one way round such an inclination, and the only idea he'd had so far—appeal to their finer natures and their care for their own necks.

"Before we enumerate all the reasons we have *not* injured Miss Knightsbridge," Edwin said, "let me point out the obvious. We have, and there is further damage yet to come. I do not believe the lady or her friends are even aware of the rumors, but they will be."

He noticed some squirming around the table and that was well. A gentleman who could not help shifting in his chair had just heard an idea that stung with the uncomfortable ring of truth.

Now, he would roll the dice on a gamble. "Further, gentlemen," he said, "we have unknowingly caused a far greater danger to ourselves in going on with this scheme."

"To us?" Grayson asked.

"What danger can there be to us?" Ashworth asked. "Even if we are known to have taken the shot, it was Miss Knightsbridge herself who provided the gun."

"That sworn statement from Longbottom or Longmoore or whatever name he calls himself is absolute rubbish and you all know it," Edwin said.

"Still," Cabot muttered, "it is sworn. That is on his head, not ours."

"And that is where you have gone so far wrong in your thinking," Edwin said. "You believe your rank protects you, but it does nothing of the sort—it exposes you. Think of how the common people will consider it when they hear of six men to be dukes of England who have sunk so low as to malign a young lady for their own amusement. Six gentlemen who have paid off a scoundrel to swear to a lie."

"It wasn't amusement," Ashworth said. "We wanted people to turn from talking of us to somebody else. *You* suggested her."

Dalton laughed. "Come now, Hampton," he said. "The thing won't be traced back to us."

"You think not?" Edwin said. "Were you her father, might you not have this Longmoore fellow hauled in front of you? Of *course* the whole scheme will come out in time. Though, whatever the viscount thinks to do about it will be nothing compared to the butcher and baker down the road."

"We are now to worry ourselves over what a baker or butcher thinks of us?" Cabot said.

"You had better," Edwin said darkly. "If there is one stupid thing you ought not be guilty of, it is ignoring what has gone before. Do you think the noblemen of France had a care for the baker's opinion? Not until the baker was happy to watch their heads roll on the guillotine."

The gentlemen at the table fairly recoiled at the idea. It was a thought that every man and woman with any sort of rank had considered in the dark hours of the night, though the idea was little discussed for fear of bringing it to life.

Englishmen prided themselves on being ever so much more civilized than the French. It could not happen here. And yet, might not it? Might there not come a time when commoners decided they did not care a fig who inherited what title and land from who? Might they not sit up one day and take a hard look at the Regent and his profligate spending and appetites? Might there not come a time when tenants simply decided not to pay their rents?

When would they all know when such a thing had begun to take hold? Would they be out one day, and some person would call them mister, rather than my lord? Or worse—citizen.

The Americans, and then the French, had sent a chilling message through the great houses of England and the continent—the privileged served at the pleasure of the common man. When the common man decided, *en masse,* that they preferred not to be ruled, the rule was ended.

"To be seen as abusing our power is to invite comment and scrutiny," Edwin said. "We, of all men in England, must act above reproach. We have not done so in this case."

Lockwood, who had so far been silent, said, "I have nothing against Miss Knightsbridge, but what's done is done. In any case, we hardly need worry that your baker is poised to storm our estates."

"No," Edwin said. "Not today. But let me ask all of you—if your doors were stormed, what defenses do you have? The days of moats and murder holes and personal armies are long gone. The truth is, your houses would fall in less time than it takes for tea."

Nobody countered that idea, as they all knew it to be true. They'd left their estates in the hands of their aged fathers and aged butlers and middle-aged stewards. Footmen were many, but not likely to risk their own person. It would not take ten determined men to seize control of any of their properties.

"We retain our privileges because all of England thinks it is right we do so. Or, if they do not feel that, they do not feel the sort of hatred that would galvanize them into action. If they ever have cause to change their minds, we will be helpless against it. We had better start acting as if we deserve such a courtesy. Revolutions do not occur because a man is run through with a sword, they begin because too many men have suffered a thousand small cuts. Do not let this circumstance become one of the cuts."

"All right, Hampton," Dalton said. "You've gone and painted a dire picture; we all regret poor Miss Knightsbridge and hope the local baker is not just now poisoning our bread. But what are we to do about it?"

"The only thing we can do about it," Hampton said. "We will aim to fill Miss Knightsbridge's dance card. We will engage her in conversation. We will speak to others of our admiration of the lady. We will conduct ourselves as if in a military campaign. We will send the clear message that whatever the world may think, *we* hold the lady in esteem. Mamas everywhere have very high hopes for their daughters just now, and they will stop their tongues if they believe they cross us."

One by one, the men nodded in agreement. The growing resolve on their features gave Hampton every confidence that they would carry out his idea. Even Dalton, who of them all might be considered the least worried over a murderous baker, was engaged.

⸻

CASSANDRA HAD RARELY been on horseback since she'd come to town. She'd been carried here and there in one of Lady Marksworth's well-appointed carriages and had begun to feel very much like a bird in a cage, looking out the bars and yearning to take flight. Now, though, she'd convinced her aunt to allow her to ride in Hyde Park.

While Lady Marksworth had been convinced, she'd not thrown all caution to the wind. The lady followed her niece in a barouche with the top down and there were two grooms besides. Cassandra, having become more closely acquainted with her aunt's modes of thinking, had broached the subject in a way she could not have devised when she'd first arrived. In those early days, she had mentioned fresh air and the glories of riding. This time, she'd mentioned her new riding habit and how many people they were likely to meet in the park. Her aunt's goal was to see her well-settled, and so thoughts of her niece in a charming blue velvet riding habit, out and about for everybody to admire, had tipped the scales in favor of the scheme.

It was wondrous to be on horseback again, to be in absolute control of one's direction. That the horse she sat upon did not equal Juno, Cassandra could not deny. Juno's sire was a fleet and agile Arabian and her dam a steady Cleveland Bay. She was by turns strong and fast, and her temperament made her ready to seize any challenge in front of her.

The horse Cassandra rode now, Butternut, was as her name would suggest—calm to the point of lazy and far too fond of her oats. Nobody would bother with a gallop on Butternut, particularly not Butternut herself. Cassandra supposed that was one of the reasons her aunt approved of the horse so thoroughly—Butternut had never done an irrational or speedy thing in her life and was not likely to begin now. Still, she *was* a horse, if only barely.

The only thing that disappointed Cassandra, aside from Butternut's staid progress, was that the park was so crowded. Blessedly, many of the carriages they passed contained ladies happening to look in the other direction, otherwise she was certain they would be forever stopping.

Always attuned to everything around her when she rode, Cassandra heard the distinct sounds of a gallop behind her. She turned her head in time to see Mr. Conners wheel in his horse. He was one of the gentlemen she had danced with at the Montagues' ball and she supposed he would pay his respects. Cassandra only hoped he had finally thought of something to say that was more interesting than inquiring about Surrey.

"Hey Ho, Miss Knightsbridge," he called. "What's say we race to the gate? I'll put twenty pounds on it."

Cassandra was momentarily taken aback. Was it the custom to make such jokes? Certainly, it *was* a joke, as nobody would think poor old Butternut up to doing anything so outrageous. Cassandra herself would not think to do anything so outrageous. Perhaps in Surrey, on Juno and challenged by an intimate acquaintance, but with a near-stranger in Hyde Park? It was unthinkable.

Lady Marksworth did not appear to see the humor in the joke. "Sir?" she asked. Though it was one word, it was said in a tone containing so much condemnation that Cassandra perceived instantly that what Mr. Conners had just proposed bordered on insult.

Before Mr. Conners could answer Lady Marksworth's one-word inquiry, Cassandra spotted Lord Hampton galloping toward them.

She felt a flutter at seeing him so, he sat on his fine Bay with such confidence and skill. She could almost envision him galloping across a field and into battle.

Lord Hampton reached them and reined in his horse. He tipped his hat to Cassandra and Lady Marksworth.

"Hampton, my good fellow!" Mr. Conners said.

Though he said it as if the two gentlemen were longstanding friends, Cassandra did not see an equal amount of familiarity on the lord's side. Lord Hampton only nodded.

"I was just challenging Miss Knightsbridge to a race to the gate, I wagered twenty pounds. Should you like to join in? Jolly good fun, eh?"

Lady Marksworth coldly stared at Mr. Conners. Lord Hampton looked infuriated. Now, Cassandra had no doubt that Mr. Conners sought to insult her. But why? What had she ever done to the gentleman? She had only suffered through a dance with him and if he had noted that she suffered, it might have taught him to become more amusing, rather than seeking to insult his victim.

"I would have a word," Lord Hampton said to Mr. Conners. The lord took the reins from Mr. Conners' hands and led him away from the carriage.

Cassandra looked toward her aunt, but Lady Marksworth still had her gaze locked on Mr. Conners. Cassandra could not hear what the two men spoke of, but could see that whatever it was, Mr. Conners did very little of the speaking. The one phrase she did hear was the last one. She was certain Lord Hampton had said, "Now clear off," before dropping Mr. Conners' reins.

For Mr. Conners' part, he spurred his horse and cantered away without taking his leave. Lord Hampton watched him go and then turned his own horse and trotted over to the carriage.

"Lady Marksworth, Miss Knightsbridge, I would apologize for my uncouth acquaintance."

Lady Marksworth softened at the sentiment. "We are glad to see you, Lord Hampton. It seems absolutely anybody might wander round the park bothering people these days."

Lord Hampton nodded and said, "I will escort you on your way to ensure that none of Mr. Conners' friends are so inclined to harass."

At that, they made their way forward. Lord Hampton was silent, as was Cassandra. It was fortunate that Lady Marksworth was not so afflicted and nattered on about where society was going when young bucks took such liberties.

Cassandra was far too busy trying to work out what Mr. Conners had thought he was about. Was it really because he noted that she was not delighted with his conversation at the Montagues' ball? It was a frightening thought, especially if there were other gentlemen who might think to insult her if they felt themselves affronted by her lack of interest. There might well be—Lord Hampton had cautioned against the gentleman's friends.

But then, she was certain she had not shown her true feelings when Mr. Conners had asked her no end of questions about Surrey. She had been quite civil. At least, she thought she had been.

Finding herself unwilling to remain in the dark on such a matter, Cassandra said, "My Lord, is Mr. Conners in the habit of proposing such ludicrous things to ladies he hardly knows?"

Lord Hampton had taken time with his answer, and finally said, "I cannot claim to know his habits, Miss Knightsbridge. I am only very casually acquainted with him. Though, having witnessed it, I will make it my business to be less acquainted with him."

It did not give Cassandra any real answer, but she found she was much complimented by the idea that the lord would cut Mr. Conners on account of an insult to herself. In truth, she was admiring of the way Lord Hampton had handled the entire situation. He had been masterful, and a lady could not be oblivious when a gentleman stepped in on her behalf.

"I applaud you, Lord Hampton," Lady Marksworth said. "It's all well and good to allow a mister or missus into one's sphere, but only if they can conduct themselves creditably in civil society. We lords and ladies must lead the way and set the example."

Lord Hampton seemed particularly struck by the idea and softly said, "Indeed, we must."

A clatter of hooves behind Cassandra made her turn her head, almost dreading that it might be Mr. Conners' friends. Instead, she saw Lord Lockwood and Lord Ashworth.

While she was glad it was not to be some other gentleman challenging her to a race, she found herself slightly alarmed to be in the company of three of the gentlemen of the pact.

The two men very civilly greeted her and Lady Marksworth. Lord Hampton said, "I was just escorting Lady Marksworth and Miss Knightsbridge. I discovered Mr. Conners acting less than a gentleman."

The three men exchanged looks between them that Cassandra could not divine the meaning of.

Lord Lockwood said, "We might all have a mind to escort Miss Knightsbridge, if Lady Marksworth is not opposed."

Cassandra knew her aunt could not be less opposed to anything. Lady Marksworth said, "We should be delighted to have your company, my lords. Though, we are nearly at the gate."

"We should not mind going all the way to Marksworth House, should we not, gentlemen?" Lord Ashworth asked.

The gentlemen all nodded as if this were the most usual thing in the world. Lady Marksworth appeared delighted. Cassandra turned her head to hide her face. What they proposed was extraordinary. It was as if she retained her own cavalry. It had not gone unnoticed, either.

Every carriage they passed contained people looking fairly agog at their progress.

What was the meaning of it? Why should the three gentlemen escort them to her aunt's house? Further, what should they do when they arrived? Invite them all in for tea?

She noticed, as she pondered it, that the three gentlemen had placed themselves into some kind of formation. Lords Lockwood and Ashworth rode ahead on either side, while Lord Hampton rode behind her.

Cassandra blushed. She might be a queen for all the care that was being taken. But why?

It sometimes felt constraining to keep oneself in the realm of polite conversation, and it certainly did at the moment. If she could have had her way, Cassandra would have said, "Gentlemen, what is the meaning of this? What is it you do?"

She could not say such a thing and was forced to ride forward as if this situation were not at all strange. That it *was* strange was evidenced by the various looks of passerby. Cassandra dearly hoped it would not lead to any unfortunate gossip.

Riding through the streets of London felt as if she were in the midst of some embarrassing procession. There was not much spoken, and the men appeared almost grim. It was only Lady Marksworth who seemed to enjoy the journey.

Though Cassandra had worried over what was to be done when they arrived at the house, she need not have. Lady Marksworth thanked the gentlemen for their consideration with such an air of finality that they tipped their hats and trotted off.

Now, she and her aunt sat in Lady Marksworth's charming sitting room, warming themselves in front of the fire. As genial as the weather had been, the early evening had grown damp and cold.

"Aunt," Cassandra said carefully, "were you not surprised at Mr. Conners' audacity? Have you ever seen such before? And why would Lord Hampton mention Mr. Conners' friends? Do they all conduct themselves in such a manner?"

"Goodness," Lady Marksworth said, "that is a lot of questions. Yes, I was very surprised by Mr. Conners. On the other hand, I do not know the gentleman or his friends, nor do I wish to. I cannot say how they all conduct themselves or whether they are in the habit of such nonsense. People such as that may have gathered up enough coin to look the gentleman, but not enough sense to act as one."

"I just thought it odd that Lord Hampton, and Lords Lockwood and Ashworth too, would view it in so serious a light as to escort us all the way home. It was as if they knew something that we did not. That there might be some further danger there, aside from the insult of Mr. Conners' suggestion."

"I had not viewed it in such a light," Lady Markswroth said. She smiled and said, "You do realize that gentlemen may pretend all sorts of things when looking to converse with a pretty face."

"But they did not converse much," Cassandra said, pressing on.

"Ah well," Lady Marksworth said, pouring the tea, "a young gentleman often wishes to converse, and then finds his nerves getting the best of him."

Cassandra did not think any of those lords prone to nerves. Certainly, Lord Hampton was no worried flower.

"There were such looks at us as we passed," Cassandra said. "It felt as if we made an unnecessary scene of it. I am afraid people will talk."

"Of course, they will talk," Lady Marksworth said. "Miss Knightsbridge escorted by three of the lords of the pact? You will be the talk of every drawing room. Really, Cassandra, you must become accustomed to receiving attention."

Though Cassandra knew herself to be, in general, averse to attention of that sort, she felt there was something even more worrying about what had occurred in the park. Something she did not rightly understand. There had been some undercurrent of over-seriousness that rankled. Mr. Conners' proposed race to the gate had been ludicrous and insulting, but when did ludicrous and insulting require an escort of three men? She only hoped the entire circumstance would be forgotten by all by the next sunrise, and that she never encountered Mr. Conners again.

Chapter Eight

THE FOLLOWING MORNING, as they sat at their usual window seat, Cassandra wondered what ailed Sybil. They had grown so accustomed to one another that her friend's demeanor felt markedly changed.

Lady Marksworth had gone out, and Racine had delivered a tea fit for a queen and resplendent with fairy cakes and almond biscuits. Cassandra knew Sybil had a particular weakness for almond biscuits. She had asked for them specially, and yet her friend had touched neither tea nor biscuit. So far, Sybil had spent more time staring out the window or over Cassandra's head than anything else.

"Come now," Cassandra said. "I feel last evening must not have been to your liking. What happened at your dinner at the Smythes'?"

"Happened?" Sybil said in a nervous tone of voice. "Why should anything have happened?"

"Sybil," Cassandra said, clasping her hands, "we are comrades in arms, remember? We go into battle together. You do not seem comfortable just now and you have not touched a biscuit—Racine will feel it a heavy blow if you do not enjoy them. Now do tell me what troubles you."

Sybil quietly sighed and said, "As it happens, I had a very strange conversation at the Smythes' dinner. Mr. Richards asked me if I were acquainted with Miss Knightsbridge. I said you were known to me very well, and then he said I ought not to continue the acquaintance on account of the three gentlemen."

"Three gentlemen?" Cassandra asked.

"Precisely what I said," Sybil said. "Then Lord Burke interrupted us and told Mr. Richards, strongly I might add, that he talked as much as an old woman and he better stop where he was. Mr. Richards turned red as an apple and moved to the other side of the room."

"And what did Lord Burke say then?"

"Nothing," Sybil said. "He would say nothing more about it other than Mr. Richards was an old woman."

Before Cassandra could properly think through what Sybil had said, a street urchin stopped in front of the house and boldly smiled at them through the wrought iron fence. He stared in quite a determined and challenging manner, and Cassandra wondered if she should call a footman to chase him off. In a moment, the boy took something from his pocket and hurled it over the fence at one of the windows.

The glass from a window on the far side of the room shattered and scattered across the rug. Racine rushed in at the noise and stared at the window.

"It was a boy," Cassandra said, gathering her wits over the sudden shock, "he's just run down the road!"

Racine hurried from the room to galvanize his footmen and it was only seconds before Jimmy and Ben raced from the house in pursuit.

Cassandra rose and stepped carefully around the broken glass to the object that had been thrown. It was a rock, covered in paper secured with twine. She picked it up.

"Do leave it alone, Cass," Sybil said from the window seat.

Cassandra untied the twine and removed the paper from around the rock, smoothing it out.

She stared at it, trying to work out what she looked at or why somebody would throw it through her aunt's window. It was an illustration of a lady on horseback, raising a shotgun at three gentlemen floating in a cloudless sky.

"Really, Cass," Sybil said, her voice frightened, "there may be poison on it or something equally dangerous about it."

In a moment, Cassandra perceived what she saw. The lady was herself. Someone at the table at the Bergrams' ball had repeated her claim to having used a shotgun. That, combined with the three lords' escort of her out of Hyde Park and through London, had been enough to compose the scene.

"There is poison here, to be sure," Cassandra said. "Just not the sort to damage one's physical person." She carried it to the window seat, careful to step around the broken glass, and showed it to Sybil.

Sybil stared at it, then looked up. "What does it mean? I do not understand it at all."

"The lady is meant to be me. I did not mention, because I wished to forget, that during my initial encounter with Lord Hampton I was rather provoked and owned to having shot bird on my father's estate. Clearly, I was overheard."

Sybil laughed, though it was rather a small laugh. "Cass, shooting? Why should you say such a thing?"

"Because it is true, though I need not have laid claim to it."

Sybil considered the idea for a moment. She said, "Taking up a shotgun is unusual, to be sure. Though, if your claim of shooting birds is the cause of this, why should the birds in the illustration be three gentlemen? Are they the three gentlemen mentioned by Mr. Richards? Who are they?"

"I am afraid they are the Lords Hampton, Lockwood and Ashworth," Cassandra said. "I had not yet had time to tell you of my encounter in the park yesterday. Mr. Conners, who I met at the Montagues' ball, approached me and proposed I engage in a horse race."

"He did not!" Sybil exclaimed.

"He did. Then Lord Hampton came on the scene and chased him

away."

"That was very good of Lord Hampton," Sybil said.

"Yes, it was," Cassandra said. "But there is more. Not long after, Lord Lockwood and Lord Ashworth arrived. The three gentlemen insisted they escort us on our way home. *All* the way home. It was strange and there were no end of people staring at us. You see? The three gentlemen in the illustration are Hampton, Ashworth and Lockwood."

"I do see," Sybil said. "Goodness, that is unfair. You have not deserved this. As well, it does not entirely explain Mr. Richards' comment on the three gentlemen. Why should one be wary of your company because three gentlemen of the pact did you a marked courtesy?"

"I do not know, nor do I fully understand why they did such a courtesy. I am perhaps most alarmed at the idea that something that occurred yesterday afternoon was so widely known that same night and a mocking of it is done today." Cassandra paused, then said, "As well, who would be so determined as to throw it through my aunt's window?"

"Lady Marksworth will know what ought to be done," Sybil said. "I expect a 'Chin up and ignore the gossip' is what she will say."

Cassandra took Sybil's hands in her own. "But you need not ignore it, my friend. I would not like to see you tainted by talk involving myself. This will not be the only copy of this print and I cannot know how many others circulate. Perhaps Mr. Richards was right, perhaps it might be best for you to stay away for now."

"Stay away?" Sybil said, with more vigor than she had displayed all morning. "I certainly will not. Lady Sybil Hayworth is made of sterner stuff than that, thank you very much."

Cassandra smiled at her friend's valiant loyalty, though she knew it might not hold. "Your mother may not feel the same," she said.

"My mother comes from a long line of lady warriors," Sybil said.

"She will not retreat in the face of difficulty."

Racine came in with the two footmen, who both worked to catch their breath. "The little blighter could not be caught," he said.

"It is no matter," Cassandra said. "I do not know what we would have done with him if we *had* caught him."

"Knock the stuffing out of him is what I would do!" Racine said.

Cassandra smiled at the idea. It appeared Racine was from a long line of warriors too.

"I think," she said, "the best thing we can do is send somebody to Mrs. Hanson's house to retrieve my aunt."

Racine nodded, though he appeared to experience some disappointment in not having the opportunity to knock the stuffing out of anybody. "Jimmy, you go. Say an important letter has arrived, nothing more until you are on your way. Ben, sweep the glass from the rug and cover the window with a cloth. I will arrange for a glazier to come and repair it."

Cassandra felt a bit better, having settled on a plan of action and seeing Racine so competent in carrying out the details. She would feel both comforted and mortified to see her aunt. She had caused talk about herself! She would need to own that she had spoken so out of turn as to mention shooting. As for the three gentlemen escorting them home, she could not have done anything about that—Lady Marksworth had quite approved it.

It was simply that the two pieces of information, taken together, resulted in a humiliating picture. She supposed that was what the people who dreamt up such illustrations sought out—combining a few disparate facts into a scene that would amuse.

Though who would have felt it necessary to hire a boy to throw the thing through a window? That was not just amusement, there was real condemnation there. Further, her name was not even on the drawing. Were both circumstances so well known, and so quickly, that whoever had hired the boy had instantly perceived who the drawing represented?

Sybil wiped her eyes. "It is so unfair!" she said.

"Indeed it is," Cassandra said. "Though I do not like to see you upset by it. You ought to go home, I know you attend the Blakeleys' ball this evening and you will not want red eyes, particularly not with a mask on—you would appear a frightful specter."

"Oh no," Sybil said, her voice resolute. "I shall not go anywhere until your aunt arrives. I will not have you sit alone waiting for her. Though, I think we'd best move away from the window. Just in case another boy comes along."

The thought of a second broken window sent a shiver down Cassandra's spine and they moved with all haste to the other side of the room.

"You were to go to the Blakeleys' tonight as well," Sybil said. "Shall you attend?"

"I will do as my aunt suggests," Cassandra said. "I very much hope she suggests we stay home, as I am in no mood for levity or for finding myself stared at. I can have no idea how many people have seen a copy of that print."

"If you do go," Sybil said, "I shall be right by your side. Let the starers note it all they like. I rather think you should go, my mama says Lady Blakeley takes a deal of time choosing the right mask for each person. I am rather terrified to see what arrives today but whatever it is, I will put it on and remain close by you."

Cassandra smiled at her friend, much cheered to find her such a stalwart ally. Sybil might not gallop off without a groom or shoot birds, but she was as steady as any soldier. As for the mask, Lady Markswort had told her of Lady Blakeley's unusual way of going on. It was not a full-dress mask and those attending did not choose their own. Two masks of some sort would arrive for herself and her aunt before the day was through.

Cassandra had looked forward to the idea, but now she would just as soon forgo donning a mask of cheerfulness or anything Lady Blakeley might dream up.

IT WAS NOT more than a half hour before Jimmy returned with Lady Marksworth. He'd somehow got her out of the house and then informed her of events as they made their way home, no doubt jogging alongside her window.

Cassandra's aunt blew into the room like a north wind, took in the cloth covering the window and her niece sitting on the far side of the room with Sybil.

"Cassandra, are you quite all right?"

"I am unhurt," Cassandra said. To claim being quite all right felt too much to own.

"And dear Lady Sybil," Lady Marksworth said, "how good of you to stay with her. You must have been frightened out of your wits."

Sybil rose and said, "Not terribly so and Cassandra was terrifically brave. In any case, as my father always says, the Hayworths stand their ground."

Sybil curtsied and took her leave amidst Lady Marksworth's thanks and Cassandra's grateful looks. Her aunt came and sat beside Cassandra. She picked up the print and stared at it.

"You will only understand part of it, I think," Cassandra said. "The three gentlemen are Lords Hampton, Lockwood and Ashworth."

"I see," Lady Marksworth said. "So the gossipmongers would make something of three gentlemen escorting a lady home. Entirely ridiculous."

"The gun, though," Cassandra said, determined that her aunt should understand it all. "That is my fault. At the Bergram's ball, Lord Hampton said something provoking and somehow I carelessly mentioned I'd been in the habit of shooting birds."

Lady Marksworth's forehead wrinkled. "Why should you invent such a bizarre account of yourself?"

"It was not an invention," Cassandra said.

"Not an invention? Do you mean to say? No, certainly your father would not… he would not have allowed his daughter. Good Lord. He did."

"He did," Cassandra confirmed. "I ought not to have mentioned it and regretted it as soon as I said it."

Lady Marksworth appeared pensive. "Well, a girl with a shotgun is strange, there's no getting round it. Though I have heard that Lady Rentworth has been known to shoot bird."

Cassandra was cheered by that idea. "So it is not entirely unknown," she said.

"Perhaps not. But the reason I have heard of it is because people speak of it and Lady Rentworth is a middle-aged spinster who has always been known as a great eccentric."

"And I am young and here for my first season," Cassandra said quietly.

"Just so," Lady Marksworth said.

The full weight of what had occurred, and what might be the result of it, seemed to come over Cassandra all at once. Was she to be stared at everywhere? Was she the subject of jokes? Was her name spoken in jest in the gentlemen's clubs? Were there those that might snub her? Of course there must be. At least one person in town had paid a boy to break her window with the news.

A tear rolled down her cheek and she said, "I ought to go home, Aunt. I have disappointed you and caused talk that will reflect on you. It is not right that I stay."

Lady Marksworth took her niece's hand. "You will do no such thing, my dear. The very worst idea is to cut and run, it would be like air to the fire. No, we shall keep to our schedule and if anybody has the nerve to stare while I am in the vicinity, they will wish they had not. In any case, while the depiction of you is odd, it in no way impugns your innocence. You have been painted as having facility with a gun and having three dashing admirers. That is not ideal, but that is all."

Cassandra thought that was quite enough but was encouraged by her aunt's stance on the matter—Lady Marksworth was all cool head and commonsense.

"In any case, if there is blame to be shared, I must take my part in it," Lady Marksworth said. "I thought it perfectly acceptable that the lords should escort us on our way if it pleased them. Together, we shall face down the talkers with grace and aplomb."

"I wondered what we should do about the Blakeleys' ball this evening," Cassandra said.

"Wonder no more," Lady Marksworth said firmly. "We will arrive as expected and let anyone dare say a word about it. You could not hope to arrive at a friendlier house. In the meantime, I will write your father of this idiocy. He will not put much stock in it, but better he knows of it if the print reaches as far as Surrey."

"Could it reach as far as Surrey?" Cassandra said in alarm. She was not worried about her father, he did not rattle easily, but she would not like to think of all her friends viewing such a thing.

"One never knows," Lady Marksworth said. "I suppose it depends upon how amusing the illustrator considered it and how much he thought he might gain by it. As you are relatively unknown, I don't expect it will go far. A print of the Regent might be recognized in the furthest reaches of England, but not so with you."

Cassandra found herself somewhat mollified by the idea. Of course, the prints must be sold to make them worthwhile, and who would pay for a print of an unknown and unnamed girl? She began to hope the pieces of paper would be few and of little interest.

UNTIL A ROCK had sailed through her window, Cassandra had looked forward to the Blakeleys' ball. They were a young couple, Lord Blakeley known for his outspoken politics and Lady Blakeley known for her forward-looking wardrobe. The lady was often in the newspapers, with breathless descriptions of some outfit or other. The last had been a red silk Japanese Kimono that she'd worn to a reception for the Persian ambassador.

There were some circles that wondered if the couple were not a little too fast for the best society, but Lady Marksworth was fond of them both. She'd known Lady Blakeley as a girl, having been friends with her mother, and had always found her lively and vastly entertaining.

Now, Cassandra was very much less looking forward to the Blakeleys' mask. She had felt on pins and needles all through the day. A rock had shattered a window, she was the subject of a joke, and she waited to see how Lady Blakeley had depicted her character via the choosing of her mask.

It was with both great relief and great trepidation that the boxes containing their masks had finally arrived. Lady Marksworth opened hers and moved aside the delicate tissue to find the face of an owl, done in feathers.

"I am thought to be wise, it seems," Lady Marksworth said smiling. "Either that or I am exceptionally cruel to mice. Now let us see what you are to be."

Cassandra gently removed the mask from the box. It was covered in a soft taupe velvet with rounded ears outlined in a cream silk ribbon. The holes for her eyes were outlined in a black silk and there was a small black nose slightly protruding.

"A fawn," Lady Marksworth said. "Both charming and appropriate. Nothing could be more innocent, gentle and deserving of care than a fawn. Well! Lady Blakeley has made her opinion known and all will see it."

LORD HAMPTON HAD sent a note to all of the gentlemen of the pact after receiving an alarming communication from Dalton. The lord wrote that his butler, Bellamy, witnessed a street urchin throw a rock through the windows of Lady Markswo rth's house and that rock appeared to have had a paper tied round it. The lady's footmen had given chase but returned empty-handed. Lady Marksworth had arrived to the house some time later and nothing else had been seen.

It had not taken much thinking to guess what had been done. Some person had decided it was time to send a stern message to Miss Knightsbridge. It was not unknown that a satirical print would be delivered via rock to some poor soul's address, though it was usually a politician who could expect such discourtesy. If the lady had been at home as the glass shattered, she must have been terrified.

He very much doubted Miss Knightsbridge would venture out to the Blakeleys' ball after having a rock thrown through her window. He was certain she and her aunt huddled together, attempting to work out the meaning of the print. If they had not been apprised of the rumor of the three engagements so far, and he did not think they had been, they would be mightily confused and alarmed by it.

In case his assumption that she would not attend was wrong, he had conferred with Lady Blakeley on the matter and convinced her he ought to know what mask Miss Knightsbridge wore. He had been well-pleased to discover it was to be a fawn, and further pleased that the hostess had heard the gossip and tossed it aside as rubbish.

After that meeting, he had sent what amounted to military orders to the gentlemen of the pact—they had all been invited and were therefore all to attend, they were to split up and do reconnaissance, and they were to challenge every scrap of gossip they heard. If Miss Knightsbridge made an appearance, she would be identified as the lady masked as a fawn and her dance card was to be filled.

He was well aware that none of the gentlemen wished to go to the mask; they had an abhorrence for such things. Especially the masks that Lady Blakeley might choose for them, as she could have quite the acerbic wit. However, he had made it their duty and they would go.

Hampton did not particularly wish to go himself. His mask this year was of an old and serious-looking clergyman, replete with a band. He supposed that was some comment on his lack of levity. Dalton was to be a pirate, and well-pleased by it. God only knew what the rest of them would be.

No matter, they were duty-bound to make every possible exertion on behalf of Miss Knightsbridge.

Chapter Nine

The Blakeleys' house in Mayfair appeared quite usual from the outside, with its stone façade and many windows. However, Cassandra was just now hearing from her aunt that the inside was less than usual.

As the carriage came to a stop in the line, Lady Marksworth said, "Lady Blakeley has always been fascinated with anything foreign, fortunately her lord indulges her fancy. I understand she's recently added a sarcophagus to the drawing room and her children are fond of hiding in it."

"Goodness," Cassandra said. "I presume it arrived empty."

Lady Marksworth laughed at the remark and said, "I am glad you are in good spirits."

"I cannot say in what spirits I am," Cassandra said. "I will perhaps have a better idea after an hour or two. However, I decided that I ought not allow myself to be defeated. I have not done anything shameful. Shocking to some sensibilities, perhaps, but nothing truly shameful. I should not blush at anything my father or my aunt have approved."

"True, though I suspect even your father cautioned you to forgo mentioning shooting birds."

"That he did," Cassandra admitted, "and perhaps this has been a valuable lesson to me. I have been in the habit of saying all my thoughts and have now discovered that only thinking them is often sufficient."

"I believe that is a lesson we all learn at some point," Lady Marksworth said. "In any case, you are right to understand that you did nothing shameful and it will not be overlong before some new idea about someone else is setting the tongues wagging. Hold your head up and go forward—after all, it was only a silly illustration. Ah, here we are."

Footmen had opened the door and they helped Cassandra to the ground.

LORD AND LADY Blakeley were a dashing couple—he tall and lean and she nearly as tall as he. They had both removed their masks to greet their guests, though Cassandra could see two footmen standing nearby, ready to hand them over. They both went as lions, his with a great mane and hers as the more delicate female. She supposed the couple wished to declare themselves king and queen of the jungle and the thought made her smile. London *was* a jungle, when it came down to it.

Lady Marksworth was greeted in all genial familiarity. Lady Blakeley said, "And this must be your charming niece, Miss Knightsbridge."

Cassandra curtsied and Lady Blakeley rose her up. Loudly, she said, "You are always welcome to my house, innocent fawn." Then she leaned in and whispered, "Ignore the cobras, they will eventually turn on each other and devour themselves."

Lord Blakeley had nodded vigorously at that sentiment. "They always do," he said.

Cassandra did not know what was in her future, but she was comforted by the idea that whatever was to come, Lord and Lady Blakeley had very publicly made it known that they were firmly in her camp.

FOR ALL HER comfort upon being introduced to the Blakeleys, Cassandra fairly quaked upon entering the ballroom. It was one thing to know that one did not commit any serious crime, and to know that the host and hostess felt the same. It was another to wonder if others present might hold a different opinion.

She could not escape the idea that at least one person had made the effort to hire a boy to throw that ridiculous print through her window. That person might well be in attendance, but how would she know? She also could not escape the idea that many people, even if they'd not seen the print, would have heard some version of what had occurred in the park. Mr. Richards certainly had heard of it only hours after the event, though she still was not clear on why the gentleman thought Sybil ought to break with her over three gentlemen escorting her home. Perhaps her facility with a shotgun had been shocking enough for the man.

Cassandra searched desperately for Sybil. Though her aunt remained at her side, she felt Sybil to be her life raft in a stormy sea. It would be hard enough to locate her friend at a ball this large, and here everyone wore a mask. How would she ever find her?

She was suddenly tapped on the shoulder. Sybil said, "I know that is you, Cassandra, I recognize the chain of white roses embroidered on the hem of your dress."

Cassandra turned and found Sybil, masked as a dove in soft grey feathers.

"Sybil!" Cassandra practically cried out, relieved to be united with her friend. "You are a dove, Lady Blakeley could not have chosen better for my friend."

"And you a fawn," Sybil said. "I believe we have done very well on that front. I have heard that the Montagues are not attending this evening because Lady Montague received a mask very much resembling a snake."

"Goodness," Cassandra said. "It would appear Lady Blakeley did not wish her to attend, as who would don such a thing?"

Cassandra found herself markedly relieved that the lady would not attend. She could not know if anything about her had reached Lady Montague's ears, but she could guess that if it had, the lady would be condemning.

On the other hand, she was rather embarrassed by her own delight at Lady Montague's misfortune. If Sybil had heard of the mask of a snake, it must be talked of widely. She was ashamed to feel relief at another suffering at the hands of gossip, even if that person was the stern Lady Montague. It was as if gossip and rumor were hunters and the *ton* was a timid herd of deer—each deer secretly hoped it would be another singled out for shooting.

Lady Marksworth had stepped away to speak with a friend and Cassandra and Sybil gazed around the ballroom.

"It is almost off-putting," Sybil said, "to not know who anybody is."

"At the moment," Cassandra said, "I find myself rather glad of it as no prying eyes know who *I* am."

"Do be cheerful, Cass," Sybil said. "I told everything to my mother and father and they stand with Marksworth House. My father said if everybody is to reshuffle their friends because of some ridiculous print going round, England is sunk. My mother stood and quite wonderfully vowed to do battle alongside Miss Knightsbridge's forces. She's got Margaret Beaufort back in her line somewhere and is quite happy to engage in an extended campaign."

"I am so grateful," Cassandra said, "you must tell them."

A gentleman masked as what appeared to be a stern old clergyman approached them and they could talk no further on the subject.

"Miss Knightsbridge," he said, holding his hand out for her card.

Cassandra had no doubt of the voice, it was rich and deep. "Lord

Hampton?" she asked, handing it over.

He nodded as he put down his name for the dance before supper. Why that dance? Was he not aware of the talk? Had he not heard of the print? Would not this cause even further talk?

He handed the card back to her and bowed before moving away.

"He must not have heard that he has caused you trouble by escorting you from the park," Sybil said. "I suspect it is not as widely spoken of as you feared. Now, I wonder why Lady Blakeley masked Lord Hampton as an old vicar?"

"*I* wonder how Lord Hampton addressed me by name before we had even spoken. How did he know it to be me?"

Before Cassandra could speculate on how Lord Hampton knew her as the fawn, a fierce-looking pirate approached and requested her card. He hastily filled in his name, quickly followed by a gentleman wearing a mask of a savage-faced boar, another wearing a mask of gold coin, then a knight, and finally a replica of a Waterloo medal. Though her card was filled in rapid succession, none of the gentlemen stayed to speak with her, though some had put down their names on Sybil's card too.

There was finally a pause and Cassandra glanced down at her card to see who they were, almost terrified she would find Mr. Conners in the mix.

She did not find Mr. Conners, but the list of names left her cold. Hampton, Dalton, Lockwood, Ashworth, Grayson and Cabot. Every single gentleman named in the pact.

Was she the subject of some joke between them? How else to account for it? She'd never even been introduced to Lords Dalton, Grayson or Cabot, and they'd not bothered to accomplish that nicety before writing their names down.

Cassandra scanned the room and noted Lord Hampton's vicar in conference with a man masked as a jester. The jester looked back at her and she turned away.

They spoke of her, she knew it. She could feel it in her bones. Perhaps she ought to seek out her aunt and they might claim an illness and leave. Whatever transpired here, it felt dangerous. She felt a sense of impending doom, though had she been asked to explain it she did not know what she would have said. Many a lady might be delighted to find such illustrious names on her card, but in light of recent events…

The jester had crossed the room in a moment and stood before her. "Miss Knightsbridge? It is Burke, of course you must have guessed the jester's mask would be my own. It seems my blasted cook and the stories I tell of him have made a fool of me."

"Lord Burke!" she said, not quite knowing what to make of it.

"May I?" he asked.

She handed over her card and Lord Burke filled in his name for the last dance that had not yet been taken. Her evening was claimed, and it was claimed by every gentleman in the room who would be a duke someday.

Cassandra did not know the meaning of it, but she was beginning to be terrified of discovering it. If it had caused talk to be escorted home by three gentlemen of the pact, what would be the result of this? It would not go unremarked. She might hide behind her fawn's mask for now, but it would come off at supper.

THE EVENING HAD seemed interminable to Cassandra. She had opened the ball with Lord Dalton. He seemed a rather intense sort of person and she began to see how he might be styled as a pirate. He did not explain himself, other than noting that had he been born without funds he might very well have taken up the profession. She had asked him if he liked masked balls, that seeming an entirely innocuous question. He'd said he did not like them but should, as it was a kindness to others that his disfigured face remained hidden. She had stayed silent after that.

Lord Lockwood had been rather frightening to behold, his mask composed of some sort of rough fur that stuck out at all angles, and frightening tusks protruding. His conversation had been far more lighthearted than his appearance. He speculated he'd been made a boar for his penchant of barreling ahead before thinking. It had nearly got him killed in the war and he still hadn't rid himself of the habit. On the other hand, he'd rather be known as a boar than a bore.

Aside from those comments, he'd asked her a few questions about Sybil. Cassandra speculated that she might even divine some interest on his part and felt sorry that Sybil was determined to avoid the gentlemen of the pact, *and* that Sybil's father had a hatred of his own father over a long past card game. If Lord Lockwood *did* have some partiality for Sybil, it was an entirely lost cause.

Lord Ashworth accounted for his mask of gold coins by claiming he was a keen gambler. His father had been dead set against it until he saw how much money his son had brought back into the estate.

Lord Cabot had appeared reluctant to account for his mask being the Waterloo medal, until finally admitting that he perhaps talked of the war and its battles a bit much for the female taste. He had seemed vastly grateful when she remarked that the impact of war could only be rightly felt by those persons who had participated in it and everybody else should not presume to comment.

Cassandra had not expected Lord Hampton to account for being portrayed as a vicar. In truth, she was rather surprised he'd come at all. Very like Lady Montague's snake, she would have thought he'd have looked at it, tossed it aside, and then sent his regrets.

As they waited their turn to move through the steps, he said, "It seems each year Lady Blakeley sets out to teach me a lesson. I suppose I am to know that I am too serious this time."

"Do you mark yourself as such?" Cassandra asked, rather surprised that she'd not had to initiate the conversation and rather relieved it was not on the subject of dogs or kennels.

"Perhaps," Lord Hampton said. "Perhaps more so since the war. Too many lives wasted in battle for any sort of frivolity to feel entirely comfortable."

"My father would agree regarding the lives wasted," Cassandra said. "He says it's all well and good to be blindly patriotic, but that is cold comfort for a farmer who's lost his only son."

"One of the tenants on my father's estate had three sons and lost them all. It makes one wonder over the rightness of having survived."

Cassandra was struck with the lord's words. She had become used to various gentlemen speaking of the war in heroic terms of this or that battle as if it were a story, or Lord Burke making it all sound like a joke.

"I suppose you do no great service to the dead by failing to enjoy that which was not taken from you."

The lord appeared thoughtful over that idea, or at least as thoughtful as one could seem while wearing a mask. Or perhaps it was the mask itself, looking thoughtful all on its own. Cassandra could not be sure. She could also not be sure how she might inquire about the various names on her card. It could not be a coincidence, and yet what could be the meaning of it? She had worried it was some sort of joke, until she thought of how unlikely it would be for Lord Hampton to joke. Still, what could she say without seeming either odd or accusing? Or worse, appearing as if she'd gone fishing for some compliment to herself?

As it happened, no further conversation was had on any subject, as it was their turn to execute the steps.

IT SEEMED LADY Blakeley did everything her own way; the entrance to supper was done in strict order by rank of the gentlemen and organized by her butler who appeared to be a regular Debrett's on who was who behind each mask. As Lord Hampton was to be a duke, they were near the front of the line. Dear Sybil was being taken in by Lord Lockwood and stood directly behind them—Cassandra had great hopes of being placed next to them at table. Lady Marksworth was escorted by a Marquess who was a dear old friend and lined up not so far behind them. If she were fortunate, she would find herself surrounded by friends and allies.

The Blakeley's dining room was a sight to behold—its length was enormous and had no trouble accommodating sixty couples. Lady Marksworth had told Cassandra that Lord and Lady Blakeley had done extensive renovations and had removed a wall adjoining a large sitting room so that the dining room now ran the length of the house. However, it was the room's decoration that struck.

An exotic silk fabric lined the walls, depicting maharajahs sitting on gold thrones under palm trees, fanned by small boys wielding marvelously large feathers. The chairs of the endless table were covered in striking red satin. The chandeliers dripped with colored glass in amethyst, amber and cobalt, hundreds of candles casting their glow through them and giving the room an air of drama and mystery. Even the plates were unusual, with a rim of vibrant red and a center depicting a multi-colored star, said to be Russian porcelain.

Cassandra was seated near the head of the table and to her great approval, Sybil and Lord Lockwood were directly across. While that was a comfort, she knew that the time would soon come when everybody was to remove their masks and that was a less comfortable idea. She'd noted the looks, particularly toward the end of the dancing, as she was led by one would-be duke after the next. She did not think her own identity particularly known, but she had the feeling that the gentlemen's identities were less secret. It would not surprise her to know that there were those who would be interested to see who the girl was that had accomplished such a feat. For that matter, she did not know herself why it should be so.

She felt her trepidation growing as the table filled, it was impossible to ignore the various glances made in the direction of the fawn.

Lady Blakeley had risen, and the table quieted.

"Good evening, my friends," she said. "As always, my dear husband has given over the pleasure of bidding you welcome as he knows well my fondness for talking."

There was gentle laughter up and down the table.

"As those of you who have attended this little soiree in years past know, it amuses me to choose the masks for my guests. Some are gentle teasing, some a small compliment, and very few a light jab. This evening I am most gratified to see such wonderful creatures as a fawn, a dove, a kitten, and a canary.

Cassandra blushed beneath her mask. Why should the lady reference so few, herself included? There were so many different masks at the table.

"Gentle creatures such as those depend upon our kindness and reward us with their innocence. One does not like to think of, or even to countenance, the individual who would be cruel to those defenseless beings."

Cassandra felt her cheeks must burn through her mask. The lady was making a point about the rumors regarding her, she was certain of it. She was scolding the diners lest one of them think to believe them or spread them.

She noted Lady Marksworth's owl nod approvingly and the idea was entirely confirmed. While it was embarrassing in the extreme, she could not help but be grateful for Lady Blakeley's pointed defense.

"Of course, we have fiercer miens amongst us and I will thank Lord Lockwood to have a care for those tusks near my china."

Laughter erupted at the table. After it died down, Lady Blakeley said, "Naturally, there are the very few who do not care for my commentary. But then, I do not particularly wish to have a snake in my house."

The laughter at that was widespread, though more hushed. It was as if those amused also worried that Lady Montague might make an appearance and strike as deadly as the snake she was meant to be.

Cassandra was in awe of Lady Blakeley's daring. She had grown used to the careful conversations of society and yet here was a woman who maintained strong opinions and would make them known. Here was a woman not the least bit afraid to take on the formidable Lady Montague.

While Cassandra knew she was not of an age or sufficient authority to dare the same herself, she could not help but admire it.

"Now, my lovelies, and you are all lovely in my eyes," Lady Montague said gaily, "reveal yourself to be who you are in the rest of your life."

Masks were slowly removed and, as Cassandra had expected, quite a few people watched her remove her own. Their attention was diverted by Lady Blakeley clapping in appreciation of the faces turned to her. She motioned to her butler, who motioned to his footmen, and an immense variety of dishes began to make their rounds like a much-practiced ballet.

As the dishes came round, Cassandra was pensive. She would very much like to ask Lord Hampton how it was that all six gentlemen of the pact had ended up on her card. She had thought it through backward and forward and yet there seemed no casual way to bring it up.

"You will be pleased to know, Miss Knightsbridge," Lord Lockwood said from across the table, "that we do not see a particular Mr. C. here this evening. One does not dare show one's face when one has discovered one's face was to be masked as a rat."

Cassandra looked down at her plate, hardly knowing how to answer the lord. There were so many thoughts swirling in her mind at once. Of course he referred to Mr. Conners. Had Lady Blakeley gifted a mask of a rat to Mr. Conners because she'd heard of his behavior in the park or for some other offense? If it had been due to the insult to herself, then did all of London know of it? If they did, then would it not have been more understandable that the three lords had escorted her home?

She did not know what to make of it.

Lord Hampton answered for her. "I think we need not expend any time discussing that particular gentleman."

Lord Lockwood seemed surprised but nodded.

"Though," Cassandra said, desperate for any bit of information, "I would like to know the cause, if the gentleman was indeed given such a mask. Was it to do with his behavior in the park, or is he in the general habit of offending?"

"The park," Lord Lockwood said, albeit reluctantly now that his friend had made clear he wished to dismiss the subject.

Cassandra did not believe she could persuade Lord Lockwood to say any more, though perhaps he'd said enough. She could not directly address the offensive illustration or the talk that went round about her, but she thought she could obliquely communicate her stance on it. And, truthfully, if she did not say something in her own defense, she might burst.

"Were it up to me, I would have painted Mr. Conners as a mouse, rather than a rat—his efforts being so weak and feeble," Cassandra said. "Though, I doubt he is alone in his ill-considered opinions. It matters little, all the mice in London may go round chattering, they will not attract *my* notice." She paused and then said, "Other than to pick up a broom and chase them out to the street where they belong."

"Well said," Lord Hampton said quietly.

Sybil beamed; Lord Lockwood appeared both taken aback and amused. As nobody had a retort to Cassandra's very definite and determined statements, the conversation turned to more usual topics.

She and the lord briefly touched on the subject of dogs again, but then blessedly landed on literature. As it turned out, Lord Hampton read as much and as widely as she did herself. As they spoke of botany, architecture, the Romans, and astronomy, Cassandra found herself speaking to a highly educated man who did more than recite facts. He had not just taken in information—he had thought about it. It was frighteningly attractive. Despite her own mental discipline on the subject, her mind kept presenting opposing arguments. Was it really so awful to be a duchess, after all? Might not a man involved in the pact have an interest that was not forced by his father? Was there another man in London with those eyes? It was not so much their color, which was very dark, but their habit of examining her as if they wished to know her secrets. She was very glad nobody could hear her thoughts doing battle with one another.

Cassandra also found herself glad she'd made her opinion known regarding the gossip going round about her. Her aunt had said it would be the worst thing to cut and run. She'd not run, she'd challenged whatever ridiculous ideas circulated about Miss Knightsbridge.

She could not have helped but notice that couples around her had been over-quiet during her forthright speech. Let them repeat her words in every drawing room in town if they wished.

Cassandra found herself, in the end, well-satisfied with the evening. It felt as if the heavy weight of the rock thrown through her window had begun to lift.

That the familiar shiver went down her spine more than once before the supper was over, she was determined to ignore for now.

CHAPTER TEN

HAMPTON SAT IN his library, the dying fire the only light in the predawn hours. At his feet, Havoc gleefully shredded the mask of a clergyman.

He had been surprised to see Miss Knightsbridge at the Blakeley's ball. He'd given contingency instructions to his friends on what to do if she *did* appear, though he never truly believed she would.

His surprise gave over to astonishment at her spirited defense of herself at supper. She'd not said it particularly softly either. Plenty at the table would have heard of the London gossipers likened to insignificant mice who might be chased off with a broom.

What courage the lady had! To arrive as if nothing were amiss, and then to proclaim her opinion so forcefully as to any talk that had made the rounds. He doubted there were many females who could have girded themselves for such a trial. Certainly, none he'd encountered during this blasted season.

Thanks to his father's demands, he'd danced with and spoken to an unending list of unmarried ladies. Those females made every attempt to display their beauty and wit, and then somewhere in the conversation, shyly present an example of their over-refined sensibilities. He was to know that they were easily shocked, that aspect of their temperament supposedly meant to be some hallmark of good breeding.

The idea nearly made him laugh. His grandmother was not easily shocked and, in fact, sometimes did the shocking herself. His mother routinely dispatched all manner of circumstances that might cause a blush in a less determined lady. Only a year ago, the duchess had discovered a housemaid in her household had been compromised and was with child. She'd wasted no time demanding to know the culprit's name and to her great lack of surprise it had been a footman. In one curt and speedy interview with the man she demanded he marry the girl, which he did, and now the foolish couple had some little shop in the village. The duchess had been no more affected by the circumstance than she would have been over viewing a cup of spilled milk. He did not quite understand how any of these young, unmarried ladies proposed to run a large house if they needed to fan themselves over every difficulty.

Then there was Miss Knightsbridge. She had no need of a fan.

What, though, did she really know about what was being said? It was likely that what Bellamy had witnessed being thrown through the window was a satirical print—he'd seen the one going round that showed her with shotgun aiming at three gentlemen floating above her, but he could not be certain that was what she'd seen. That she knew *something* was evident, else she would not have made such a pronouncement at supper. Whatever she knew, she did not know all. To know all would be to know his hand in it.

He'd felt such a fraud, sitting there so apparently above reproach while Mr. Conners' inappropriate proposition had been alluded to. He'd done far worse. Far, far worse.

At the mask, he, Lockwood, Dalton, Ashworth, Cabot and Grayson had set out to quash any talk about Miss Knightsbridge, and there had been plenty to occupy them. The ridiculous story of three suitors still made the rounds, and sometimes four suitors or five. There was talk of her having shot a farmer she did not care for just for amusement. *Now*, there was even the suggestion that her own father was terrified of her and rued the day he'd allowed her to take up a gun.

One particularly acerbic little miss masked in dark feathers that very much resembled a magpie had even had the temerity to wonder aloud how a gentleman might be quite comfortable in marriage to such a lady. After all, she'd said, he might never know when he'd provoked her ire until shots rang out. He had informed that charming lady of her deficiencies in judgment and left her near tears. He'd not been sorry for it, though he realized that if such talk went on much longer, it would be no time at all before Miss Knightsbridge was known as a veritable Genghis Khan.

He'd hoped the words Miss Knightsbridge had spoken for herself might mitigate some of the worst ideas being passed round, as it had been clear enough that she'd been overheard. Rather, before he left the Blakeley's he heard one lady say to the next, "Apparently, if she deigns not to shoot you, she will chase you with a broom. One wonders how there is anybody left alive in Surrey."

That, in regard to a lady so composed, so stalwart, and so well-educated! He'd discovered that evening that she was well-read. Truly well-read, not like some others who claimed to be great readers and had nothing to show for it because all they read were French novels. Miss Knightsbridge had a deep knowledge of botany and architecture, two subjects dear to his heart. Then, of course, she had already displayed her marked good sense regarding dogs and their kennels.

He smiled ever so slightly as he recalled the first evening they had met, and her hint that not everybody in the world was eager to know him. He'd been in such high dudgeon over it! Now, he could see that he had deserved the comment; he'd been rather rude. In truth, he'd been in a bit of a sulk, no better than a ten-year-old boy discovering his favorite toy broken.

In repayment for his well-earned comeuppance, he'd been the source of the gossip that now plagued her. If only he could go back! He might have realized he danced with an exceptional lady. He might have put aside his aggravation with his father to behold what was in front of him.

Hampton paused. He did not like where his thoughts led him. It was one thing to admire Miss Knightsbridge, but his admiration could only go so far. As with any other lady, he did not wish his admiration to be in any way singular. He had already recognized he would be in danger if he did not keep himself in check—how any other gentleman had escaped the charms of that heart-shaped face he did not know. But, that was to be put in the back of his mind and not considered again. Still, when she looked up at him as she discussed Palladian columns, he could not help but be aware of its effect.

Ah well, it was most likely his guilt that made him more admiring than he should be.

IT WAS BOTH a week of quiet and a week of busyness and confusion. Cassandra and her aunt did not have many engagements. The Hedleys' ball had been cancelled at the last minute as Lady Hedley had fallen ill. Cassandra could not say that she was sorry for it—sorry for Lady Hedley's illness of course, but not sorry to have missed her ball. The lady was known to be great friends with Lady Montague and that particular person had instilled a dread in her.

They had made various calls, but their timing was invariably off and they did not find many of their acquaintances at home.

On the other hand, the preparations for the ball at Marksworth House were in full swing. Racine led them all with a cool head, even when facing certain disaster.

The musicians who had been hired months ago had underhandedly accepted another job for more money. They would not say by who, nor would they be swayed by an increase in payment. Replacement musicians had to be speedily procured.

The ballroom floor had needed polishing, but one of the footmen had poured so much linseed oil on it that it was temporarily as slippery as a frozen pond.

The merchant who supplied their ices suddenly died and his son knew nothing about the order.

While Cassandra felt an uncomfortable flutter and Lady Marksworth noticeably paled at each alarming development, Racine only shook his head gravely and said, "I will see to it, my lady." Somehow, that remarkable butler *did* see to it, and each new disaster was speedily dispatched.

Sybil came to see Cassandra three days before the ball. The fear of any more flying rocks having left them, they cozied up on their window seat overlooking the garden. Sybil said, "I was certain I would see you at the Hedleys', did you have some other engagement?"

"The Hedleys'?" Cassandra asked. "We did not go because Lady Hedley was taken ill."

"She did not appear so," Sybil said. "How would you have heard such a thing?"

Cassandra felt as if her insides had taken flight and fought to break free of her. "We heard it from the lady's secretary," she said quietly. "A note was delivered."

Cassandra and Sybil stared at one another. Sybil said quietly, "As it was not Lady Hedley herself, perhaps the secretary made a mistake?"

"That would be very odd, would it not? A secretary is not likely to mistake her lady as ill and notify only one guest of it," Cassandra said. "No, if I had to guess, we were disinvited by way of excuse on account of the rumors and that stupid print."

"But who could believe any of it?" Sybil cried.

"Lady Hedley is much in the company of Lady Montague, and I suspect I am not held in high regard in that lady's eyes. She maintains strict opinions of the comportment of young ladies. I presume being talked about will not be one of her approved attributes."

"I do not like Lady Montague," Sybil said. "Not at all."

"I suspect neither Lady Montague nor Lady Hedley will make an appearance at my ball. I cannot say I am sorry for it."

Sybil's face grew an alarming shade of pink and she balled up her tiny fists. "If I were a man, I'd challenge them all! I'd throw down the gauntlet and meet them at dawn!"

While Cassandra was much disturbed at discovering that she and her aunt had been purposefully excluded from the Hedleys' ball, she could only be admiring of her brave friend. "There now, Lady Margaret Beaufort, I should not like to think of you shot at sunrise on some lonely expanse of green."

Sybil's fists unclenched. "Goodness, I am a goose. No matter, whether that note you received was or was not a mistake, you did not miss anything extraordinary."

Sybil paused, seeming to think of something. "Oh! I had meant to tell you before I began thinking of duels I will never fight, that both Lord Lockwood and Lord Hampton were at the Hedleys'. Lord Hampton asked about you very specifically."

"Asked about me? Why? Why should he ask about me?"

In truth, Cassandra was not certain what she thought about that. She was flattered, she supposed, that he might inquire about her. On the other hand, why should a lord be asking about a lady who did not attend? Did it not point to some singular notice?

"He asked how you got on," Sybil said. "Naturally, I said you were quite well. Then, he hinted that he had seen the print that had gone round. I said, it was such a lot of nonsense that whoever had so wronged Miss Knightsbridge ought to be drawn and quartered."

"You did not say such a thing," Cassandra said.

"I did," Sybil said, nodding vigorously. "I suppose I shan't be surprised if some print is made out of *that*."

"What did Lord Hampton say to your rather bold pronouncement?" Cassandra asked.

"He appeared thoroughly shocked and only nodded in agreement," Sybil said.

"Heavens, perhaps I am glad that I did not attend," Cassandra said.

"And here is another thing," Sybil said. "Lord Lockwood would insist on taking me into dinner again. I fear his attention was too marked and, if that was not uncomfortable enough, my father viewed it in a very dim light."

"That is three times he has taken you in," Cassandra said.

"Yes," Sybil said, "though I hardly count the first as he only rescued me and had not much to say for himself."

"Do you like him, Sybil?"

Sybil reached for an almond biscuit and chewed it determinedly before she answered. "Truly, I have not allowed myself to consider it. There is too much against it—he is a gentleman of the pact and even if he were not, my father abhors his own father."

"That is true, and in any case, if you wish to be a duchess whilst avoiding that ridiculous pact, you might marry Lord Burke. He is not so burdened, and you would be very merry at table as he regales you with stories of his cook."

Both ladies dissolved into laughter at the thought of it. Though, under Cassandra's laughter, there was intense trepidation. She and Lady Marksworth had been snubbed by the Hedleys, and she feared there might be more snubs to come.

Cassandra began to get the sickening idea that perhaps more snubs had already come. When they had made their calls and found ladies not at home, *had* they been at home? Had some of Lady Marksworth's acquaintance refused her card? The excuses they had been given had seemed reasonable, one lady had been called away to care for a sick aunt, another attended a wedding breakfast. But what if those reasons had been invented?

She could not know. She would never know. But the very idea was stinging. It was not so much for herself that it stung, it was for her dear aunt. The idea that she might have been a catalyst to causing her aunt pain and embarrassment was too awful to think of.

THE DAY OF the Marksworths' ball had passed by in frenetic activity. Cassandra had felt a charge in the house, as if lightning had come through the windows and sparked its way through every room. Even the unflappable Racine had a look about him that she likened to a wary fox catching the scent of hounds. Cassandra had gone to no end of balls and had not had the first idea of what a hostess must go through. She would be more appreciative of their efforts in future.

Despite the atmosphere that had at times bordered on doom, all had been arranged. The musicians had arrived, the ices had arrived, hundreds of beeswax candles had been lit and the preparations for supper were well on their way in the kitchens. The ballroom itself, usually dark and empty, was ablaze with light and servants running this way and that while attending to final details.

Cassandra marveled at her dress. Lady Marksworth had spent a deal of time working with the dressmaker to achieve what she had in her mind and it was glorious. White satin, the skirt overlaid with the palest of pink gauze. Large white rosettes lined the hem of the satin and showed charmingly through the gauze. Smaller rosettes circled the sleeves and bodice. It was not overdone or overwrought, it was elegant in every respect. Having only so recently been a young girl racing round her estate and muddying up her clothes, she wondered at finding herself so attired.

Her nerves were at once heightened with excitement and trepidation. She knew herself to be an object of curiosity and so would be on display. But her own ball! At a ball such as that, the young lady would be the focus of the evening. Anybody wishing to stare might do so without risking disapproval. Of course, there were those who would likely not come because of the unwanted attention she had received. She knew the dreaded Lady Montague had been issued an invitation and even indicated she would attend, but that had been weeks ago. Cassandra felt certain the lady would not come now. Not with the talk that had gone round. Not Lady Montague. She also expected that Lady Montague's friend Lady Hedley would not appear. She could not say that she would miss either one of them. But then, there might be others who would snub her.

All the gentlemen of the pact had said they would attend, a fact that Lady Marksworth had not informed her of until that very morning. Her aunt saw it as a particular compliment—it was not every hostess who could claim that six would-be dukes attended their ball. In fact, seven, as Lord Burke had accepted too.

For Cassandra's own part, she was not certain what she thought of it. She could not say she would be sorry to have further conversation with Lord Hampton. Their last had been truly engaging and felt more effortless than the usual conversations she'd had with various gentlemen. She'd convinced herself that she enjoyed talking with him so thoroughly because he proved himself well-educated. She'd nearly given up denying her attraction to him, though nothing would come of it.

Having heard from Sybil that he had asked after her gave her an unnamed feeling. Worse, that he had obliquely referenced the embarrassing print, which she'd prayed had faded into obscurity by now.

She had the highest hopes that it *had* fallen out of favor as the latest gossip. Lady Marksworth had told her that she'd heard from a friend that Lady Montague's refusal to come as a snake to the Blakeley's mask was on everybody's tongues just now. Cassandra, having experienced it herself, could not wish anybody to come under such scrutiny. Though, if somebody must, she could not weep over it being Lady Montague.

Lady Marksworth met her at the bottom of the stairs and led her to the hall. There they would stand as the carriages rolled up, greeting each and every guest. She expected she would be exhausted by the end of it, though the dancing would not even have begun.

"You could not look lovelier, my dear," Lady Marksworth said.

Racine nodded as if seconding his mistress's opinion.

They heard the distinctive clip-clop and stop of a carriage arriving and Racine threw open the doors.

The cold air rushed in and Cassandra was glad that Racine had the foresight to place braziers all around the hall.

Lord Dalton was the first to arrive and Cassandra could only be surprised by it. Of all the gentlemen of the pact, she would have expected him to be one of the last, pirate that he viewed himself to be.

She was much cheered to see Sybil and her mother and father, who had no need of a carriage as they were directly next door. Cassandra was certain that dear Sybil had hurried her parents along, knowing how nervous her friend must be on such a night.

Sybil squeezed her hand tight as they walked through.

Lord and Lady Sedway arrived and her old friend Anne looked just as elegant as ever. Cassandra began to calm her nerves; it was comforting to find so many friends already in the house.

Lord Lockwood and Lord Hampton arrived together. Cassandra began to think they must be particular friends as she had seen them so often together. Lord Hampton had appeared exceedingly reserved, even for him, and Cassandra had felt some sort of embarrassment at seeing him, though she could not pinpoint her feelings exactly.

Lords Cabot, Ashworth and Grayson all arrived on horseback. Lady Marksworth looked victorious—all six gentlemen of the pact had arrived, and they had arrived in good time. Cassandra, now that she viewed it, thought there was something odd in it. They had indeed arrived promptly. Why should these gentlemen be so eager to arrive? It was generally understood that a lady's friends and family come at the designated hour and the rest of the guests begin arriving sometime after that. Single gentlemen were notorious for coming in at the last decent moment, all the while striking terror into their hostesses' hearts. Why were they all so early?

Before she could contemplate it further, Lord and Lady Blakeley arrived. He appeared as dashing as ever, she wore a marvelous turban decorated with bright colored jewels. Though Lady Marksworth viewed the gentlemen of the pact as the coup of the evening, Cassandra thought it the reception of the Blakeleys. It was understood that they did not accept every invitation that came their way, they were the sort of couple that were so sought after that they could not, even if they'd wanted to. It was a testament to Lady Marksworth's longstanding friendship with Lady Blakeley that they'd chosen to accept *her* invitation.

There was a lull in the arrivals which gave Cassandra a moment to catch her breath. She noticed a footman jogging up the steps. The boy handed a note to Racine, who brought it to Lady Marksworth.

She opened it and Cassandra noted her brow furrow.

"What is it, Aunt?"

Lady Marksworth said, "Lady Montague writes that she cannot attend after all. I am not surprised by it, or even disappointed, but I *am* surprised by her wording."

"Why?" Cassandra asked in alarm. "What surprises you?"

"That she would have the nerve to reference gossip for one thing," Lady Marksworth said, "and for another, she addresses me overly formally considering our long acquaintance. The thing is meant to insult and I believe I may cut her the next time I see her."

"May I?" Cassandra asked, holding out her hand.

Lady Marksworth handed over the note and Cassandra scanned its contents.

Lady Marksworth,

In light of recent unfortunate events, it is of course impossible for me to attend you this evening. My sincerest regrets,

Harriet Downing

Cassandra understood the lady's intent instantly. The words *recent unfortunate events* were clearly a reference to the gossip. Lady Montague wished to say that she could not see her way clear to notice a girl who had been so talked of.

Though she had been certain Lady Montague would not attend, and equally certain the lady would not approve of her, seeing it so clearly spelled out on paper was humiliating.

"Never mind, Cass," Lady Markswooth said. "Do not allow bitter old Harriet to ruin your evening. She has spent a lifetime ruining countless evenings for countless other people and I should not like you to join that sad company."

Cassandra considered her aunt's view and was cheered by it. It was true the note was humiliating, but it was not public. Nobody would miss the lady, and nobody would know what she'd written.

The clatter of horses at a fast trot caught Cassandra's attention. A carriage barreled down the road, the coachman pulling on the reins in front of the house. Lord Burke jumped down to the road before the vehicle had barely come to a stop.

He bounded up the steps breathless.

"Dear Lord Burke," Lady Marksworth said, laughing. "Do not hurry so, you are in good time."

"My haste is for good reason, Lady Marksworth," Lord Burke said. "I must insist on a private interview with you and Miss Knightsbridge this instant. It is quite urgent."

Cassandra felt her knees go weak. Never had she seen Lord Burke in such earnest. "Is it my father?" she cried.

"No, God no, nothing like that," Lord Burke said hurriedly. "Where can we speak privately?"

Lady Marksworth paled. Racine said, "The small drawing room, my lady. I will make your excuses at the door and show your guests to the ballroom."

Her aunt nodded, and Cassandra dazedly followed Lord Burke and Lady Marksworth into the small drawing room. After the door was closed, Lady Marksworth said, "Whatever is it, Lord Burke? Do not keep us in suspense."

Though the lord had been in such a hurry to get them away to the drawing room, now that he had them away, he seemed not to know where to begin.

"It is not my father or any other terrible news from Surrey?" Cassandra asked. News that her father had been taken ill, or worse, was the only news she thought could absolutely terrify her. Though the lord had already denied it was so, she must have a confirmation.

"I have had no news at all from Surrey," Lord Burke said, rubbing his hands and looking decidedly uncomfortable. "I come on another matter entirely. One that I was apprised of only a half hour ago. My mother sent for me and showed me a note that was delivered to one of her friends. That friend is not as highly placed as she, was terrified of its contents, and planned to acquiesce to its demands."

Lord Burke pulled a folded piece of paper from his pocket and handed it to Lady Marksworth. Cassandra leaned over and read it along with her aunt.

Jemima,

As I have informed others of my acquaintance, anybody being so reckless as to pay notice to a girl who has involved herself in three engagements behind the back of her father can no longer be noticed by me. I have full confidence you will not attend the girl's ball at Marksworth House.

Harriet Downing

Chapter Eleven

CASSANDRA LOOKED UP from Lady Montague's note. "What does it mean?" Cassandra said.

"It means," Lord Burke said, "that Lady Montague has set out to ensure that very few people attend this ball. She knows she cannot hold sway over those such as the Blakeleys or my own mother, but she *can* hold sway over many. Though my mother had not planned on attending this evening, as she rarely attends balls, she sent for me to say that she would attend if necessary, to stand firm against Lady Montague's scheme. I counseled that it would be best to take another course. Lady Marksworth, we must invent a ruse to cancel the ball immediately. It will be the only way to avert disaster."

"Lord Burke," Lady Marksworth said, "Nothing Lady Montague could get up to would surprise me, but we do not understand the note itself. What three engagements?"

Lord Burke paled. "Good Lord. You have not seen the print that has been everywhere."

"If you mean the ridiculous illustration of the three gentlemen in the sky, we have seen it. It was thrown through our window, in fact. However, that is a reference to Lords Hampton, Lockwood and Ashworth choosing to escort us from the park after a certain rude gentleman made a coarse remark to my niece. It has nothing at all to do with any engagement."

Lord Burke appeared thoroughly confused. "Hampton, Lockwood and Ashworth? No, Lady Marksworth. That is not who the gentlemen are meant to be. It is said that Miss Knightsbridge was secretly engaged to three gentlemen in Surrey, and that the three all met on the road to her estate. When they discovered each other, all three broke off with the lady."

If Cassandra's knees had felt weak when Lord Burke had first arrived, now they positively could not hold her up. She sank down onto a sofa.

What was this? What three gentlemen? What engagements?

Lady Marksworth held herself straight. She appeared furious. "I see. And do we know who the author of this wretched business might be? I am certain her father would call the scoundrel out at dawn."

"That I do not know," Lord Burke said.

"Is there any other story associated with this nonsense?" Lady Marksworth asked.

Lord Burke turned his face away.

"I see that there is," Lady Marksworth said. "Out with it, if you please, my lord."

Lord Burke heavily sighed. "As is the nature of gossip, at times there is talk of there being four or five gentlemen, rather than three. And, it is said, that Miss Knightsbridge has a particular facility with a shotgun and her father is terrified of her."

Now it was Lady Marksworth's turn to sink to the sofa. "And Lady Montague has seen fit to take full advantage of these malicious stories."

"My lady," Lord Burke said. "I know what I have communicated has come at a great shock, but we must act quickly. The later it gets, the more apparent that Lady Montague has succeeded."

Lady Marksworth straightened her back, as if firming her resolve. "What do you suggest we do?" she asked.

"It is just this—I will run from this room and claim that Miss

Knightsbridge has fainted and does not wake. I will tell your butler to send down a lady's maid. We will send for a doctor, my own man who I can trust. Lady Marksworth, you will make the announcement that the evening is cancelled. It is the only way forward."

Cassandra thought it might not be a lie to say that she had fainted and would not wake. She very much wished that it was so. The truth of what had occurred was so terrible that it could not be faced—oblivion would be a blessing.

All along, she had thought the gossip that swirled round her had to do with shooting a gun and the three lords escorting her home. But this was a thousand times worse! It spoke to her character!

"Truly," Lord Burke said urgently, "there is not a moment to lose."

Lady Marksworth stood. "I believe you are right, Lord Burke, and I thank you for assisting us at this terrible hour. As soon as the lady's maid arrives, I will inform the guests. Do insist on Clara, not Peggy. Go and do your work."

Lord Burke looked much relieved and fairly flew from the room. Cassandra could not hold her feelings back longer and began to sob.

Her aunt sat by her and put an arm round her shoulder. "There now, you must not give in to your feelings this moment. There will be plenty of time later, but just now we must play our parts."

Cassandra nodded and willed herself to stop her tears. Lady Marksworth was right—there would be endless amounts of time to cry, but not right now.

"Lay down and close your eyes. You must appear in a faint in case anybody sees you when the door opens to admit Clara. Do not worry about my maid, she can keep a thing to herself. Peggy, I am not so sure of, and so I advise allowing her to know nothing."

Cassandra nodded, and then closed her eyes.

AS EVENTS TRANSPIRED outside the door, Cassandra lay there with Clara holding her hand, hearing bits and pieces of it. She distinctly heard Lord Hampton suggest he send for his own doctor, only to be denied by Lady Marksworth. Sybil asked if she might come in, but Lady Marksworth said it would be time enough on the morrow for a visit.

Had they all heard the story? It seemed impossible that the six gentlemen of the pact had not heard all that had been said. It must be the talk of every gentlemen's club. Had they come with an eye toward amusement? It would not surprise her to know that they were well aware of Lady Montague's salvo and had come to see how it would all unfold. They would look upon it as a jolly bit of fun to be discussed the following day. Certainly, that was the cause of their very early arrival, they would not wish to miss anything of this disaster.

Suddenly, she understood Mr. Conners' untoward behavior in the park, his bizarre challenge to a race. He'd had the nerve to treat her as less than a lady as he believed she'd conducted herself as less than a lady.

How had this all happened? When she'd thought the three gentlemen depicted on the print were Hampton, Lockwood and Ashworth, it had only seemed as if some person had put two disparate ideas into one illustration. She'd owned to skill with a gun and the three gentlemen had escorted her from the park. But where on earth had the idea of the three engagements in Surrey originated? There was no truth that could account for it, even if that truth were to be stretched beyond recognition.

Cassandra felt she would truly faint. She wished it with all her heart. Anything to be away from this dreadful scene.

EDWIN HAD BEEN alarmed at the news of Miss Knightsbridge fainting.

Not so much because she fainted, ladies had ever been in the habit of doing so, but because she would not wake. He had some vague idea that a waving of smelling salts was all that was required to bring a lady back to the present.

His alarm had reached new heights after speaking with Burke. Hampton had directed all the gentlemen of the pact to turn up in force. He'd thought it would send a clear message to all who attended Lady Marksworth's ball.

He'd never imagined that most others would not attend due to Lady Montague's directive. He'd never imagined Lady Montague would dare *issue* such a directive. She was a spiteful old thing and feared by enough of society to have her will. That she did not dare attempt to influence him or his friends came as no surprise, Lady Montague wielded her iron fist down, never up.

Burke told him Miss Knightsbridge had barely held up upon hearing what was said of her. Until this very night, she'd had no idea of any talk of three broken engagements. The further blow delivered—that very few would come to her ball—had felled her and she did not wake. All along, Burke said, she had thought the print to be representative of a meeting in the park with Hampton, Lockwood and Ashworth after Mr. Conners' untoward suggestion of a race. That might have been upsetting, but in no way reached the heights of the humiliation of the real story that had gone round.

Now, she knew the truth. What a poison they had unleashed upon the lady!

What was to be the end of it? The rumors he'd thought they could counter with some effort could not be subdued. Lady Montague's stance was determined and there were few who would dare to cross her.

Miss Knightsbridge would receive dwindling invitations going forward. Even less marriage proposals. Perhaps no marriage proposals at all. What gentleman, even if she had the means of meeting him at a gathering, would gladly suffer the notoriety of finding himself the fourth gentleman engaged to the lady? What gentleman would risk being ostracized by Lady Montague for marrying her? What family would welcome it?

Through their own selfishness, he and his friends had ruined a lady. *He* had ruined the lady.

The truth must come out. They must own what they did. He and his friends were low and self-interested—all should know that they were the worst sort of people, regardless of what titles they might hold.

Edwin paused. They must do more than just own being the cause of this disaster. They must atone for it. *He* must atone for it. But how?

He knew how. He knew the only certain thing he might do to reestablish Miss Knightsbridge in society. To give her a rightful place in it. To ensure that she was treated with the respect she deserved. To firmly and finally shut the mouths of Lady Montague and her ilk.

He must marry Miss Knightsbridge.

What a pass he had come to! This terrible circumstance had begun with a hope to avoid the state and now he was honor-bound to accomplish it.

Still, if he was to live with himself, it must be done.

THE HOUSE HAD grown very quiet and Cassandra had been carried up the stairs by two footmen under the watchful eyes of Racine and Clara. Peggy had been sent below stairs, the girl too prone to talk, while Lady Marksworth attended Lord Burke and waited for his physician. Cassandra understood the physician would be told the truth, that she had no illness but that of spirit, but he could be trusted and would be seen coming and going—it would bolster the idea of her sudden illness.

Where had the story of the three engagements come from? She'd had no particular suitors in Surrey. She'd bestowed no singular interest on any gentleman.

Was a lady to be ruined simply because some mean-spirited person decided to invent a tale? How was that possible? Who would do it? She had not made enemies of anybody that she knew of.

Yet, there was someone out there who harbored a hatred of her.

Cassandra had known London was another world, that she would need guidance to wend her way through. She had never imagined it was a sea of piranhas, though it appeared that was precisely what it was. She had waded in and sharp teeth had torn her to shreds.

As she'd lain on the sofa, gazing at the hem of her gown and waiting for the few guests who had arrived to take their leave, her aunt had spoken to her in soft and gentle tones. Lady Marksworth had mulled over various steps to be taken, but in the end, Cassandra had her way. She wished to go home. She wished to go on the morrow at first light.

Lady Marksworth would take her in her carriage and Peggy would stay behind to pack up her things. It was essential that she leave this horrid town. She must see her father and her dog and have all the familiar comforts of home surrounding her. She would miss Sybil, but she suspected that was all she would miss of this place. In any case, had she decided to stay, she must part with Sybil. The rumors had gone too far to allow her friend to be tainted by them, as brave and stalwart as that friend was.

Clara helped her out of her dress and Cassandra turned away from it. She could not bear to see that gown—it had represented everything hopeful and happy only hours ago.

RACINE HAD NEVER seen a more sorrowful morning at Marksworth House since the master died. Lady Marksworth had been grim as she made the arrangements for the carriage to come round at dawn. Miss Cassandra had been pale, an almost ghostly figure, seated quietly on a sofa and waiting to depart.

Neither had taken much breakfast, though he had left out every interesting morsel to be found in the kitchen. As the ball had not come off, the kitchens were groaning under the weight of the food that was to have comprised the supper. Racine had been careful to leave all of that alone, there could not be any reminder of the disastrous evening that had just passed. Still, Miss Cassandra could not even be persuaded to take an almond biscuit to break her fast.

The soft clip-clop of horses' hooves, muffled by the morning mist, had signaled the arrival of the carriage. His mistress and her niece had left almost silently, as if they joined a funeral procession.

He could hardly take in the events of the night before! First, the offensive note from a certain Lady Montague, then Lord Burke rushing in and revealing the nefarious plot afoot.

Miss Cassandra was to be ostracized! It was outrageous. That good, young girl had never done a wrong thing in her life.

If he had his way, he would set off to locate this Lady Montague and knock the stuffing out of her.

As it was, he could not knock the stuffing out of anybody, except perhaps Miss Cassandra's maid Peggy, who still snored in her bed. He would see to it that Peggy packed up her mistress's things in an orderly and neat fashion and that she kept her opinions to herself. He'd already grown tired of the girl's opinions and now he was downright done with them.

Hours later, as he watched over the house and its inhabitants with a careful and somber eye, he heard the clatter of a horse reined in and a pounding on the door.

Fearing it would be news of an accident on the road, he rushed to answer it.

Lord Hampton stood on the steps, seeming out of breath as if he'd galloped his way across London.

"Is Miss Knightsbridge at home?" Lord Hampton asked. "Or Lady Marksworth? Or both? Perhaps both would be better."

"I am afraid, my lord," Racine said, "both Miss Knightsbridge and Lady Marksworth have retired to the country."

"To the country?" Lord Hampton said. "My God, what time did they set off?"

"At first light, my lord," Racine said.

"But surely… she was not well. Is it wise that she travel so soon?"

Racine had not been prepared for the question, but that was of little matter. His years as a butler had trained him to always be ready to answer any question in a manner befitting the house.

"The doctor was here and examined Miss Knightsbridge. He pronounced her fit for travel and charged Lady Marksworth to get her into the country air as soon as possible."

"Where do they go? Surrey? Or to Lady Marksworth's estate?"

"They go to Miss Knightsbridge's father in Surrey," Racine said gravely.

Racine watched in some amazement as Lord Hampton fairly stumbled down the steps. It seemed the lord took a singular interest in the health of Miss Cassandra.

He could not say whether he approved or disapproved of the idea. Though, if the lord did take such an interest, he might make himself useful by discovering the whereabouts of Lady Montague and knocking the stuffing out of her.

UNBEKNOWNST TO CASSANDRA, Lady Marksworth had the foresight to send a letter via fast horse to Trebly Hall the night before, preparing her father for their arrival and the circumstances surrounding their sudden decampment.

Cassandra had slept a deal of the way, sleep now being her welcome escape. She woke and found the sun high overhead and, out the carriage windows, the familiar scenes of her neighborhood. It was comforting to view Mr. Jenkin's fields kept in good order as they had always been. The grand old willow that draped its greenery so close to the road stood as it ever had. Two rough and tumble boys stuck their tongues out at the passing carriage, as boys had always been wont to do.

It was as if time had stood still. So much had happened to her, but nothing had happened to Surrey.

Then, finally, they rumbled through the gates and Trebly Hall rose in the distance. Its fine stone façade and glorious tall windows standing as it had ever stood these past hundred years.

The carriage rolled to a stop and, much to her surprise, her father was there to greet them.

Lady Marksworth leaned over and said softly, "Your father knows all—I wrote ahead."

Cassandra was helped down to the gravel. Though her father had always been exceedingly kind, she did feel some trepidation over how he would view this particular disaster. She'd been sent to London to conduct herself creditably and somehow come home in disgrace.

The viscount gently took her arm and said, "There now, I hear you have been through the wars, but there is no war here. Come in and be at peace in your home."

This was so generous that Cassandra found herself sobbing. Her dear, dear father! What a change from those sneering, talking people of London!

She was led indoors as her father talked beside her. "You will need refreshment before you go above stairs to change. Come into the library, a certain ridiculous dog awaits you there. Further, Maidencraft has had Cook working like a demon to see that your favorite biscuits appear on the tea tray."

The library doors were thrown open. Mayhem, as she had heard the commotion outside, was just behind the door and prepared to throw herself into the fray, whatever the fray might be. The mastiff flung herself at Cassandra, nearly knocking her over. Then, she proceeded to race around the library to show her wild approbation over this unexpected arrival. She snatched a book off a shelf for good measure and tossed it in the air, before coming to a stop at her mistress's feet.

"My wonderful May," Cassandra said quietly. "How I have missed your innocent enthusiasm."

She led May to a sofa near the windows. It was known to be for the exclusive use of the dog, May having claimed it as a puppy and it being generally so covered in dog hair as to make it unsuitable for human use. Cassandra did not particularly care about covering her traveling dress in dog hair and happily ensconced herself on it. May leapt up and flung her heavy head on her adored mistress's lap.

The viscount and Lady Marksworth sat together on the other side of the room, talking quietly.

Cassandra only heard bits and pieces, but from what she could gather, neither her aunt nor her father could fathom where the rumor of the three engagements had come from. Lady Marksworth suggested that Cassandra stay in Surrey for a year or two—perhaps her niece would meet a local gentleman who would suit.

Her father, however, had other ideas. He'd already made inquiries into hiring an investigator. He would discover the culprit. That person would be punished, Cassandra's name cleared, and her rightful place restored to her.

Finally, there was some hushed talk of a certain Lady Montague until her father said, rather loudly, "I do not care who the lady thinks she is, I'll go to London and straighten out the harridan myself if I have to."

Cassandra could not say if she cared one way or another what was done. She was home and there was a feeling in the house of being cushioned from all harm. No matter what went on out in the world, that awful world could not encroach upon Trebly Hall. All the whispers and unkind words could stay where they were—they would not gain entrance here.

The night before, as she had stared into the darkness and considered her future, she'd nearly decided that she would not marry at all. Why should she? Her father's estate was not entailed. She would inherit all of it. Of course, he'd had the idea that she would have sons and one of the younger might take it over, rather than choose the military or the clergy. But might she not manage on her own? She thought she knew enough of the estate's business to do so—she understood animal husbandry and planting and how to manage a tenant. She had taken over the supervision of the apple orchard and the subsequent cider-making some years ago. She might get on very well and if she took that course, she would not answer to anybody. The wags in London might talk until they were breathless, but they would not be heard.

She might give up trying to be a perfect little lady and, instead, pick up a shotgun whenever she liked. She might simply be who she always was. It would come as a relief, really. She would never have to step foot in that poisonous town again.

She would, of course, miss Sybil terribly. The lady had been such a stalwart ally! Still, she could write and once Sybil was a married lady she might visit, assuming her husband did not condemn the connection.

Cassandra pushed away an idea that kept inconveniently surfacing in her mind. It was becoming more and more uncomfortable to imagine what some people might think of her upon hearing of the three engagements. In particular, what Lord Hampton might think. Had he and his friends all arrived early to her ball, knowing of impending disaster and wishing to see how it unfolded? It stung to think so, as she had begun to believe that they developed a friendship through their mutual interests. But perhaps he had only toyed with her and found it amusing.

She was confounded by his face persisting in her mind. His dark hair and darker eyes and his… she did not really know what it was about him. They had not met well, but then somehow had got on well. He'd paid her marked attention and his attention felt a bigger compliment, as it was not easily earned. Now, she felt a fool for having wondered if he would take her into supper at her own ball. He could not admire her, not after what he would have heard.

The pang of it was deep and awful.

May interrupted her thoughts with a large lick to her hand, meant to remind her that her dog was very fond of an ear scratch.

Chapter Twelve

Edwin had been more than surprised to discover Miss Knightsbridge had decamped to Surrey so precipitously. According to the butler, she and Lady Marksworth had left at dawn.

If he had not fully comprehended the disaster that had befallen the lady, a rushed departure before the town woke must reveal it in all clarity. He did not know *what* would be said in every drawing room in the days to come, only that much would be said.

He'd had the inclination of rushing to Surrey to see Miss Knightsbridge there, but he had paused. He had not any connection to the viscount and, if he were to simply arrive unannounced, what should he say? My lord, I have been the architect of your daughter's destruction and would now propose that we wed?

Any decent father would not hand over a daughter under such bizarre and unseemly circumstances. Any decent father might propose a private meeting at dawn instead, accompanied only by their respective seconds.

If he were to approach the viscount, and he was determined to do so, he must arrive better prepared. He must admit what he'd done, but then he must also explain what he'd done about it.

He'd felt that he and the other gentlemen of the pact had carried out all that could be done to counter the talk against Miss Knightsbridge. Now, he saw that was not so. Now, there must be more urgent steps taken. The first of those steps began at Lady Montague's door.

He gazed around at the lady's overdressed drawing room, it fairly bursting with Greek statuettes, portraits of those long dead, and strategically placed books meant to make one seem intelligent. It fairly screamed façade, and he supposed that was fitting. Had Lady Montague not been born high, he supposed she might have made a living on the stage.

"Lord Hampton," the lady said, breezing into the room, "what a welcome surprise! I do not believe we have seen you since my ball."

Edwin kept his face neutral, though he was always irritated by the lady's use of the royal we.

"I hear you were in attendance at Marksworth House last evening?" Lady Montague continued. "A shame the lady was taken ill, but then it would not have been well attended in any case. I should have thought to alert you to the rumors before you sullied your person in that house, I do apologize for my carelessness."

My God. He'd thought he'd have to bring up the topic himself, but the lady was eager to speak of it. She even appeared proud of her handiwork.

"I am well aware of the rumors, Lady Montague, as the gentlemen of the pact started them," Edwin said. "We wished for some little trifle to go round to take eyes off of us. Unfortunately, more than a trifle went round, it's all nonsense, and I am determined to rectify it."

Lady Montague nodded approvingly. "You are very gallant, my lord, attempting to rescue the lady's reputation. Sadly, it will not do."

"Madam," Edwin said, "it must do, as it is the truth. Further, I am aware of what you did to ensure low attendance at the lady's ball."

Lady Montague shrugged. "Friends must be warned, my lord."

"Your friends, if that is what you think they are, were threatened."

At this, Lady Montague began to comprehend that Lord Hampton might not be entirely in agreement with her way of thinking.

"Surely not," she said with somewhat less confidence.

"Surely so," Edwin said. "Were you a reasonable lady, I would task you with correcting others' opinions of Miss Knightsbridge as those opinions are patently false. The lady has been unjustly accused and everybody of any sense must know it. As it happens, I have never found you reasonable and would not trust you to do it creditably. Rather, I think you would make it your business to defend your initial opinion, as you so little care to be wrong. Therefore, you and your lord will absent yourself from London as soon as you can pack your cases and no later than the morrow."

"But the season—"

"I insist," Edwin said.

"I am not so certain that you *can* insist," Lady Montague said petulantly.

"I can. And I do. If you refuse me, my friends and I will make certain that all the best houses shut their doors against you. You are not the only individual who can hold sway over the *ton* and I wager we can bring to bear a lot more force than you have at your disposal. I will make you a pariah and the people who fear you now will cut you on the street."

Edwin's speech had been well thought out and composed to strike fear into the heart of a lady who valued her place in the world above anything else. He had no doubt he'd accomplished what he set out to do, as Lady Montague sank down to the sofa.

"Good day, madam," he said, "I will eagerly anticipate hearing the news that the Montagues have decamped to Yorkshire."

THE MONTAGUES DID indeed leave for Yorkshire the following day, Lady Montague developing a cough that only her home county could cure.

While the Montagues' carriage barreled out of London, Edwin called the gentlemen of the pact to Dalton's house, determined they develop a plan of action.

"Lady Montague has been sent packing," he said. "Now, we must have everybody understand that we are the authors of this pack of lies going round about Miss Knightsbridge. It is the only way to put an end to it."

"Fall on our swords, eh?" Cabot said.

"More like fall on a hundred swords," Dalton said drily.

"What of our fathers?" Lockwood asked. "They will lose their minds over this."

"They well may," Hampton said. "But we are gentlemen and must face the consequences."

There were various sighs and foot shufflings and lookings askance, but Hampton could see that they would do it. The news would fly through London unimpeded by Lady Montague's naysaying. Miss Knightsbridge would be recognized as the innocent victim that she was. They would all be hailed as scoundrels, and a well-earned moniker it would be.

News of it would surely travel to Surrey one way or the other, and that was the one aspect that worried Hampton exceedingly. He would not be on hand to personally explain what had happened.

"In any case," Dalton said, "it will get you off the hook. No need to marry the girl if we've set her to rights. No further need of rescue, I think."

"Well, as to that..." Edwin trailed off. In truth, he was not certain he wished to answer those comments. As soon as he had resolved to marry Miss Knightsbridge, it had begun to seem a pleasant idea. After all, where was another like her? She had beauty, she had wit, and well... she was rather extraordinary.

In truth, it had become more than a pleasant idea. With him hardly realizing it was happening, marriage to Miss Knightsbridge had begun to feel a *necessary* idea.

"That's right," Ashworth said, "she'll come back looking the tragic heroine and then marry some fellow."

Edwin stiffened. As if Miss Knightsbridge should waste herself on some fellow! She was born to be a duchess. She had all the fortitude of his mother and grandmother, not like all those simpering misses who fanned their faces to keep themselves upright. Then of course, there was that face…

She was smashing in every respect. Marry *some fellow*, indeed.

"Even if we are successful," he said carefully, "I may still find I owe her a debt."

"Good Lord," Grayson said, "you have fallen. You are in love with Miss Knightsbridge."

"Nobody spoke of love," Edwin said. Least of all himself, though it sat in front of him like a waving flag.

He stood. "We know our duty, let us carry it out. Now, I am late for an appointment." He left Dalton's library as fast as his legs could carry him.

LADY MARKSWORTH HAD left Trebly Hall and returned to London. She wrote regular letters, both to the viscount and Cassandra, informing them of what was being said in town. These letters differed entirely from the regular letters Cassandra received from Sybil, who worked painstakingly to avoid any topic that might cause grief and so generally described the weather in minute detail.

For some weeks, Lady Marksworth's letters held nothing of particular note, excepting that most people were very much relieved that the Montagues had gone home. Lady Marksworth said that while nobody would claim it outright, the general feeling was that all wished Lady Montague's cough to be rather serious.

Then, on a bright and sunny morning, a letter arrived that turned Cassandra's thoughts on their head.

My dear niece,

As I have written your father, the investigator here still has not tracked down where this terrible rumor began. However, a most interesting development has occurred. The gentlemen of the pact all now claim that it was they who invented it. They say it was to take scrutiny away from themselves. A flimsy story, at best. Nobody believes them for a moment, but all the talk revolves around how admiring they are of Miss Knightsbridge to attempt such a rash scheme to explain away the gossip. It is said that Lord Hampton is particularly vocal with the story and has been announcing it to all and sundry.

Though the idea is not considered creditable, I will say that I think it has softened opinion toward you. After all, how is a baron's wife or an earl's daughter to condemn a lady held up as blameless by six gentlemen who will one day be dukes of the realm?

It also does not hurt that Lady Montague is away from the scene, as many are better able to form their own opinions when she is not nearby to correct them.

I would not say the tide has turned in your favor, but I think it ceases to rise.

All my Love,
Aunt Catherine

Cassandra dropped her aunt's letter, then swiftly picked it up again before May could chew it to bits.

If the gentlemen came to her defense, then they could not have arrived to her ball simply to observe a blossoming disaster. Perhaps they'd seen the disaster coming and came to support her side?

But why should they defend her so vigorously? Why should Lord Hampton do so?

She could only think of one reason, and it gave her a shiver to think of it. Might it be true that he had some interest in her that was marked?

Since she had been home, the lord's face had been somewhat relentless in presenting itself to her mind. She had all but given up attempting to chase it away. Rather, if she were never to marry, surely there was no harm in living a romance in her imagination. Nobody should know of it but herself, it might be her own private world she could retreat to when she felt too alone. In fact, it might be the best of all worlds, as an imaginary gentleman could never disappoint her. He would act just as she wished and they would always be in the first blush of love.

She'd tried the idea on any number of faces she'd seen in London. Lord Burke had seemed a likely candidate, but she found her thoughts always going to jokes and stories, there was no romance in it. Lord Lockwood was too… something. Others were… not quite right. It was only the imaginary Lord Hampton that caused a flutter. And, the more she thought of him, the more she felt it.

It had all been a pleasant dream. As she reread her aunt's letter, she determined she should not see anything in it. She must not begin to hope for some reality that would begin to match her wild imagination. Daydreaming was perfectly fine, but she would set herself up for even more heartache if she allowed herself to hope for anything in the real world.

For all that, though, it was gratifying to know that she was defended.

CASSANDRA'S FATHER HAD hired two investigators who worked together—one canvassing London and the other making inquiries in Surrey. The viscount was determined to discover who had launched the rumors against his daughter.

Cassandra wished he'd give it up. She did not think he would ever find success and each time he met with Mr. Cringle or read a letter from Mr. Shanks it brought all the first bursts of outrage back upon him.

Mr. Shanks had written a rather victorious letter about the gentlemen of the pact confessing their crime against Miss Knightsbridge, only to have to be told that it was a ridiculous fiction that nobody believed. The viscount began to question Mr. Shanks' judgment—if the man could not see through such a ludicrous account, how was he to recognize the truth when he found it?

Mr. Cringle turned up every Wednesday, his meetings with the viscount were not long and her father was never happy at the end of them. Everybody in the neighborhood had heard the rumor and it seemed agreed upon that the notion had begun in Surrey. Different theories floated about the environs of Trebly Hall with no more sense in them than ducks bobbing on a lake. There was much finger pointing and the circumstance began to be used whenever a person wished to accuse an enemy. It had devolved to such ridiculous degrees that two elderly women having a dispute over a basket of washing had accused each other of having invented the tale. Cassandra's friend, Lily Farnsworth, did her best to hush the talk, but with little success.

Lily visited and did her level best to cheer Cassandra but did not have much success. Cassandra had determined that she would not rejoin local society. At least, not yet. Dinners and balls held little attraction just now and she had no wish to find herself the object of interest at a neighbor's table.

If there were any little thing that had given Cassandra pleasure, it was the gifting of two of her evening dresses to Lily. With very little alteration, she'd already worn one to a local assembly. It pleased Cassandra to know her friend wore new dresses, instead of refurbishing old ones with various bits and bobs.

Lily had been hesitant to take such a gift, but Cassandra reasoned she'd have little use for those gowns now. Privately, she thought all hope of redemption was lost and she'd best accept her lot, such as it was. There would be no schedule of London balls needing dresses.

Her father did not at all agree and would persist with the investigators.

Aside from his dealings with the investigators, the viscount had made every effort to see that his daughter was comfortable. He suggested outings but acquiesced when she declined. She spoke to him of never marrying and he took the news with seeming equanimity, though Cassandra did not think he believed in the idea. She told him she was done attempting to be a proper little miss and would return to her old ways of going on, shotgun included. The viscount was highly approving of that idea, as he'd never disapproved of her ways and felt that at least it would draw her from the house, shotguns being known for their unsuitability indoors.

She had then begun to go out, though only on her father's estate. Some mornings she slipped out at dawn and rode Juno as wildly as she liked over the grounds. Flying over fences, it made her laugh to think of poor old Buttercup plodding her way through Hyde Park. There was something rejuvenating about feeling the wind on one's face on a windless day, the breeze created by one's own speed.

Other days, she went out in the afternoon with two grooms and practiced her aim. They'd devised a target practice by using dried balls of clay launched out of a slingshot from the top of a hill while Cassandra aimed from the valley. They brought two guns and once Cassandra had fired one, she'd toss it to a groom who'd in turn toss her one loaded. The footman at the top of the hill shot off the clay balls rapid fire and it was a thrill to see how many she could take down. Her already good aim had improved markedly and when pheasant season came, she would take more than any man.

That particular afternoon, she'd been out riding most of the morning and sat pleasantly tired with May on her designated sofa by the window. As it was a Wednesday, she was not at all surprised to see Mr. Cringle's coach lumbering up the drive.

It sometimes amused her to examine Mr. Cringle's expression as he descended the stairs from his coach. He was a long and thin man with pinched features, always looking as if he were pained by something. He usually paused and looked at the house before knocking on the door, and if Cassandra imagined his thoughts, they must be along the lines of "let us get this over quickly."

The coach came to a halt and to her surprise, Mr. Cringle leapt down from the carriage with an expression she thought might be glee. The corners of his lips had turned strangely up and he had a very animated look about him.

Mr. Cringle turned and pulled another man from the coach.

Cassandra sat back from the window. It was Mr. Longmoore. What on earth was that scoundrel doing at Trebly Hall?

Whatever this conference was to be about, it was nothing usual. She was determined to hear what was said.

Maidencraft let the two gentlemen into the house and Cassandra heard them announced. She suppressed a smile: Maidencraft had said Mr. Longmoore's name as if he had just apprised the viscount that a virulent plague had arrived at his doors.

Cassandra tiptoed to the north drawing room, May following closely behind and bumping into her skirts. The north room was not much used as it was generally cold, but it shared only a wall of bookcases with her father's library. She would have no trouble hearing what was said from that vantage point.

"He is the author of it all!" Mr. Cringle fairly shouted.

"He?" the Viscount asked. "How could a drunken shopkeeper have created this misery?"

"I am not always drunken," Mr. Longmoore said quietly. "Only often."

"Tell him, man," Mr. Cringle said. "Else I'll make good my threats against you."

There was silence for some moments. The Viscount said, "If you have anything to say, Mr. Longmoore, I bid you say it. Though, Mr. Cringle, I am becoming weary of these goose chases."

"This is no feint, my lord," Mr. Cringle said. "And you will know it when you hear what he has done, why he has done it, and how he has done it."

Cassandra pressed her ear harder against the wood. Could it be true? Could Mr. Longmoore have really had anything to do with her situation? It seemed as incomprehensible to her as it did to her father.

Cassandra paused. A sudden memory flashed across her mind. The slap to his cheek at the assembly in Guildford.

If Mr. Longmoore did have something to do with the rumors, then she could not know how, but she could very well guess *why*.

"Speak, Mr. Longmoore," the Viscount said gravely.

"Dash it," Mr. Longmoore said, "she slapped me. Did she tell you that?"

"Do not propose to excuse yourself before you have even admitted what you have done," Mr. Cringle said sternly.

"All right!" Mr. Longmoore cried. "A man plied me with drink and encouraged me to tell a story of Miss Knightsbridge and then somehow it got away from me. I might have mentioned we were engaged, and then I had to call it off on account of there being two other gentlemen in the same condition."

"To the tune of fifty pounds," Mr. Cringle said.

"That's all gone now!"

Cassandra nearly lost her breath. That drunken sot had ruined her for fifty pounds! She briefly considered retrieving her shotgun and blowing his head off, but then decided she would not hang for the scoundrel.

"Tell him who the man worked for," Cringle demanded.

"He said he was in the employ of a highly placed gent," Mr.

Longmoore said. "As he was leavin,' he mentioned a Lord Dalton, though I don't think he knows I heard it. I committed it to memory in case..."

Cassandra sank down on the sofa. Lord Dalton?

"Never mind what that case might be," Mr. Cringle said, "as I am certain it would have something to do with blackmail when you found yourself once again short of funds."

"And you believe this account, Mr. Cringle?" the viscount said. "I enquire because I do not think Mr. Longmoore has been in his right mind as of late."

"It was the guilt that drove me mad!" Mr. Longmoore cried.

"I do believe his account," Mr. Cringle said. "I have had corroborating evidence from our man in London. He has confronted Mr. Tuttle, the gentleman who approached Mr. Longmoore and one we both know well, and Tuttle refuses to confirm or deny. If it were not true, he would most certainly deny. Further, the gentlemen of the pact are putting the story about themselves. They have not been believed, but they should have been. Those gentlemen sought to divert gossip from themselves and Miss Knightsbridge paid the price for it. It seems they now attempt to rectify their villainy with little success."

Could it be true? She had been ruined because six gentlemen did not wish to be talked about?

Of course it could be true. All the pieces of the puzzle began to fall into place. They had seen they'd gone too far and so suddenly they filled her dance card and they arrived early to her ball. It had not been kindness or admiration; it had been shame.

She had been such a fool to believe that they showed her such marked attention because the gossip had been about three of them escorting her from the park. She'd realized she had not grasped something when she understood the real gossip that made the rounds. She could not understand why they had rallied round her then. Now, she understood.

She felt tears sting as she remembered all her ridiculous imaginings of Lord Hampton. All along, he'd known the truth. He'd presented himself as a gentleman, all the while betraying her in the worst fashion. It had been a betrayal of Leviathan proportions, there was nothing worse that could be done to a lady beyond ruining her reputation and standing in the world.

In a terrible voice, the viscount said, "If this is so, Lord Dalton will answer for it at a dawn not too distant."

Cassandra jumped from the sofa. Whatever was to happen next, she could not allow her father to fight a duel. She could not lose her father, and if he challenged Lord Dalton, she most certainly would. The man was hardened from the war, he'd be an expert shot.

She ran from the north room and burst into the library. "Father, please!" she cried. "Do not let the end of this be that I am here alone. I could not bear it."

She crossed the room and threw herself into her father's arms and sobbed.

The viscount stroked her hair and said, "Do not cry so."

"But I must," Cassandra said, nearly choking on her words. "I cannot stand to think of it!"

"My dear," the viscount said softly, "what else am I to do? I am a man of honor, I cannot let this pass."

Cassandra pulled away from her father and glanced at Mr. Longmoore. She said, "First, we will deal with *that* person. Later, we will decide what to do about Lord Dalton. In any case, it will not be just Lord Dalton. All of the gentlemen of the pact orchestrated this disaster and you cannot fight them all."

"Miss Knightsbridge speaks the truth," Mr. Cringle said. "Lord Dalton might have done the paying, but they all had a hand in this despicable business."

Cassandra turned to Mr. Longmoore and said, "You, sir, will pack up your things and go to I know not where, nor do I care. If you do not absent yourself from this county, I will shoot you myself."

Mr. Longmoore looked pleadingly at Mr. Cringle. "She would not!"

"She very well might," Mr. Cringle said. "Then I would be forced to claim witness to the tragic accident."

"But it would not be an accident!" Mr. Longmoore cried.

"So says you, though as you bled into the ground you would have no ability to claim it. Go and wait in the carriage, you sinner."

Mr. Longmoore fairly fled the room. Cassandra had no doubt that he would leave as he was bidden.

"I must have justice," the viscount said. "If I am not to kill them all, what am I to do?"

Chapter Thirteen

Mr. Cringle rubbed his chin upon considering what the viscount might do, excepting killing all the gentlemen of the pact. "The gentlemen have owned to the misdeed. If only there were some way to convince society of their veracity. If that were accomplished, Miss Knightsbridge might go back to town with her head held high while they would be castigated. I have already got a sworn statement from Longmoore recanting everything he said."

Cassandra reined in her roiling thoughts. It was a moment for practicality. She must attend the situation at hand. Whatever was to be done, she must ensure that her father remained safe. Those idiot gentlemen might have taken her reputation, but they would not take her father.

"I do not particularly wish to return to town," Cassandra said. "Though I do not like the idea that I am prevented or that people still have my name on their lips. I would be satisfied if those gentlemen are recognized as scoundrels, and you must be too, papa."

"One powerful person taking up the position that the gentlemen speak the truth might sway the rest," Mr. Cringle said. "I do not suppose you could call upon the Prince Regent?"

The viscount rubbed his eyes. "I would not call upon that fat bumbler to lace my boots."

Poor Mr. Cringle appeared deeply shocked by the sentiment. Cassandra supposed he was not so used to the viscount's opinions on royal persons who did not appear to accomplish much aside from spending coin in the most profligate manner possible.

"Though," the viscount said thoughtfully, "there is one person who might wield such power. Delilah Weston, the Dowager Duchess of Carlisle."

"But, is that not—" Cassandra sputtered.

"Lord Hampton's grandmother," the viscount said. "Even if she cannot lend assistance, I am determined she understand what her grandson has wrought upon this family. If I know Delilah, that stupid young man will pay a heavy price."

Cassandra could not say she was against causing Lord Hampton and his friends any little amount of trouble, but most importantly, the idea had turned her father away from thoughts of a duel.

She must keep that imperative at the forefront of her efforts. She could not allow her father to slip back into the idea of a duel. She must dwell on that, and not on the knowledge that she had daydreamed of Lord Hampton, unaware that he'd been her undoing. She felt her heart slowly turn to stone against him, bathed in hardening rage.

HAMPTON SAT IN his library, sharpening a quill and pondering what to do next. He'd told everybody he'd come into contact with that the gentlemen of the pact had been the authors of the lies spread about Miss Knightsbridge. He'd sought to convince that none of what had been said was true and the lady was entirely innocent.

He could not be certain what effect it had, but for the most part he'd not been believed.

He and his friends admitted to being the worst sort of scoundrels and only kept getting congratulated on their chivalry for attempting to defend the lady!

He really was not certain what to do now, though he thought he ought to go to Surrey and attempt an interview with the viscount. He would own what he did, what attempts had been made to rectify it, and then offer his hand to Miss Knightsbridge.

He could not guess how he would be received, but if the gentleman was of a practical turn of mind, he might see the marriage as a solution.

Would *she* forgive him, though? Even if he managed to get past the father, would his daughter accept him?

He did not know, but over the days he'd become more and more determined to win her over. In truth, over the days, he'd realized that there would be no other for Edwin Weston.

She no doubt knew by now that they'd owned their crime, but could she find a way to look past it? Then, even if she could, did she even like him a little? She did not even wish to become a duchess, she'd said so the first night they'd met.

It felt a steep mountain to climb, but climb it he would.

Dreyfus softly knocked on the door and opened it. "The dowager duchess to see you, my lord."

Edwin dropped his quill. His grandmother? Here?

Before he could gather his wits, the dowager stormed the room. "You reprobate! You absolute reprobate!"

"Duchess," he said.

"Silence!"

THE NEXT HOUR of Lord Hampton's life was filled with the sort of vitriol and condemnations that one would expect from a judge to a murderer.

The dowager, as it turned out, was a particular friend of Miss Knightsbridge's father. They had kept up a correspondence for going on twenty-five years. The viscount had recently apprised her of Miss Knightsbridge's misfortune and who was to blame for it.

Edwin attempted to speak once or twice, but it was all for naught.

His grandmother would hear of no excuse, no explanation, no justification. He must bear the full weight of the crime on his shoulders and he should carry it with him all of his days. Once a soul had been stained in such a manner, it could not be washed clean again.

Finally, Edwin stood and yelled, "I'll marry her!"

The dowager paused in her diatribe. "What did you say?"

"I'll marry her, if she'll have me," Edwin said. "That is the only reparation that I can think of."

The dowager examined him with a critical eye. "I see. So, heaped upon what you have done already, you would propose to lock the poor girl into a loveless marriage in order to assuage your conscience."

Edwin did not answer, though he was certain his face flamed red.

"Or is it," the dowager said thoughtfully, "that you do love her?"

"As it happens," Edwin said stiffly.

"Good God, man," the dowager said. "It is bad enough to impugn a lady's honor but why on earth would you so damage a lady you admire?"

Edwin looked down at his desk and muttered, "It was all rather complicated."

"Apparently," the duchess said, drily.

"I was planning to go to Surrey and speak with the viscount. Own everything, and then offer my hand."

"There is hardly a need to explain anything to the viscount at this point," the dowager said, "the man is already perfectly aware of your part in it. As for a marriage proposal, you may cool your heels here for the time being. It is I who will go to Surrey."

Edwin did not know what his grandmother intended to accomplish, nor whether it was right for her to go, rather than himself. It mattered not, as once the dowager had set her mind on something, everybody else must just jump out of the way.

⋙⋘

THE AFTERNOON BEING bright and warm, and Jimmy having spent days rolling up and drying a respectable-sized stack of clay balls, Cassandra determined to go out for shooting practice. The more she used her shotgun, the more she liked it. In most other things she was powerless, but with a shotgun she felt the mistress of her own destiny. She found it rather pleasant to silently name the clay balls before she shot them out of the sky, and she had blown the head off Mr. Longmoore, Lady Montague, and all six gentlemen of the pact repeatedly. Perhaps none more so than Lord Hampton.

She rode Juno down the country road that led to their usual hill and dale, that bit of land well-suited to get the balls high in the air for her to shoot. Johnny jogged along with two baskets filled with the balls on either side of a stick resting on his shoulders. He would set up the slingshot on the ridge. Jimmy trotted on a sturdy pony, carrying the guns.

They'd set up in good time, both Jimmy and Johnny so well used to the activity that they did not need to be directed. Cassandra thought they were rather fond of it, as it got them out of the house and away from Maidencraft's stern and watchful eye.

Cassandra had already shot half of the balls they'd brought along when she heard the distinct rumblings of a carriage approaching. She held up a hand to Johnny at the top of the hill to pause him in his launches and motioned for Jimmy to follow her in stepping behind the wide trunk of an old oak tree.

Though she was determined to live as she pleased, she would not give any nosy passerby the satisfaction of being able to go round telling the tale of having seen Miss Knightsbridge shoot.

A well-equipped carriage came into view. It was driven at a reckless speed and Cassandra thought they'd better slow to make an upcoming turn or they might well tip over.

She squinted and saw the driver madly whipping the horses. What an idiot! Nobody should treat their horses so. She supposed some thoughtless young buck had given his coachman the impossible task to be somewhere they could not be if they were to drive sensible.

Suddenly, three riders came into view, gaining on the coach.

Cassandra took in a breath. That was no careless driving for the sake of it, the carriage fled from highwaymen!

She grabbed her gun and untethered her horse from a tree branch. She whispered to Jimmy, "Follow on the pony and make certain the other gun is loaded."

Cassandra leapt on her horse and galloped toward the fleeing carriage. As she approached, she saw the men had got ahead of it and forced it to slow. It had finally come to a stop.

Cassandra spurred Juno and, as they neared it, she wheeled in her horse. She raised her shotgun at the men on horseback and yelled, "I'll take one of your heads if you do not clear off!"

The three men had initially appeared confused to see a lady aiming a fowling piece at them, but then they began to laugh.

"See that!" one of them cried. "We are to be shot at by a lady! Who here fears being hit?"

"Not I," called one.

"Only if I were much fatter and presented a bigger target," the other said.

Cassandra could see that they were not afraid of her gun because it was inconceivable to them that she could shoot it. Jimmy had reached her on his pony. She whispered, "As soon as I fire, we switch guns and you reload."

Jimmy nodded. Cassandra turned to Johnny standing on the ridge and signaled him to launch a clay ball, hoping he would do as she asked, despite the situation he now viewed.

Johnny only hesitated a moment, and then loaded the slingshot and let loose a ball high into the air. Cassandra watched its trajectory and took in the wind direction, aimed and fired.

The clay exploded into a thousand fragments and fell to the ground.

Cassandra threw her gun to Jimmy with one hand and caught the loaded gun he threw with the other.

"Well?" she called, as Jimmy reloaded the gun she'd just fired. "Your heads present a far larger target than that which I have just blown out of the sky."

The three men seemed to hesitate.

"I have two guns and remarkably good aim. That means only one of you will have the chance to escape while I reload. Who is it to be?"

Cassandra leveled her gun and motioned it back and forth, as if deciding who she ought to shoot first.

The man who had spoken first was the first to turn tail and run. The other two, seeing they were no longer to wonder who would be shot and who would not, as there were sufficient bullets for them both, quickly did as their leader.

Cassandra found herself breathing heavily as the three highwaymen clattered off through the trees. Now that the danger had passed, she felt as wobbly as a newborn foal. Though she had aimed at no end of birds and clay balls, this was the first time she'd aimed at a man. She really did not know if she would have had the courage to shoot and thanked the heavens she'd not been forced to find out.

A curtain drew aside and an elegant, older lady leaned her head out the window of the carriage. "You are Miss Knightsbridge, I think?"

Cassandra felt a little wave of irritation pass through her. She supposed her reputation had become such that any lady seen with a shotgun in her hands was instantly recognized as Miss Knightsbridge.

She nodded, remembering she'd vowed to be as she was and never mind the naysayers. Those that did not approve of her habits could very well not look at them.

The lady said, "I am the Dowager Duchess of Carlisle, just now on my way to see your father."

"Your Grace!" Cassandra said, her thoughts all in a muddle. Why should Lord Hampton's grandmother have arrived? Her father had said nothing of the visit. Though they had corresponded these many years, the lady had never come to Trebly Hall.

What a time for her to come! She presumed the lady arrived in response to her father's letter outlining what had occurred and Lord Hampton's hand in it. But why come? Why not simply respond by letter?

The dowager turned to Jimmy and said, "What is your name, young man?"

Jimmy looked as if nobody in his life had ever inquired into his name. "Jimmy, Your Grace," he stuttered.

"Jimmy," the Dowager said, "might you and your friend up there on the hill manage to take back the horses so that Miss Knightsbridge may ride with me?"

Jimmy, appearing to receive this request as any knight given a noble commission, nodded enthusiastically. "Me and Johnny will see to it, Your Grace. We'll see to it all efficient like."

"Excellent," the Dowager said.

Cassandra did not see what else was to be done but acquiesce to the dowager's arrangements. She dismounted her horse and handed her gun to Jimmy.

"My dear Miss Knightsbridge," the Dowager said. "Perhaps bring a gun with you. Loaded, of course. One never knows if a scoundrel who's run off might find his courage lying about in a heap somewhere and decide to return."

Cassandra thought that idea full of good sense, though she was rather surprised that the elegant elderly lady should wish to have a girl with a gun in her carriage.

"Yes, Your Grace," she said.

"Ma'am will do," the dowager said. "No need for the daughter of my old friend to stand on ceremony."

Jimmy handed back her gun and Cassandra made her way to the carriage. As she got in, the Dowager called to her coachman. "Well, Bradley, have you recovered enough from this adventure to carry on?"

Bradley, though he still appeared rather shaken, tipped his hat. It was not a moment before they were on their way to Trebly Hall.

The Dowager's carriage was richly appointed, the seats a fine leather and the sides padded beneath silk coverings. There were all manner of fur throws folded on the seats. Seated on one particular pile of blankets was a cream-colored Pomeranian, its eyes bright and staring at her.

"That is George," the Dowager said. "Lovely company but entirely useless against highwaymen."

Upon hearing his name, George let out an appreciative yap toward the coach's roof, having no idea his usefulness against highwaymen had been so recently disparaged.

"You, however," the dowager said, eyeing Cassandra, "have proved mightily helpful against those devils."

Cassandra supposed the dowager both grateful and shocked that a girl should wield a gun. "I know it is not usual—"

"I care nothing for usual, Miss Knightsbridge. Usual, in my opinion, is highly overrated."

Cassandra was gratified by the dowager's view but could not help continuing to wonder why the lady had come. "Pray, ma'am," she said, "has your visit been long planned?"

"You mean, does your father know I am set to descend upon his house? He does not. But then, he's made the mistake of repeatedly writing that I should come any time. Any time, it appears, has arrived."

Cassandra's mind raced at all that should be done to accommodate a duchess. A room was not even ready!

"Miss Knightsbridge," the dowager said, "I would dislike having any mystery or words hanging unsaid between us. I am certain you will have guessed I come in response to your father's letter about what has befallen you, and my grandson's hand in it."

Cassandra nodded, but that was all she could muster for an answer.

"I might wax on about my fury, or what fury I heaped upon my grandson's head, or how sorry he is about the whole thing, but none of that would be particularly helpful to you."

At the mention of Lord Hampton, Cassandra found she could not keep her emotions in check. Each day that passed had seen her rage harden it into something vengeful. And yet, underneath her anger was still a yearning she worked to stamp out.

She said, "It *is* rather helpful, Ma'am, to know that somebody has heaped fury upon him. For myself, I have begun the habit of imagining the clay balls I shoot out of the sky are your grandson's head."

Cassandra instantly regretted her words. So far, the dowager had been kind, but if she were forced to side one way or the other, of course she must side with her grandson. Images of him being shot out of the sky could not be welcome.

Rather than appear annoyed, the dowager laughed heartily. "As well you should, and as well I would if I were you. Fire away, Miss Knightsbridge, if it brings you any sense of satisfaction. However, I think of enacting a scheme which you may find more satisfying than that."

Cassandra looked with interest at the dowager, and then tried not to laugh upon noticing George appeared just as interested—ears up and unblinking.

"I speak of bringing you back to London in triumph, my dear. And, as if my little scheme was not wonderful enough, I may now add that Miss Knightsbridge, through her uncommonly good sense, has saved my life and my jewels."

Though Cassandra was gratified that the dowager took such an interest in her, she could not wish for any scheme enacted upon her behalf.

"I would rather not return to London under any circumstances, ma'am," Cassandra said. "It is a poisonous place."

The dowager patted her hand and said, "Well, we'll talk about it."

TO SAY THAT the viscount was surprised by the Dowager's arrival had been an understatement. However, her father never stayed in a shocked state for long and so quickly recovered himself.

It was Maidencraft who was nearly struck down by the news. Cassandra could sympathize—had their stalwart butler been apprised in advance, all manner of preparations would have been made. As it was, he'd sent maids running one way and footmen another to patch things together as best they could.

Mayhem, always ready for any new development, stared fascinated at the little Pomeranian that had trotted in behind the dowager as she entered the house. George, always conscious of his diminutive size and determined that it should not be held against him, had marched up to May and growled ferociously.

May was both delighted and amused and placated her new friend by throwing herself on the floor and rolling on her back. George, having been satisfied that he was to be in charge, wagged his tail.

After seeing that the dogs got on well and tea would be sent in, Cassandra had excused herself from the drawing room so her father and the dowager might speak privately.

The dowager waited for Jimmy to close the door behind him. She poured tea for the viscount and said, "Never in all my years did I think my own grandson would cause damage to your daughter. I am sorry for it and I am determined to rectify it."

The viscount took his tea and said, "It was no fault of yours."

"Perhaps not, though I wonder if I did enough to guide him, that he would have fallen into such a situation. Did you know he is in love with her?"

The viscount set his teacup down with a clatter. "What?"

"It is true," the dowager said, "and he wishes to marry her. From what I can gather, he initially fooled himself into thinking he did his duty by marriage. That it would atone for what he'd done. But, as it happens, he's quite smitten."

"The marriage would restore Cassandra to her rightful place," the viscount said slowly.

"Indeed so," the dowager said, "though she'll never agree to it. Not yet, at least. Did you know she shoots his head off for target practice?"

The viscount laughed despite himself. "I did not, but I cannot claim to be surprised by it."

"She is furious, and rightly so," the dowager said. "I do not know if there is a possibility of feelings on her side, but I do know there is no room for love when one seethes."

"Perhaps time will cure her of it," the viscount said. "It has cured me of considering lining them all up and challenging them to duels. That, and Cassandra pointed out she would be left quite alone after I was shot up."

"I rather think neither duels nor time are what is required. We must give Cassandra her revenge. She must have revenge on the gentlemen of the pact, and on that awful Lady Montague. *She* must be the belle of London and *they* must become pariahs. Only then will her anger be appeased and we will see what lays beneath it."

The viscount leaned back in his chair. "Do I dare inquire how you mean to accomplish it?"

"Leave it to me," the dowager said. "Though it may take some time. I am likely to be under your roof for at least a fortnight."

Chapter Fourteen

EDWIN STARED INTO the fire, then swept up his grandmother's letter and read it again.

My dear awful grandson,

As you know, I made my way to Surrey in all haste after becoming apprised of your base actions. Approaching Trebly Hall, I was set upon by highwaymen. Fortunately, Miss Knightsbridge was nearby and able to rescue me by way of two shotguns and very good aim. I am lucky to have survived the ordeal and remain in her debt.

To do what I can to repair the situation you and your idiot friends have created, I will spread this tale far and wide and make clear to all of my acquaintance that you are to be believed when you own your crimes. I expect to hear the welcome news that you are widely denounced sometime in the coming weeks. Miss Knightsbridge, I will affirm, has been blameless in all of it and has been the hapless victim of plotters (you) and gossipers (Lady Montague).

I am of a mind to bring Miss Knightsbridge back to London and sponsor her personally. At the moment she refuses, but I think I will wear her down eventually. As for you, Miss Knightsbridge is in the habit of blowing off your head while she practices her aim at shooting. This may sound dire, but I am of the mind that one does not experience that sort of rage unless there are other feelings lurking underneath. You had better hope so, in any case. You would be very fortunate to win such a lady, though I have my doubts about whether you deserve her.

I expect your father and the other dukes have heard of this fiasco by now and so I will not be surprised to hear you are living in Cheapside sooner than expected.

Regards,
Your disappointed grandmother

Aside from the stinging retribution, which Edwin felt was well-earned, he could not but help wonder if his grandmother was right. *Did* Miss Knightsbridge harbor any feelings for him?

He did not know, but as the days passed he knew he would not marry another, even if he did have to spend his days in Cheapside, warming his own toast in front of a fire.

What a lady! To think, she'd fought off highwaymen to save his grandmother. It was extraordinary.

If ever there was a woman who ought to have influence and power, it was she. If ever there was a woman who could crush his future happiness, it was also she.

THE DUKES HAD gathered at White's, all rushing to London when word reached them of what their sons had been about.

"Those blasted ne'er-do-wells," the Duke of Gravesley said.

The Duke of Wentworth stared at his gouty foot, that appendage more swollen than ever. "Viscount Trebly is an honorable man, I am surprised he has not shot them all."

"The dowager writes to me that my son is willing to marry the girl, but she won't have him," the Duke of Carlisle said.

"Marriage would fix the thing up," the Duke of Dembly said hopefully.

"But she won't have him," Carlisle answered.

"We owe the viscount a debt," Gravesley said. "We must do what we can to appease him."

"What can we do, if she won't have Hampton?" Dembly said.

The dukes considered this conundrum in silence, until one of them muttered, "The scoundrels."

"Hear, hear," the rest answered.

They were quiet for some minutes, until Carlisle said, "The dowager had an idea, though it is rather...extreme."

THE DOWAGER HAD settled herself into Trebly Hall as if it were her own house. She'd taken over the library and hired a secretary. Mr. Brown was a short and pudgy sort of fellow, but he could write like the wind and so was suited to the lady's purposes.

The dowager had made it no secret that she fired off letters that were to pepper London and rain down on all of England. All were to know of Miss Knightsbridge's innocence and the gentlemen of the pact's guilt. Most of the letters read the same, hence the use of a secretary to copy them all out. Some the dowager wrote herself, in particular a rather scathing missive to Lady Montague filled with veiled threats of that lady losing her place in society.

Cassandra was pleased by the letter to Lady Montague, it amused her to think of how hard the lady would cough upon reading it. It, and all the other letters, gave her a sense of vindication, though she still resisted the dowager's ploys to get her to London. Rather, she would carry on riding and shooting in Surrey, well away from the talkers.

The dowager was an energetic sort of person and Mr. Brown found his hours filled, beginning at nine in the morning. At eleven, he was sent to the kitchens to rest his writing hand and have tea and biscuits, while Cassandra joined the Dowager in the library for the same. Her father sometimes joined them, but mostly left them to themselves.

On just such a morning, the dowager said, "I suppose you both look forward to children and are terrified of what one must go through to bring them into the world. I remember the horror I experienced the first time I was with child, contemplating a person growing in my belly. Nobody ever talks about it, but there it is."

Cassandra smiled, having become accustomed to the dowager bringing up subjects that nobody else in England would dare allude to. "Whatever my difficulties may turn out to be," Cassandra said, "childbearing will not be one of them. I have decided I will never marry."

"There now," the dowager said, "make no such decision. If you are to be a spinster, so be it. However, I think you would find yourself unhappy with the state. Guns and horses will not be enough for a strong beating heart such as yours."

Cassandra could not say if that were accurate or not. She *had* wondered how she should like the isolation of never marrying. Her father would not live forever and someday she would find herself quite alone in the house. Invitations would be few, nobody ever knew what to do with a spinster. And then, no children. She was not the least fearful of childbirth, she'd seen enough animals born in the barns and stables to be inured to the idea, and she'd often imagined being surrounded by her own. Still, after what she had been through, spinsterhood seemed the safest course.

Any mention of marriage, or of gentlemen in general, sent her thoughts racing in one direction. That she still could not entirely remove Lord Hampton from her mind felt the worst betrayal. He had no business there and she both loved him and hated him. She loved the lord that had lived on in her mind, her own creation of goodness with a handsome face. She hated the real lord, who'd so glibly changed her life. She would not risk her heart again. She would never allow herself to be vulnerable to another's schemes. Trebly Hall was safety and that was where she would stay.

To waylay the Dowager in her talk of marriage, Cassandra said, "I know my father was in a debt to you in his youth, but I wonder what the circumstances were."

The dowager laughed and said, "I see he has failed to expound upon the subject. Well, I suppose there is no harm in telling you, it is ancient history."

Cassandra listened in fascination as the dowager told the story of a long-ago card game.

It had all begun at a house party at the Duke of Gravesley's estate. As was often the case at such house parties, there were too many women and not enough gentlemen and so a few fellows nobody knew well were scrounged up. Gravesely brought in Mr. Shine, a gentleman known to both he and the Duke of Dembly through various business ventures.

Cassandra leaned forward. She knew the Duke of Gravesley to be Lord Lockwood's father and the Duke of Dembly to be Lord Ashworth's father. Cassandra thought back to Sybil's tale of her father despising both the Lord's fathers. Certainly, the circumstance must be connected.

She asked, "Was Lord Blanding there as well?"

"Indeed, he was a principal player in the drama," the dowager said. "How did you know?"

"Just a guess," she said.

The dowager continued with her tale.

All might have proceeded in the usual fashion of a house party if it had not been for the weather. It poured rain for days and the gentlemen, having no recourse to shooting, began to gamble their time away. At first, it was for small sums, but Mr. Shine kept pushing the bets ever higher.

The dowager, then the Duchess of Carlisle, had pressed her duke to withdraw. They played *vingt-et-un,* a game too reliant on chance to risk great sums. Her husband, being older than the other players, was therefore equipped with more sense and did end his time at the table. The dowager had felt, initially, that her work was done. She'd rescued her husband and that was the entire realm of her responsibility.

But then, she could not ignore the play, and the stakes, and in particular a young viscount who was taking a drubbing. She saw all too clearly that he should withdraw from further play, and just as clearly that he would not. There is nothing so foolish as a baron or a viscount of tender years attempting to impress.

She began to watch the game more closely, and her sharp eyes picked up what others could not. Someone had very cleverly marked the cards. She had marched over to the card table and said, "Goodness, you all really ought to get a new set. These have been in the hands of children, I think. See here how the crown has one extra jewel on the right side, shaped very like a seven, and then there embedded in the crest, the smallest heart? Some little blighter has a fine hand and is fond of a good joke—I would guess that card is the seven of hearts."

She need not have said more. Everybody at the table comprehended that the cards had been marked. Naturally, they all had their suspicions, and those suspicions were confirmed when, hours later, Mr. Shine departed the house under darkness and was never heard from again.

Mr. Shine had not got away entirely scot free. The dowager had felt he might abscond and had waylaid him before he did. She'd recovered the money the viscount had lost.

That should have been the end of it, but Lord Blanding got the idea that Gravesley and Dembly had known Mr. Shine was a card sharp, both of those gentleman's estates being on shaky footing at the time. He began to give the vaguest hints that the three were in league.

The Dowager could see a storm coming and persuaded her husband that they ought to depart, rather than get swept into a feud. She'd also convinced him to bring along the young Viscount Trebly.

"Your father was quite spirited about it," the Dowager said now. "He thought he ought to stay and see the thing through. I counseled that he'd better get in my carriage and he would thank me later."

"And so he did thank you," Cassandra said, "when he realized you had removed him from an argument that I believe still goes on to this day."

"Just so," the dowager said. "I understand that after we left there were various threats of duels. Fortunately, they all had a care for their own person and did not carry through with it. Lord Blanding left in a fury and I hear he still mentions the event from time to time."

"Goodness," Cassandra said. "It is so extraordinary to think of my father as being young and getting himself embroiled in such a situation."

"Ah, but that is youth, is it not? Mistakes are made, judgments are faulty. It is only with age that one can reflect back and see it was all a lot of nonsense. If only one could comprehend it at the time, there would be far less heartache in the world."

Cassandra had the uncomfortable feeling that the Dowager no longer referred to her father. She felt the Dowager attempted to tell her that the uncomfortable situation she found herself in now would fade with time. That when she was older, it would not seem as significant. She did not know if that were true, but it seemed impossible that she would ever look upon this period of her life with any sort of equanimity.

THE MANY LETTERS the dowager and her secretary shot off descended upon London and its environs like a flock of birds settling on tree branches. All those who had been swayed by Lady Montague had initially fallen to her wishes because they perceived her as powerful. Lady Montague had been thoroughly trumped by the Dowager

Duchess of Carlisle.

As often happens with the downtrodden, those who had acquiesced to Lady Montague's demands harbored a deep resentment over it. Now, having been given leave to overthrow those earlier forced opinions and a shield to hide behind by way of the dowager, they took full advantage of it.

The talk in various drawing rooms generally unfolded as, "I was never really convinced of the story, you know. It seemed a bit too contrived."

"Indeed! And now that I hear the real circumstances, it bears the ring of truth."

"To think, Miss Knightsbridge saved the dowager's life! I would not go in for my own daughter picking up a fowling piece, but nevertheless..."

"Yes, nevertheless."

There were, perhaps, only a handful of people in England whose judgments went absolutely unquestioned—the Dowager Duchess of Carlisle's were one of those. It was generally accepted that Miss Knightsbridge had been wronged, and while unusual that she shot birds, that skill *had* saved the dowager.

Equally interesting to the *ton* was the role the gentlemen of the pact had played. There was outrage and caution. Every mama was torn—on the one hand, those gentlemen remained eminently eligible. On the other, did they dare allow a daughter to fall victim to them? Miss Knightsbridge had been fortunate that the dowager had stepped in on her behalf. Would another girl be so lucky?

If the gentlemen of the pact had been stared at before, it was nothing compared to what they experienced now.

Lord Dalton took himself off to the seaside. Lord Cabot conveniently decided to visit his family's estate in Scotland. Lord Grayson was suddenly inspired to visit an old aunt in Sussex. Lord Ashworth remained in London, but removed himself to a notorious gambler's house, so he might direct all his efforts to gaming rather than dancing.

It was only Lord Hampton and Lord Lockwood who stood firm. Lord Lockwood felt a peculiar need to attempt to explain himself to those he encountered, in particular, Miss Knightsbridge's friend Lady Sybil. That the explanation did not suit the lady, he should have known. Though, he'd been rather surprised when she said that if she were a man, she'd challenge him to a duel.

Lord Hampton made the rounds to bolster the dowager's claims. While he had not been believed when he'd first owned the deed, he was believed now. He got the feeling that had he not been in line for a dukedom, many a hostess would have thrown him out on his ear.

Still, he did not care much for that. He only waited to hear from his grandmother the news from Surrey.

All of the gentlemen of the pact, though choosing to take different routes at that particular moment, had waited with dread to hear from their fathers. It was impossible that the old men remained unaware of what had transpired. There was even the suggestion that they'd all arrived to London. And yet, the silence was deafening.

Edwin felt it was rather like waiting for the ax to fall. He did not know when, but fall it would.

CASSANDRA WAS IN the drawing room, watching with mirth as George took May's favorite blanket and dragged it around the floor with an air of superiority. Poor May appeared helpless in the face of this gambit. Though both dogs must be aware of their relative sizes, George's bold determination and out-sized confidence had overcome the giant mastiff at every turn. He'd gleefully lie down in the middle of May's sofa, and May would squeeze to one side rather than pick up the Pomeranian by the scruff of the neck and throw him off, as she was perfectly capable of doing. George would find the sunniest spot on the carpet and stretch out his full length, lest May find any bit of sunshine to warm herself. George regularly stole a biscuit off the tea tray, a crime May would never dream of committing, and then gleefully chewed it up while staring into the mastiff's eyes. George had become the master of the house and May served at his pleasure.

Cassandra heard the clatter of horses on the drive and walked to the window. She was escorted by both May and George, George muscling his way past May to jump on the sofa for a better view.

A fine coach emblazoned with a coat of arms in gold had stopped at the door. Cassandra took a sharp breath. A lion and a unicorn—it was the royal coat of arms.

What on earth?

Before she could speculate on why such a vehicle would have come up their drive, she remembered the dowager. Of course the lady was connected everywhere and would be well-known to the Prince Regent.

But goodness! Were they to have a royal visitor? Maidencraft would collapse in a heap over it.

The door to the carriage opened, but the only person to emerge was an exceedingly tall and elegantly attired footman.

The young man made his way to the door. Cassandra noted the hint of surprise in Maidencraft's voice when he opened it and viewed what had arrived on the doorstep. If Cassandra hoped for anything further she was disappointed—no sooner had the footman got out of the coach but he was back in it again and the carriage clattered away.

Maidencraft entered the drawing room bearing a silver tray. He appeared pale, as she would have expected him to after encountering a royal carriage so near to his person.

He walked toward her and Cassandra said, "The dowager is in the library. Surely you might interrupt her to deliver the letter? I am sure she would not mind it."

Maidencraft cleared his throat and looked about and finally said, "It is addressed to you, Miss Cassandra."

Cassandra laughed. "Surely not."

As the butler did not seem to be engaging in any sort of levity, Cassandra quickly crossed the room and examined the paper. It was indeed addressed to her.

"Why?" she said. "Whatever for?"

Maidencraft did not appear to have an answer for the peculiar circumstance, but merely held the tray out and when she had taken the letter, bowed and closed the door behind him.

Cassandra sank down onto a chair, while George and May settled round her feet. She opened the letter.

The royal crest topped the paper. Underneath, she read:

It is the Prince Regent's pleasure to request the attendance of the Dowager Duchess of Carlisle, Viscount Trebly and the Honorable Cassandra Knightsbridge to an evening ball to be held on 16th of April at nine o'clock at Carlton House in recognition of Miss Knightsbridge's service to the crown upon defending our Dowager Duchess of Carlisle at great risk to her own person.

The ball is further sponsored by the dukes of the realm: Carlisle, Gravesley, Dembly, Bainbridge, Wentworth, and Glastonburg.

George P R

The paper fluttered to Cassandra's lap. Before she could think through what the invitation meant, the dowager herself barreled into the room.

"Maidencraft informs me we have had an unusual letter delivered?" she said. "He was so overcome by it that I almost sent a footman for smelling salts."

"I might need them myself," Cassandra said quietly.

The dowager crossed the room with her usual energy. "Let us see," she said.

She scanned the invitation. "Most excellent," she said softly.

"But it is not excellent!" Cassandra said. "I have no wish to be made a spectacle of. It is most strange that the Prince Regent should think of such a thing. As well, why should the further sponsors, as they are called, be the fathers of the gentlemen of the pact? I do not even know what the term *further sponsors* means!"

"It means nothing at all," the dowager said, "other than to apprise people of the support you have garnered from those gentlemen."

"I will have to send my regrets and certainly my father will wish the same. Of course, I am honored that such a great personage should take an interest in me, but I could not bear it."

"My dear," the dowager said kindly, "one does not send one's regrets to the Regent. This is less an invitation and more a summons. I am afraid you have no choice but to attend."

Though Cassandra knew the dowager was correct, she still searched her mind for a way out of going. It was one thing to know that letters flew hither and thither proclaiming her innocence, but she did not feel up to presenting herself for inspection.

"Now, I would like to have a look at your dresses before we make our way to London. Oh, and I'd rather not go to the bother of opening up my house and I have no particular wish to stay with my grandson at this moment. Do you suppose Lady Marksworth would mind my staying at Marksworth House? Will you see to it, my dear?"

Despite Cassandra having no wish to go to London *or* Carlton House, it seemed she would go. The dowager raced ahead with plans and it rather struck her as a galloping horse. There did not seem to be a way of slowing the lady down.

At least she had a week before she must go and face down the *ton*.

Chapter Fifteen

The gentlemen of the pact who had found it convenient to absent themselves from London had all been tracked down and been delivered a directive. It was not one that any of them could have anticipated, its bizarre nature too far removed from any kind of prediction.

They had gathered at Dalton's house to see what could be done about it, though Edwin was certain nothing could be done. Once Prinny got an idea into his head, it was near impossible to get it out, and the Regent did enjoy a good joke.

The gentlemen who had gathered round the table in Dalton's library generally enjoyed a good joke as much as their Regent, though perhaps not as jovially when the joke was upon themselves.

"It cannot hold," Lockwood said. "I expect that once he's had his amusement, we will be delivered of the real invitations."

"It will hold," Edwin said. "Mark me, it will hold."

"It's outrageous," Dalton said, downing his brandy. "How is an earl expected…"

"Just like the rest of us, I would guess," Ashworth said.

"Perhaps we should cease wallowing in our misery and be grateful that the Regent has taken up Miss Knightsbridge's cause," Edwin said.

"She hardly needs it at this point," Cabot said. "She's been proved an innocent victim, we are condemned and, if that were not enough, suddenly she's a heroine!"

"That's right," Grayson said. "One minute she's to be censured for wielding a shotgun and the next it seems the height of good sense!"

"She *did* rescue my grandmother with that gun," Edwin said drily.

"I'm all for supporting Miss Knightsbridge and taking upon me any condemnation," Dalton said, "but this crosses a line."

"Perhaps," Edwin said. "But we will do as we have been commanded. There's no escaping it. Have you seen the real invitation? The one sent to everybody else? Our father's names are on them."

"They are all in league!" Lockwood said.

"Apparently," Edwin said. "Though we all must have known that the silence from our fathers must portend some incoming disaster."

"I, for one," Cabot said, "plan on drinking a vast quantity of wine."

"That will not be wise," Edwin said. "We will have much work to do."

"I still say we should consider burning down White's," Lockwood said.

As nobody concurred with that daring plan, Lord Lockwood drained his brandy.

THE VISCOUNT HAD been out on the estate, making his rounds to various tenants, and so it had been some hours before he arrived back to the Hall and was apprised of the remarkable invitation that had arrived from the Prince Regent.

Now, Maidencraft oversaw the footmen serving dinner, as the viscount said, "I'd rather shoot them all, but I suppose a ball will have to do."

"I think it will do very well," the dowager said. "Though, my dear viscount, I pray you will not let on your views of our Regent?"

"That he is a fat fool?" the viscount said.

There was a clatter of a serving spoon, but Jimmy quickly recovered.

"I'll say nothing about it," the viscount said. "In any case, it appears he finally does something useful."

"You will return to town victorious," the dowager said to Cassandra. "Though I know you are not particularly enthusiastic over the idea."

Cassandra had used the day to think over going back to face the *ton*. While she could not say she was enthusiastic, her opinion had somewhat shifted.

"It is true I do not relish the idea," Cassandra said, "but it occurs to me that I have been hiding here. To be hiding means I must be frightened. *That* is an idea that does not suit. Cassandra Knightsbridge is not to be frightened off by wagging tongues. I can ride like the devil and shoot better than most men, I will not be cowed by words."

The viscount smiled with pride. Maidencraft was so struck by the speech that he stood motionless holding a bowl of peas.

The dowager said, "Brava, Miss Knightsbridge."

THE FOLLOWING MORNING, Cassandra received a letter from Sybil. She curled up on the sofa with May on one side and George on the other.

My dear Cass—

In my prior letters I was careful not to write anything alluding to your misfortune as I did not wish to cause you further distress. Now, though, I may speak freely. You are the toast of the town! All anybody talks of is how Miss Knightsbridge was wronged, how bravely she faced it, how she saved the dowager duchess and how the Prince Regent and six dukes throw her a ball. An invitation to the ball is much sought after and much discussed. Some that have received it mention it everywhere as if it were a badge of honor. It is said that

Lady Montague fumes in Yorkshire as she has received no such invitation. I have even heard that the Dowager Duchess of Carlisle has scolded the lady severely via a terse and condemning letter and many suspect Lady Montague of distributing that awful print that was thrown through your window. One wonders if she hired the urchin to throw it, though I suspect we will never know.

I and my mother and father will be in attendance at the ball and ready to support you through it, as I imagine you must be in a state of nerves over it. My mother likens it to the Battle of Bosworth—it will be the decisive victory. For myself, I wonder if the six gentlemen of the pact will attend. Nobody seems to know, and there have been hints that they may have been snubbed. On the one hand, that would be quite right. On the other, I would be interested to see how Lord Hampton would conduct himself. Of all the gentlemen, he has been the most industrious in claiming fault. Further, he has seemed to go out of his way to speak to me about you—have I heard from you, how does Miss Knightsbridge do? I do not know whose very stupid idea this rumor was, and those things always do start with one before they are taken up by others, but he certainly appears the most sorry over it.

Lord Lockwood has twice attempted to explain himself to me, but I will have none of it. I told him, most emphatically, that if I were a man I would meet him at dawn. I apprised my mother and father of this and they were most amused—my mother said she would provide the dueling pistols and my father said he'd load them. So that is an indication of their solid support for Miss Knightsbridge. Lord Lockwood may try all he likes to make himself pleasant, but I cannot overlook what he has been a part of.

That is all for now, I find myself at the window often, hoping to see the carriage that brings you back to us.

Your friend,
Sybil Hayworth

Cassandra laid down the letter. She could not help but be relieved that the truth was now known and widely accepted. She could not help but be grateful for Sybil's staunch support, not to mention Lord and Lady Blanding's. She also could not help feeling the light wings of a butterfly against her heart as she read of Lord Hampton. It was unfair that he should have any effect upon her at all, other than anger and disdain. He and his friends had hurt her badly and it was only through other's efforts that she was being restored.

She at once hoped he would attend the ball and dreaded it. What on earth could he say to her by way of apology? And yet, did she not wish to hear what he would say? But then, how could she countenance a gentleman who had so materially damaged her?

The more she thought of the likelihood of seeing him there, the more she was convinced she would not. The ball was being held in her honor, it would be absurd for the very perpetrators of the scheme to be welcomed.

She patted both May and George on the head. "Well," she said, "I will be forced to meet their fathers, but I am fairly certain I will not see *them.*"

CASSANDRA RODE IN the dowager's carriage as it barreled toward London; her father would follow them on the morrow. The dowager had chosen one of Cassandra's dresses for the ball as being suitable, but she had in mind some small alterations and so was determined to set off earlier than planned.

Cassandra hoped her letter informing Lady Marksworth of their imminent arrival had reached her in time. It was not only their changed schedule that need be communicated, there was also the fact that May accompanied her on this trip.

The dowager very much approved of her little dog's friendship with May and thought George should not be parted with his companion unnecessarily soon.

Cassandra sat next to the dowager while on the seat across, George stretched out and May curled herself tight in the little room left to her.

"You see how George takes up as much space in the world as he can manage?" the Dowager asked.

"Indeed," Cassandra said, "I have noticed his habit of it, while my own great beast of a dog squeezes herself into a corner."

"Precisely," the dowager said. "Size, as we can see, has nothing to do with it. George takes what he believes is due him. May is convinced George ought to have more space than she *because* George is utterly sure of it. That is what you must do, my dear. Be convinced of your right to your place in the world. The talk now goes in your favor and you must cement it there by how you carry yourself and receive those who have offended."

"I pray you do not mean the gentlemen who have caused all this," Cassandra said. "I am perfectly amenable to meeting with those who heard a story and passed it on, but not those who invented it. Have I been wrong to assume they would not be invited?"

"Oh, they will not be guests, that I can assure you."

Cassandra felt a great amount of relief to have it confirmed. Though there was a part of her that wished to hear from Lord Hampton, there was a part of her that still wished to blow his head off. In any case, as the day of the ball grew near, she'd found herself dreading any sort of encounter with him. She would have enough to contend with on that particular evening.

They had entered the confines of London and Cassandra thought of the dark morning she had left it. The streetlamps had glowed through the dawn mist and it had seemed as if there could never be sunshine again. Yet, here was town in all its bustle, the sun shining down upon it all.

LADY MARKSWORTH HAD been most gracious in receiving the dowager. That she'd not got word of their early arrival was not evident, as the lady was too composed to let it show. That she'd not got word that there would be two dogs to contend with might also have been covered up, had not Racine stared so balefully at them.

Cassandra thought the butler had been somewhat mollified at being told the dogs would sleep in their respective owner's bedchambers, as he must have wondered what he was to do with them. Mollified, perhaps, but not exactly approving.

Still, Racine had never foreseen that he might one day make arrangements for a dowager duchess and Cassandra imagined it was one of the crowning moments of his career. At least, the amount and diversity of cakes on the tea tray must hint at it.

Lady Marksworth poured tea and said, "All of Cassandra's friends are most grateful for your efforts, Your Grace."

The dowager waved her hands and said, "There is nothing to be grateful for, as my own wretched grandson was at the very heart of the scheme."

"Nevertheless," Lady Marksworth said, "I have been waiting and hoping that the tide would turn and it has most decidedly. There is a stack of invitations in the hall, all wishing to host a dinner or a rout for Miss Knightsbridge."

"Please, Aunt," Cassandra said, "do not accept them. I feel as if I have enough ahead of me in considering the ball."

"We need say nothing yet," Lady Marksworth said. "We will see how you feel once you've been through the worst of it. I know how little you like to be stared at."

Racine entered and said, "Lady Sybil to see Miss Knightsbridge."

Sybil had not waited in the hall nor sent in her card; she had been in the house so often that all ceremony had fallen by the wayside. She rushed in and Cassandra leapt to her feet.

"Cass!" Sybil cried. Then, noting the dowager, she instantly halted.

"Dear Sybil," Cassandra said, crossing the room to her and clasping her hands. "How good it is to see you."

She took Sybil by the arm and walked her to the tea table. "Dowager Duchess of Carlisle, may I present my dear friend, Lady Sybil Hayworth."

Sybil deeply curtsied. "Your Grace," she said.

"Lady Sybil," the dowager said, "I understand you are a stalwart and uncompromising ally of Miss Knightsbridge."

Sybil rose and said, "If I were a man, I'd have… well, it's no matter what I'd have done."

"You'd have shot them all, I suspect," the dowager said good-humoredly. "No less than they'd deserve, though for my grandson's sake I am glad it will not come to it."

"Your Grace," Sybil said hurriedly, "I did not imply any harm to Lord Hampton, I only meant that I—"

"I comprehend you perfectly," the Dowager said. "You are very like your mother—I see the Beaufort blood runs strong in your veins. Now do sit down, I understand you are fond of almond biscuits and Racine has brought enough to feed all of London."

A very merry tea followed, as Cassandra noted that the dowager had an uncanny ability to put one at ease. She supposed it was that the dowager herself was at ease and did not stand on ceremony. She had always thought that highly placed persons were as grim and staid as the marchioness—following strict rules of protocol. There was nothing grim or staid about the Dowager Duchess of Carlisle. Rather, the lady showed who she was, not who the world thought she should be.

Cassandra had a mind to do the same.

THE NEXT DAYS at Marksworth House had the same feeling of energy that Cassandra had felt during the preparations for her wretched ball. The door was forever being answered, sometimes to admit Sybil and more often to receive yet another invitation. Some of the invitations did not even come with a date—Miss Knightsbridge was to choose whatever day she deemed most convenient.

The dowager had chosen a dress for Cassandra while they had still remained in Surrey, it was a white silk with very little adornment. Cassandra assumed the dowager chose it for its message of youthful innocence. Peggy had boldly suggested the pale blue gauze overlay, however upon noting the Dowager's cold stare, had curtsied and bowed herself out of the room.

Cassandra had not seen the dress since it had been unpacked. The Dowager had taken it from her and then a seamstress had arrived and various boxes along with her. What the alterations were to be, Cassandra did not know.

To Racine's dismay, George and May had firmly decided upon the sofa at the far end of the drawing room as being their own. Its blue velvet was continually covered in dog hair and as much as Racine ordered it cleaned, it was just covered again. Most of the shed hair belonged to George, as he maintained his dominance over May and claimed most of that piece of furniture. The two dogs spent their days thoroughly entertained—they relaxed on the sofa until somebody arrived at the door, then raced to the door practically knocking over Racine, then relaxed on the sofa again. To spice things up, there was always the diversion of launching at the windows to bark at passing carriages.

The viscount had arrived, and Cassandra felt him to be a great calming influence over the house. Whether it was his steady temperament or his utter lack of care for the opinions of the *ton* she could not say.

Cassandra had finally given in to her curiosity and sat down with the pile of invitations that had languished on a tray in the hall. Most she did not care about, one way or the other, but there was a very kind invitation from Lady Blakeley. She and her husband would be gratified to see them at a dinner on Tuesday next. *That* invitation she did tell her aunt to accept. Lady Blakeley's kindness in making her a fawn and positing a defense of her at the Blakeley's ball had been marked. There might now be dozens of people firmly on her side, but there was not then. Lady Blakeley had bucked the convenient current.

As much as Cassandra wished the day of the ball would either not come, or come and go as speedily as possible, time ground on as it always had. It would not be hurried, nor would it be late.

The day had dawned bright and Cassandra had forced herself to eat breakfast. It would seem an eternity before she was home again and the ordeal finally over and she must have the strength to face it.

Sybil and her mother and father had arranged to leave the house at the same time Cassandra and her party left, and they would follow her carriage closely. All would arrive a united army to Carlton House, the dowager leading them all as an undaunted general. It gave Cassandra some comfort to think of, though she still felt a nervous fidgeting she could not rid herself of. How many awkward conversations would be got through? How many stares must she pretend not to notice?

EDWIN STARED AT Havoc, who had utterly destroyed one of his boots and now looked back at him as if he had no idea how it happened. Fortunately, he owned a dozen pairs, as he was well-used to losing a pair whenever his dog managed to get into his dressing room.

The ball was only hours away. He was to be humiliated, debased, and defamed in the worst manner. Though he could not say it was undeserved, he realized that he'd never been humiliated by anybody in his life. The eldest son of a duke was not often crossed.

He'd not really understood his own power until the moment he was stripped of it. It gave him pause to imagine what it must be like to always be subject to others' whims. It gave him a greater understanding of how people like Lady Montague did their business—she struck terror into already terrorized hearts. If the *ton* were a great sea, it was uncomfortable indeed to find oneself an inconsequential lamprey surrounded by fearsome pike. One mistaken move and one might disappear into the pike's jaws, never to be heard from again.

Of all those who would view his nearing humiliation, it was Miss Knightsbridge that preyed on his mind. Would she be satisfied that the debt was paid? Or would she simply find mirth in it and keep her anger as hot as it must now be.

His grandmother had written to say there was, at this moment, absolutely no chance of her agreeing to marriage. Miss Knightsbridge was still inclined to shoot his head off and, through lengthy practice, her aim was much improved.

He could wait, he could bide his time. Time might soften many a strong feeling. As long as she did not marry another, he could wait.

But might she not marry another? She had become the reigning queen of the season; she would be invited everywhere.

It would be a cold justice if he had ended up creating the very fame that led to numerous proposals for the hand of Miss Knightsbridge.

CASSANDRA HAD BEEN in her dressing gown when the Dowager had entered her bedchamber. She'd been followed by Clara, carrying her dress wrapped in paper. Her maid Peggy had been sent elsewhere, as the Dowager found her an irritating sort of person.

"Now, my dear," the Dowager said, "we have a gown truly befitting you."

Clara laid the dress on the bed and unfolded the paper.

Cassandra took in a sharp breath. The gown was not materially changed from what it had been, with one striking exception. Small diamonds cut in an unusual square shape had been affixed by crosses of silver thread to a white gauze overlay. It sparkled in the candlelight like all the stars in the sky.

"Duchess!" Cassandra cried. "How can it be? I could not accept—"

"Of course you can accept my modest little changes," the dowager said.

"But those are not real—"

"My late husband was an interesting gentleman and made many investments I found bizarre, certain he should ruin us. The one investment I never quibbled over was a diamond mine in Brazil. It has given me an endless supply of jewels and I have even employed a jeweler who invents new cuts. I'm very fond of this square cut."

"It is far too valuable..."

"Trust me to have the sense to know where my own diamonds should go. Now, dear Miss Knightsbridge, it is time to dress for the most important ball of your life."

Chapter Sixteen

As Cassandra rode in the carriage toward Carlton House, she felt almost in a dreamlike state. It was as if she existed somehow distant from those around her. Her dress sparkled in the darkness and all she could think of was that she sat on enough diamonds to buy her father's estate.

The dowager very kindly held her hand, her father was a comfort across from her, and her aunt nodded, as if to say, "All will be well."

Sybil and her parents followed behind in their own carriage and Cassandra occasionally glanced out the window to assure herself that they had not become separated.

Carlton House was lit like blazes from within, though the drive itself was only illuminated by a few torches. Cassandra could see a cadre of footman waiting at the ready in the dim light. She took a long, deep breath. The moment she had been wishing speedily gone had now speedily come.

The horses came to a halt, the door opened, and the steps were let down. The dowager was helped out first and Cassandra heard the lady say, "Quite fitting."

Lady Marksworth went out next, and Cassandra was certain she heard her aunt whisper, "Goodness."

As Cassandra took the footman's hand to descend the steps, a deep voice said, "Miss Knightsbridge."

Cassandra would have known that voice anywhere, and yet she must be confused. She glanced up at the footman as she stepped onto the drive.

It seemed as if all the air in the world had vanished and there was nothing left to breathe. The footman was Lord Hampton.

She said nothing, as she was incapable of words. Why was the lord dressed in livery?

As her father exited the carriage, Cassandra noticed the line of footmen standing stiffly on the drive. All six of the gentlemen of the pact were in livery.

Was it a joke? Was there some further joke to be played against Miss Knightsbridge?

In an instant, Cassandra realized it was not so. She remembered questioning the dowager about whether the lords would attend. The lady had been very precise in her answer—they would not be guests. Then, when the dowager had seen her grandson dressed as a servant she'd said, "Quite fitting."

This was no joke on her, it was a punishment for the gentlemen.

Cassandra was not certain what she thought of it. She was at once pitying of their ridiculous state, and not at all sorry for them. Perhaps it was well they feel the sort of sting they had been so careless to inflict on others. She supposed it *would* sting—their dignity was just now thrown to the four winds.

"My dear?" the viscount said, holding out his arm, "shall we go in?"

Cassandra shakily took her father's arm, realizing he would have no way to know that these footmen were the very men who'd caused his daughter so much grief. She did not know what other shocks might be ahead of her, but she would soon find it out.

The distinguished butler of Carlton House, a man starched from head to toe, announced them with all the pomp that only a royal household could carry off. Before her stood the Prince Regent and a line of six formidable-looking gentlemen that could only be the dukes.

Cassandra curtsied low to the prince.

He raised her up and said, "Miss Knightsbridge, the heroine of the hour. We are most grateful for your assistance on that terrible day when our dear Duchess found herself in peril."

"It was nothing, Your Highness," Cassandra said.

"You see," the dowager said to the Prince Regent, "Miss Knightsbridge is not only brave, but modest, too."

"Charming," the prince said.

Cassandra felt the introduction had come off well and, as she made her way down the line, she kept an ear open for her father's encounter. She was much relieved when nothing along the lines of "fat fool" came up in their blessedly brief conversation.

The dukes were all very civil and complimented her without directly mentioning what she had suffered at the hands of their sons. Did they know their sons were out of doors, dressed as footmen and helping guests from their carriages? Cassandra could not be sure, but it pleased her to think they did.

The last in the line was the Duke of Carlisle, Lord Hampton's father. Cassandra could not but help feel more of a curiosity toward him than the others.

"Miss Knightsbridge," the Duke said.

His voice was very like his son's—low and deep, and only a bit scratchier from age.

"Your Grace," Cassandra said.

"Address me as Duke, if you will," he said.

Cassandra knew that to be the honor it was intended to be—she was in no way on an equal footing with a duke, but he would make it so.

"I am determined to be direct, Miss Knightsbridge," the duke went on. "My son and his friends are idiots. They know it and we know it. I am not in the least surprised you rejected him. One cannot be expected to tie oneself to a gentleman with so little sense. Perhaps if he reforms himself you might reconsider. In the meantime, they are tasked with a role they highly deserve—may they be run off their feet this evening."

Cassandra felt the blood drain from her cheeks. She was gratified that the duke condemned his son, and that he approved of their punishment. But, what did he mean, that she had rejected Lord Hampton? No offer had been made. No offer had even been hinted at. Surely, he was misinformed.

"Perhaps you are determined to be *too* direct, Henry," the dowager said behind Cassandra. "Now come, my dear, we do not wish to hold up the line and I believe there will be quite a queue. Everybody lucky enough to be invited will attend."

Cassandra was led off by the dowager, all the while attempting to work out what the duke had alluded to.

They passed a remarkable set of stairs that swept up as if floating in the air and were led to a cloakroom. Cassandra was handed her dance card and saw with trepidation that the prince had taken the liberty of filling in the first. She had thought her interaction with royalty would begin and end at the door, that a successful introduction would be all that was required. Now, she was to open the dance with the Regent?

A footman who was blessedly not one of the gentlemen of the pact led them into a large, rectangular room decorated in an ornate fashion. Its walls were red silk and its vaulted ceiling an ornate plaster done in cream and gold. For all it spoke of wealth and splendor, Cassandra could see the telltale demarcation where wood not protected by a carpet had been lightened by the sun. A royal personage might live a very different life from the rest of England, but they must roll up their carpets for a ball, just as the rest of the nation did.

The musicians were smartly dressed and looked as serious as undertakers while they tuned their instruments. Cassandra thought they must take their part in the evening to be a high honor.

All of Cassandra's party had arrived to the room, and Sybil was not far behind. She joined her friend and clasped her hands.

Cassandra had much to say to her friend and so pointed at a picture on the far side of the room and led Sybil there.

"The dress, Cassandra," Sybil said. "It is the most marvelous gown I have ever seen. Really, it is fit for a princess."

Cassandra had almost forgotten it. She looked down and took in a breath once more. It truly was remarkable, the jewels catching the candlelight and shimmering at her slightest movement. Still, she had more weighty ideas than diamonds to discuss with Sybil.

"You have seen them?" Cassandra asked. "The gentlemen of the pact?"

"I have," Sybil said, "Lord Lockwood helped me out of my carriage. I nearly fell over. What is the meaning of it?"

"I believe it is meant as a punishment," Cassandra said.

"Ah! Yes, that would explain it. And richly deserved, in my opinion."

"But Sybil," Cassandra said, feeling in a rush to say all she would say before they were interrupted, "the Duke of Carlisle said he did not blame me for refusing Lord Hampton."

"Refusing what?" Sybil asked. "Oh, refusing his apology, of course. But, has he made one? Was he so bold as to speak to you on the drive?"

"No, he has not apologized and that was not what the duke spoke of. He said I could not be expected to tie myself to a gentleman of so little sense."

"Tie... you mean he thought Lord Hampton had proposed?"

"Yes. No. I do not know. It was a remarkable thing to say."

"Indeed it was," Sybil said thoughtfully. "Though if his father is not entirely mistaken, then perhaps Lord Hampton plans to. What shall you say? Would you consider it?"

"Certainly not," Cassandra said with perhaps more finality than she actually felt.

"Well, then, I suppose it matters little what the duke thinks or what Lord Hampton plans to do. In any case, I suppose the lord will be too busy opening doors and taking coats to inconvenience you."

"I do not know how we are to act," Cassandra said. "Do we ignore them?"

"I plan to," Sybil said, sticking out her chin, "they are nothing to me."

Cassandra was inclined to agree with her friend, though she could not claim the gentlemen were nothing to her. Particularly not one of the gentlemen.

The idea that he'd planned to propose! If it were true, it was both thrilling and horrifying. How was she to agree to wed a man who had done such damage to her? If he had truly paid for his misdeed, she might soften somewhat. However, she did not believe acting as a footman for one evening would quite suffice.

And yet, there was that Lord Hampton that had lived so pleasantly in her imagination. What she would not give to marry *that* Lord Hampton, if only he were real.

No matter, she was at Carlton House at a ball given in her honor. She must do everything she could to get through it creditably and she would simply ignore any footmen milling about.

Now that she had resolved upon a point of view, she turned to look at the room. Lord Burke entered and made his way to her.

"Miss Knightsbridge!" he said, approaching them. "Lady Sybil. Miss Knightsbridge, I could not be happier to see you here and in good spirits."

Cassandra said, "My aunt and I owe you quite the debt, Lord Burke."

Seeing he looked confused while glancing at Sybil, she said, "My dear friend knows everything of that awful evening and the great service you provided."

"Ah, I see. For my part, I have discussed it with nobody but my mother. She is delighted that you are to be honored this evening, and even more delighted that Lady Montague has been run out of town."

Cassandra could not but help laugh at the notion. Though she had resolved to pity anybody coming under threat from gossip and further decided she would never be the means of spreading it, Lady Montague had been the lynchpin of her near destruction. Cassandra might wish to be good, but she did not aim to be a saint.

"May I?" Lord Burke said, holding his hand out for her card.

As he wrote his name in, he said, "I see you open the ball with the prince. An honor indeed, if your toes survive the experience."

"I shall remain watchful of heavy feet coming in my direction," Cassandra said, laughing.

In a lower voice, Lord Burke said, "I have heard the gentlemen who caused you such distress will not be among the prince's guests this evening."

Cassandra glanced at Sybil, who pressed her lips tightly together to hide a smile.

"Goodness, Lord Burke, did you not note the footmen lingering out of doors and helping guests from their carriages?" Cassandra asked.

"Footmen?" Lord Burke asked, clearly puzzled.

"Indeed," Sybil said. "All six of them. There is one, just standing at the door."

Lord Burked turned and took in Lord Dalton, scowl on his face and dressed in livery.

"Now that is a joke," he said softly.

The room began to fill with chattering guests and it seemed as if Cassandra were their north star. All began to drift toward her and the next half hour was filled with conversation. Some complimented her dress, some referred obliquely to what had occurred, though they claimed now to have never believed a word of it, others congratulated her on her daring rescue of the dowager.

Cassandra felt as if she were surrounded by friends, though she did not forget how quickly they had once turned from her.

It was with relief and pleasure that Cassandra was approached by one she was certain she could count on as a real friend—Lady Blakeley.

"My dear Miss Knightsbridge," she said. "How charming you look. If I must guess, I would say the dowager has been raiding her diamond mine again."

"Indeed, she has," Cassandra said, "though I did protest it was too dear."

"Nonsense," Lady Blakeley said. "The dress is fitting for the times, I think. An innocent has been washed clean and sparkles like the sun. Meanwhile, the cobras have turned on each other. I understand a certain snake in Yorkshire has been firing off letters in every direction, and yet most of those letters go sadly unanswered."

Cassandra knew this to be a reference to Lady Montague and her precipitous loss of influence.

"One hopes, though," Lady Blakeley went on, "that forgiveness can be found for some others. It is one thing to be thoroughly bad, and another to have done a bad thing."

Though Lady Blakeley did not explicitly say so, Cassandra guessed this was in reference to the gentlemen of the pact. She supposed she would be expected to at least pretend that their having been forced to act as footmen had been enough. She was not convinced it was. When what had befallen her played out in her mind, she thought she might only be satisfied if they were all made footmen forever.

"It is rather remarkable that the dowager should have come personally to see you in Surrey and taken such a marked interest," Lady Blakeley said. "It is not everybody who could inspire her to part with so many diamonds."

"Oh," Cassandra said, "well I suppose it is due to her friendship with my father—they have long been correspondents."

"Ah, and that is all, you think?"

With that enigmatic question, Lady Blakeley drifted away without waiting for her answer and a new crowd circled round her.

What did the lady hint at? Cassandra did not know but had little time to think of it. She was besieged with questions on the happenings the day the dowager's carriage had been attacked.

It was not at once that the people in the room began to realize that the gentlemen of the pact acted as footmen. It would perhaps have taken more time than it did, had not Lord Dalton's scar and his obvious contempt for his situation given them all away.

If Cassandra had wondered about how the rumors regarding herself had made their way around London, now she had a direct view. Once the true identities of the six footmen were known, there were glances and whispers and subtle pointings out. There were heads together and stifled laughter and rushes to tell a newcomer who may not have heard. The news of the gentlemen's fates blew through the room like a brisk autumn breeze.

Cassandra laid a hand on Sybil's arm and whispered, "I'd best tell my father about the footmen before he hears it elsewhere."

Sybil had nodded and Cassandra made her way across the room. "Papa," she said, taking his hand. She leaned close to his ear and whispered the facts of the case.

The viscount's brows knitted. "Serves them right," he said. "They will be lucky if I do not run them off their feet this night."

"Quite right you should do so," Cassandra said. "It is just what the Duke of Carlisle hopes for."

The room had now thoroughly filled and Cassandra watched as the Regent entered, followed by the six dukes. The newly-made footmen were lined up on either side of the door and their fathers appeared fairly contemptuous of them as they walked past.

The Regent and the dukes made their way to the top of the room, the prince kindly offering his arm to Cassandra. The footmen were left at the door, presumably to cater to anybody's needs. Should fingers snap, they would be expected to come running.

The crowd hushed as the Regent stood facing them.

"Welcome, my dear guests," the prince said. "It is my privilege to host a ball in honor of our own Miss Knightsbridge, accompanied by her father, the esteemed Viscount Trebly, and her always charming aunt, Lady Marksworth. One hopes, with this circumstance before us, that we have all learned a valuable lesson on the nature of gossip and will refrain from that unsavory activity. Though, if one should wish to natter on about the state of my footmen on the morrow, *that* particular subject has my royal approval."

Laughter spread across the room. Cassandra noted the gentlemen of the pact appearing stoic at the jab, with the exception of Lord Dalton, who looked on his way to murderous.

Lord Hampton seemed the most stoic of them, and the least offended. Cassandra supposed he'd decided to take his lumps. Why should he not? It was a rather easy payment for having almost ruined a lady. He might flush a few times before the night was through, but he'd wake up as a lord, whole again as if nothing had happened. Society might laugh at his expense tonight, but they would give him his due on the morrow.

"Miss Knightsbridge embodies all the best of England," the prince went on. "With courage and a true heart, a combination nobody can best, she prevailed over dangerous highwaymen to rescue our dear Dowager Duchess of Carlisle."

"Hear, hear," the crowd murmured.

"Now," the prince said, "before we open the ball, I believe the dukes may have something to say."

The prince led Cassandra to the side and the dukes stepped forward.

The Duke of Gravesley said, "I speak for all of us when I say that we are honored that Miss Knightsbridge has consented to be our guest this evening. We are grateful that the viscount does not cut us or plan to meet our offspring at dawn. We are embarrassed by the actions of our own sons and we propose to make amends at the Viscount's convenience and preference."

"Hear, hear," the crowd said louder.

The Duke of Carlisle stepped forward and said, "The Duke of Gravesley has expounded on our sentiments eloquently. For myself, I am not gifted with speeches and so will only say a word to the ridiculous footmen in the back of the room—you are idiots, down to a man."

Laughter and clapping rose up in the room and dozens turned to see how the gentlemen of the pact would receive the condemnation.

Cassandra could not help but look. That the gentlemen had been humiliated was not in doubt, even Lord Dalton had the good grace to stare at his boots.

"Miss Knightsbridge?" the Prince Regent asked, holding out his hand.

Cassandra took it and the musicians struck up.

It became apparent, as they began the steps, that she and the Regent would execute the first steps alone.

She felt her cheeks flame to see so many people with their eyes trained squarely upon her. She was comforted by the idea that this moment, which would pass, was likely the worst of the evening.

Remarkably, the prince was nimble on his feet. Though he looked ponderous, he moved with a lightness that did not seem to match his size.

As Cassandra danced, her eyes took in the surrounding faces. Her father, Lady Sybil, the Dowager, Lady Blakeley. And then, among them, the approving looks of the others. All of those others who had mercilessly laughed at her and pretended to be shocked by her. They were all her friends now.

She would accept their friendship for what it was, hollow and convenient. She thought she had learned two hard lessons from the trial she'd been through—one could not place one's opinion of oneself in the hands of others, and society was comprised of frightened people terrified of losing their place. The terror ran so deep that it was a relief to them to understand that it was someone else in peril and not themselves.

Cassandra felt older, and wiser, too. She did not know if being who she was with no pretense would always be so approved of, but she was determined not to care. The ton had no more hold on her.

As for Lord Hampton, she wished she could say he no longer had a hold on her, either. She was determined it be so and supposed only time would assist in that endeavor.

Chapter Seventeen

Edwin had felt as if his face flamed like a fire ever since he'd donned the livery. His valet had almost fallen over when he saw it. Mackly had picked up the coat and stared at it, then said, "You go to a mask, my lord?"

"I wish it were so," he'd answered.

Of course, Mackly's reaction was nothing compared to his butler. Dreyfus had looked positively offended when he'd descended the stairs. His own footmen had looked on in astonishment—he'd no doubt they'd laughed into their sleeves as soon as he'd left the house.

He did not know what he'd expected to occur at Carlton House, he'd had some idea that they'd be paraded around, forced to serve something to somebody, and then allowed to go home. That had not been the case.

Upon arrival, they'd not been greeted by the prince or their fathers. They'd not even been let in the front door. Rather, they had found themselves taking orders from a butler, a certain Mr. Grimes, who informed them in the most condescending terms possible that they were to assist with the carriages. For a start.

He'd had to restrain Dalton from attacking the man, though Grimes had looked down his long nose with amusement and disdain. Whatever their standing in society had ever been, for this night they were nobodies that were to be lorded over by the prince's butler.

Miss Knightsbridge's carriage had been the first to arrive.

The dowager had descended and taken great pleasure in his predicament. There would be no sympathy from that quarter. The viscount had never set eyes on him and so took no more notice of him than he would any other footman in any other house. Though, he doubted that would hold through the entire evening.

Edwin knew Miss Knightsbridge would see him eventually, he had thought to keep his head down and avoid being recognized by her as she exited her carriage. It was bad enough that he would be seen indoors, but to be seen standing on the drive?

Though he had planned to avoid her gaze, he found he could not. When she'd been framed in the door of the carriage, as beautiful as ever and dressed in a stunning diamond encrusted gown, he had spoken.

He wished he had not. Her expression told him all—the last person in the world that Miss Knightsbridge was interested in encountering was himself.

He could, at least, be satisfied by her reception at Carlton House. The room was filled with admirers of Miss Knightsbridge. It seemed the damage had been repaired, though he could not take credit for it. His grandmother and father and the Prince Regent had seen it done.

Edwin had almost got used to the humiliation of standing around in livery, having become a servant who had been used to being served. However, the dukes would not let it be so. His father, in particular, would not let it be so.

The Duke of Carlisle could not let stand Graveley's rather civil remarks. No, his father must pointedly call them idiots, down to a man.

That they *were* idiots, he was already too well aware. He could easily ignore the laughter at his expense, it was Miss Knightsbridge's serious expression that cut far deeper.

Now, Miss Knightsbridge danced with the Regent as the rest

looked on. She was glorious in that gown. Edwin could not be certain where all those diamonds had come from, but he suspected his grandmother. He would have gone to Brazil and dug them up himself if it pleased Miss Knightsbridge.

Perhaps the only bright spot to think of was his tête-à-tête with Lady Blakeley earlier in the day. That kind lady had summoned him to her house and forced him to own all. She had guessed that he had a singular interest in Miss Knightsbridge and thought it just as bizarre as his grandmother had that he'd participated in the ridiculous scheme to create gossip about her. He attempted to explain as best he could, though he'd been well aware it had sounded ludicrous. Lady Blakeley had viewed the disaster with more humor than his grandmother had and seemed more certain that all might not be lost.

Lady Blakeley was to hold a dinner on Tuesday next. Miss Knightsbridge had accepted the invitation, and one was then given to him too.

CASSANDRA HAD DANCED all evening, of course the lady the ball honored would have her card filled and many turned away.

The supper had been lavish and might have been enjoyed immensely had it not been for the gentlemen of the pact bumbling their way through the service. It provided vast amusement to the onlookers, but it had only made Cassandra uncomfortable each time she became aware of some gaffe.

Worse, Lord Hampton seemed always to be standing behind her and it made the back of her neck feel prickly to know it. She did not understand why he would persist with it, particularly because the butler kept berating him about it.

Cassandra had been taken into dinner by the Duke of Carlisle, Lord Hampton's father. She was aware it was meant to be a high honor, but she would have much preferred the easy jokes of Lord Burke.

The duke spoke to her on a variety of subjects, but did not hit upon the one she was truly interested in. What had he meant when he said that she had rejected Lord Hampton?

Though she searched her mind, there had not been any way to recall him to the subject.

She did find, though, that the duke had a modern way of thinking, perhaps more modern than his son. He was not opposed to her shooting, and even hinted that the dowager had taken up a fowling piece here and there in her youth, though they had all forgone speaking of it.

He had expounded on his opinions by saying, "I sometimes wonder if we do not put young ladies too much in a cage. They must at once come off as a delicate flower, and then when they run their own house, must transform themselves into a formidable lady with an iron fist."

The duke had concluded with, "Of course, our Miss Knightsbridge is in no danger of requiring a constant supply of smelling salts."

She did not know when she had become the duke's "*our* Miss Knightsbridge" but could only agree on the smelling salt front.

Now, happily, she was home, safe in her bedchamber with just a single candle to light the room. She had got through the ball and had been restored to her place. Her father could relax and dismiss forever any ideas of a duel—he'd been well satisfied with the gentlemen's humiliation in their livery uniforms. In fact, he had been rather gleeful in his attempts to run them off their feet. Cassandra had noticed him accepting a cup of something, then frowning and sending it back, more than once.

That *she* had not been entirely satisfied with the gentlemen's humiliation Cassandra would keep to herself. There did not seem much point in demanding anything further, as she knew she would not get it.

Cassandra was determined to enjoy the rest of the season. She would judiciously accept invitations from the pile that had continued to grow. She would only attend those events that struck her as genial. She would have a care for her person and not allow herself to become anybody's trophy at a dinner or a rout.

She had already accepted Lady Blakeley's dinner invitation, but that was the only one she had answered with any eagerness. The rest could wait.

Cassandra blew out the candle and drifted off to a well-earned sleep.

THE FOLLOWING DAY should have been one of leisure, Cassandra's party had not returned from Carlton House until after three. The morning hours *were* quiet and leisurely. Cassandra, Lady Marksworth, and the dowager breakfasted late on an enormous spread arranged by Racine. Her father, she knew, would stay abed with his breakfast and a proliferation of newspapers Jimmy had no doubt been sent out to fetch. He would leave for Surrey after he'd risen and he would not like to be rushed.

Racine appeared to consider the prince's ball a victory for the house and was in quite the jolly frame of mind. More than once, Cassandra heard him softly say, "Yes, indeed."

Lady Marksworth said, "My dear Duchess, you do know you need not descend for breakfast. We can most easily have something sent up."

"No, Lady Marksworth," the dowager said. "Once I was apprised of your own habit of coming down so that Miss Knightsbridge does not dine alone, I was determined to copy the habit. I find I rather enjoy it—it is ever so much more cheerful than staying alone in my room while Jates huffs and mutters over the state of my clothes."

"I am grateful for the company of you both," Cassandra said.

"For myself," the dowager said, "I am grateful that the ball was such a success. Miss Knightsbridge is restored to her proper place and those gentlemen of the pact, including my own grandson, were put in *their* proper place."

Cassandra had studiously avoided any mention of the gentlemen who had caused her harm, and who were shown as ridiculous the evening before. She said nothing now.

"Today is your day at home, Lady Marksworth?" the Dowager asked. "I expect you will have various visitors encountered at Carlton House coming to mark their approval of Miss Knightsbridge."

Cassandra had entirely forgotten that it was her aunt's at home day. She hoped the Dowager was mistaken and they should only be visited by Sybil and some of Lady Marksworth's closest friends. Though she had been out in the world once again, she was not in the frame of mind to be back out again so soon.

CASSANDRA HAD HOPED to only see the most well-known acquaintances in her aunt's drawing room and had worried that she should see more than that. However, she could not have imagined how many cards would batter the door like bats who had lost their way in the night. The street became choked with carriages as one person after the next was shown in.

Cassandra tried her best to get through it in good humor, though she was rather hard-pressed when a lady would boldly inquire if Miss Knightsbridge had found time to examine an invitation recently sent. Sybil was of great assistance in that regard, as she invariably stepped in to explain that Miss Knightsbridge had only recently returned to town and was still getting settled.

Cassandra was not flattered by the attention she received, as she knew all too well from whence it came. Those various ladies so eager to find Miss Knightsbridge at their table only ever sought to put another feather in their cap. She was another thing to boast of, no more important than a new china set.

Racine took the chaos of the day in stride, pressing the cook to produce ever more tea and biscuits and announcing each card that arrived with such gravitas that he could trounce the prince's own butler.

The only aspect of real amusement was the various encounters of May and those visitors newly arrived. While one might have expected a dog of that size to be banished to another part of the house, the dowager insisted that George stay and as May was his faithful follower, she must stay too. Cassandra had the distinct impression that the various small shrieks emanating from ladies viewing her darling beast for the first time entertained the dowager as much as herself.

Now, Racine had come into the drawing room again, card in hand, just when Cassandra had harbored high hopes of saying goodbye to the last of the callers.

"Viscount Hampton, my lady."

Cassandra froze. Why should Lord Hampton come?

In a moment, she divined why. He wished to show all the world he was forgiven and that it had not been such a great crime after all.

The audacity of that man! All these people had turned up to use her for their own purposes, and here was one more. Here, in fact, was the worst of them.

Cassandra glanced at the dowager and then her aunt and shook her head no. If Lady Marksworth would not refuse him entry, she would leave herself. She would not help him along in his rehabilitation. She was very sorry that she must treat the dowager's own grandson in such a manner, but she felt rather iron-willed about it.

The dowager picked up George and settled the dog in her lap. She said, "Quite right, Miss Knightsbridge. Bar the doors."

Cassandra breathed a sigh of relief. Lady Marksworth nodded and said, "Do tell Lord Hampton that, unfortunately, we are not at home."

The few callers remaining in the drawing room looked on, their expressions filled with fascination. Cassandra thought that was well. Despite the prince's admonition to avoid gossip only the night before, they would talk of Lord Hampton's refusal everywhere. It would be known that Miss Knightsbridge was not eager to reacquaint herself with the gentlemen of the pact.

EDWIN BROODED IN his study, while Havoc slowly and quietly shredded the pages of a book at his feet. He'd seen the dog stealthily take the book off a shelf and should have roused himself to rescue it, but he'd not had the will.

Lady Marksworth had refused him entry. She was not at home. He knew perfectly well that he'd been refused with his grandmother's consent.

He'd not even meant to go, but somehow had been led there. First, it had been the idea of visiting Dalton so he might look out the window to Marksworth House.

Then, all of those carriages coming and going had seemed to beckon him. At that moment, Miss Knightsbridge was greeting people, just inside the doors.

He'd resolved to go over, though Dalton had done everything possible to stop him, including threatening to tie him to a chair.

Edwin had not been convinced that Miss Knightsbridge would even be civil to him, but he *had* expected to get inside.

And then, that butler of hers! Folding his arms like a potentate and seeming very satisfied that Lady Marksworth was not at home. He'd said, "*Sadly*, Lady Marksworth is not at home." The man had said "sadly" as if he'd never been happier in his life. He supposed servants held all kinds of opinions, though he'd never considered the idea until he'd found himself a footman. Apparently, this butler had developed very firm opinions on those who had nearly ruined Miss Knightsbridge. He supposed he shouldn't condemn the fellow, as he happened to be right.

All of these ideas prompted him to consider the rightness of attending Lady Blakeley's dinner. The lady had fashioned it as a surprise, but would it not be more of an ambush?

Still, he did not see when else he might have the opportunity to speak with Miss Knightsbridge. He'd already become aware that numerous invitations had been issued to her that very pointedly excluded him and his friends. If he could not speak to her, he would never be able to even attempt to soften her views.

Those views, he knew, were hardened like lead at the moment. Though he'd placed himself nearby her as often as he could at Carlton House, he might have been an actual footman for all the notice she took of him.

He'd stared at her lovely hair, ignoring the butler attempting to direct him, while she kept her back turned. She'd acknowledged him no more than she would a fly beating against a glass.

WITH VERY FEW exceptions, Cassandra had declined the dozens of invitations sent to her. She and the dowager had been through them together, Lady Marksworth happy to leave it in their hands and the dowager in agreement with Cassandra that she was not to be paraded about like a prize cow.

Though the dowager had approved of her attending Lady Blakeley's dinner, she would not do so herself. She had arranged for a quiet evening of cards with some old friends and considered that vastly superior to a formal dinner.

Cassandra had broached the matter of the diamonds twice, certain they ought to be removed from the dress and returned to the lady. The dowager would not hear of it, rather, she said that every woman should have some sort of stockpile of her own. That way, no matter the winds of fate, she would not find herself entirely without means. The dowager had kept her own cache of jewels in a locked case throughout her marriage, in case her lord made one speculation too many and they found themselves fleeing to the continent to escape the debt. Cassandra was to remove the diamond encrusted overlay and tuck it away somewhere safe, as her own little bank against financial difficulties.

Cassandra still could not feel it was right, but faced with the lady's fortitude on the subject, she'd personally wrapped the overlay in paper and stored it away. There would be time in future to determine what to do.

Now, she was dressed in a charming pale pink silk with the palest overlay of blue gauze giving the skirt a lovely lilac color. Earlier, Peggy had begun to suggest the yellow satin dress but had stopped herself when she noted her mistress's expression. Cassandra thought she had learned more than one thing from the dowager, she had finally learned how to quell her maid.

She'd not been out since the ball at Carlton House and had rather enjoyed her time in. She, Lady Marksworth, and the dowager had grown very comfortable together and spent many an hour in the drawing room. She and Lady Marksworth sewed, but the dowager said she'd given it up long ago. Publicly, she blamed her eyes, but she admitted she just did not like it.

Sybil had come every day, with various reports of her previous evening's activities. Cassandra was still hailed all over town as the innocent victim of a plot and the heroic savior of the dowager. Sybil also mentioned that she had not seen any of the gentlemen of the pact and had the idea they were not yet welcome most places. Cassandra hoped that would hold, those gentlemen ought to go home to the country and trouble her no more. She willfully ignored the flutter inside of her when she thought of one particular of those gentlemen—her mind could not be held responsible for what her feelings insisted on doing.

During this time of peace and quiet, Racine had been a veritable magician—always coming into the drawing room at just the right moment with biscuits and fairy cakes. The dowager was particularly fond of York biscuits and Racine made certain they were offered in abundance. It was well he did, as George appeared equally fond of them and had no compunction over stealing them off the tray.

Racine had got in the habit of taking George and May out to the back garden for exercise. They followed him so dutifully that Cassandra was fairly sure there were York biscuits in his pockets. Cassandra sometimes watched them romp down the paths and around bushes, George attempting to run with an oversize branch in his mouth and May gamely trying to take it from him but rarely succeeding.

It had been days of peaceful domesticity, but now it was time to venture out once more. Cassandra took a deep breath as she stepped over the threshold of Blakeley House.

Lady Blakeley, dressed in a magnificent royal blue kimono, rushed to greet her and her aunt.

"Lady Marksworth, Miss Knightsbridge," she said, "I am so pleased you've come. We are honored, as I imagine your front hall filled to the brim with invitations."

"As it happens," Lady Marksworth said, laughing, "but Cassandra wished to accept only a few and I happily obliged."

"I was determined only to see my real friends," Cassandra said.

Lady Blakeley nodded. "Indeed. Those that sway with the winds are not to be depended upon, though they may be pitied for their lack of internal fortitude. Now," she said, taking Cassandra's arm, "let me take you in. We are to be a fairly small party this evening."

At the drawing door, Lady Blakeley leaned close to Cassandra's ear and said softly, "Remember what I said at Carlton House—there is a difference between those that are thoroughly bad and those who have done a bad thing."

At first, Cassandra did not know why Lady Blakeley should have chosen that moment to repeat her admonishment. She soon did, though.

Lord Hampton stood in the drawing room, staring at her intently. In fact, he was the only person there.

He made his way over to her. "Miss Knightsbridge," he said.

The lord was as handsome as he had ever been, and once more Cassandra felt a pang that he could not be that lord she'd invented in her mind—selfless, kind and brave. That melancholy feeling gave way to the simmering rage that was as a boiling pot of water. It was the burning rage that was always there, if sometimes lurking under the surface of her thoughts. She worked to keep her expression neutral. She would not allow him to discompose her.

Lady Blakeley had disappeared back to the front hall. Cassandra turned to Lady Marksworth. "Aunt?" she said.

Lady Marksworth, having got to know her niece much better over the season, and holding her own personal opinions of the gentlemen of the pact, said, "You do not need to speak to him if you do not wish it. I will inform Lady Blakeley that he is not to take you into dinner."

Cassandra nodded. Lord Hampton said, "If I might just have a word. That is all I ask."

While Cassandra knew the proper thing would be to say nothing and take herself off to some corner of the room, the anger that had festered for all these weeks would not allow it.

"A word?" she said. "What possible word could you have to say to me that I would be remotely interested in hearing?"

"Please, I ask you to only give me a moment. Lady Blakeley was kind enough to give you the time as a half hour early so I might accomplish it."

Cassandra was rather shocked that Lady Blakeley would be his conspirator. Rather shocked that she would have invited him at all.

"You have no need to ever look upon me again, if you would just allow me this moment," the lord said.

Cassandra could see he was intent on being persistent. She could also feel that the lord might not be the only person with something to say. In truth, she thought she might have quite a few things to say before they parted forevermore.

She allowed herself to be led to the far side of the room. Lady Marksworth called after her, "I shall be right here for you, Cassandra."

At the pianoforte, Lord Hampton said, "You must know how deeply sorry I am for what occurred. I have no excuse for it, except to say I had never imagined it would grow so serious and took every step I could think of to stop it."

None of this was particularly striking to Cassandra. It was precisely what she imagined he would say.

"Before my grandmother went to you," the lord went on, "I had resolved to go to Surrey and apply to your father… apply to you. You see, I had thought I might—"

"You thought you might gain absolution and go on your merry way," Cassandra said. "It is fortunate you did not arrive, my lord. I was much in the company of a gun and might have removed your head from your shoulders."

There. She'd said it. She'd got the opportunity to say what she really felt. All the burning rage that had sat in her like a stone, wrapped up in a very neat picture for him to consider. It felt as a great relief, as if she had been in danger of bursting if she did not give voice to it.

Lord Hampton appeared taken aback and Cassandra suppressed a smile. She very much doubted anybody had ever spoken to him of removing his head from his shoulders.

He quickly recovered himself. "I sought to propose marriage," he said. "It would have restored you to your rightful place."

Cassandra's breath caught. It was as the duke had hinted, though the duke had been under the impression his son had already asked and been declined.

Still, as handsome as he was, and as genial as he had been in her imagination, the thought of tying herself to this villain... well, it was impossible. She would not be his alibi, his convenient exit from shame.

"My lord," she said quietly, "thanks to your grandmother, the prince and a collection of embarrassed dukes, I no longer need restoring. Furthermore, if I had needed such a service, I would no sooner tie myself to the author of my travails than I would throw myself off London Bridge. Your vanity and conceit know no bounds. I once informed you that not every lady is eager to know you; I am surprised you did not heed the idea. That is all that need be said on the subject."

Cassandra turned and marched back to her aunt, leaving the lord at the pianoforte.

Lady Markswort whispered in her niece's ear. "If you wish to leave, I will make our excuses."

Cassandra said, none too quietly, "It is the gentleman who should remove himself."

Lord Hampton hesitated a moment, then he bowed, and left.

Chapter Eighteen

Having gained her aim and driven Lord Hampton from the house, Cassandra thought she should feel more satisfied than she did. She had made her point and forced the man out and yet… she did not know what she thought about it.

The idea that he would offer himself up in marriage as a penance. It was precisely what she and Sybil had sought to avoid—becoming trapped in a loveless marriage and left behind in the country for all her days. Surely, that was what he'd intended. He might proffer his hand and then glory in the sacrifice he'd made and take congratulations all round while she idled alone in some cavernous house with no nearby neighbors.

Shortly after Lord Hampton made his exit, Lady Blakeley came in. "He has told me everything. Please do not be angry, he is so heartsick I could not help it, though you find you cannot forgive him."

Cassandra stared at Lady Blakeley. Heartsick? He was not heartsick. Why should she say so? Lord Hampton, heartsick? No, certainly not.

Was he? Had she misread his intentions? She really assumed that he offered his hand as some noble gesture he could think upon with pride. Had it been otherwise? Would it matter if it had been otherwise? That, she could not answer.

"It is no matter, Lady Blakeley," Cassandra said in the steadiest voice she could muster. "You did what you thought to be right, and so did I."

"Very well," Lady Blakeley said more cheerfully. "I hope then, that you can forget the little encounter that has just occurred and manage to enjoy the evening. Lord Burke will come, and I will have him take you into dinner. If anybody can amuse, it is him."

Cassandra felt rather numb, as if she had fallen through the ice on a vast lake and somehow been pulled out. She sank down on a sofa, not particularly sure if her legs could hold her up at the moment.

She scolded herself for it. She must recover her spirits. It was true that Lord Burke could not fail to amuse anybody who wished to be amused. She must make a very great effort to be amused. She could think of Lord Hampton later. Or preferably, not at all.

EDWIN DID NOT go immediately home. Rather, he trotted his horse through the dark streets, the gloom suiting his mood.

Lady Blakeley had been so set on the idea that Miss Knightsbridge's feelings must soften, but she had been mistaken. The lady's feelings were as iron and included shooting off his head.

His father was right, he was an idiot.

He'd begun the season bemoaning the directive to choose a wife. He'd been determined to do everything in his power to outfox the old man and remain a comfortable bachelor.

Edwin laughed bitterly to think of how hard he'd been willing to work to avoid falling prey to a lady. Now, he'd worked equally hard to gain one, all to no avail.

His debasement as a footman had not been enough for Miss Knightsbridge. His apology had not been enough either. If he were honest with himself, there was likely not anything he could do or be that would be enough.

Some other lucky gentleman would win the lady. Someday, he really would have to marry and then he would be forced to look upon that unwanted lady, always comparing her to what might have been. His wife would be an ever-constant reminder of what he'd destroyed.

Still, he'd brought himself to this pass and could not blame another. He must just become accustomed to unhappiness. Perhaps it would fade to a dull regret over time.

A rat scurried underneath his horse and it startled, sidestepped and then reared, nearly forcing him off. Regaining control and coming back to the present, Edwin looked about.

He no longer traveled on cobblestone, but rather a wet clay squelched under his horse's hooves. Narrow streets ran off in every direction, the houses that lined them seeming to lean toward one another as if ready to collapse. The air was heavy with the smell of refuse and smoke. No lamplighter had dared enter the neighborhood to shed illumination on his surroundings, though if they *had* Edwin was certain he would have seen gaunt figures huddled in doorways.

He had wandered into the Seven Dials unarmed.

To find himself so foolhardy was as cold water on his face.

What was he doing, wandering into a thieves' den as if he preferred to die by rusty knife? He was not a maudlin sort! He'd been through the war, for God's sake. This was to be another war. He may have lost a battle, but he had not yet lost the war.

Edwin turned his horse and cantered toward home, passing lurking shadows who no doubt admired his purse and wished he'd slow down. There was no time to accommodate those wretches—it was time to devise a campaign.

CASSANDRA HAD WORKED hard to regain her composure after Lord Hampton had left Lady Blakeley's house. At least, to regain the appearance of composure. That effort had been helped along by Lady Blakeley herself.

While the hostess may have mistakenly invited Lord Hampton to her dinner, the rest of the guests were all friendly faces to Cassandra. It was a small party and composed of those that she thought she could trust. Sybil and her parents, Lord Burke, and some others, in particular Miss Penny Darlington, that she did not suspect of glorying in gossip.

They were a cozy party of fifteen sat round a circular table in a smaller dining room. Cassandra presumed a sixteenth chair for Lord Hampton had been hastily removed and the place settings adjusted to the new number.

Lady Blakeley rose to make a toast.

"My dear friends, I bid you welcome to my table," she said. "When you look about, you will notice how few real friends I think I have, as nobody but a true friend is allowed in here. This is my favorite room in the house, for it is where my husband and I gather the people we truly like. We are at once delighted to receive Miss Knightsbridge back to her proper place in the world, and thrilled that a certain Lady M has found her own proper place far to the north."

Laughter overtook the table and Cassandra could not help but join in. It was spoken of widely that Lady Montague continued to fire off letters from Yorkshire and had taken to blaming Lady Blakeley for any slippage in her influence. Everybody was perfectly well aware that it was the dowager duchess that Lady Montague ought to complain of, though she did not dare it.

"Let us all be merry this evening, for I have ordered a sinful amount of wine," Lady Blakeley said before sitting down.

After the "hear, hears" had died down, Lord Burke turned to Cassandra. "Might I depend upon our friendship to be so bold as to skip the pleasantries and ask you directly how you've fared through this trial?"

Cassandra smiled. Lord Burke could always be depended upon to say something surprising. Further, it was almost a relief that she might speak honestly, rather than engage in another of the conversational minuets she had so often been having since her return to town.

"I am both gratified to be exonerated and furious at the gentlemen who caused my need to be exonerated," she said. "I suppose I should be more gracious and claim all is forgiven, but I have discovered I am not so gracious."

Lord Burke nodded. "It is a hard thing to forgive, especially considering that it all might not have turned out so well had the dowager and the Regent not stepped in."

"While I lived at my father's estate in disgrace, I had decided not to marry and would run the estate myself after he passed. I was to become a hermit in Surrey and ignore all the fanciful rumors of Miss Knightsbridge. So you see, I was determined to survive, if nothing else."

"And now?" Lord Burke asked.

"Now, I cannot claim to know," Cassandra said.

"I am certain you are weary of gossip; however, I think you should be aware that there has been some talk about Hampton," Lord Burke said.

Cassandra froze. "What sort of talk?" she said slowly.

"They say he is smitten with Miss Knightsbridge. What else could account for him muscling his way into every drawing room these past weeks to proclaim your innocence and his own guilt? Then, his father was overheard to say you could not be blamed for rejecting him." Lord Burke laughed and said, "Apparently, his father will not cease informing people that his son is an idiot, that is why the duke does not blame you for turning his son down."

Cassandra took in a deep and slow breath. Carefully, she said, "As always, the gossip is invented. Lord Hampton has not asked me such a question."

Lord Burke appeared thoughtful. "I had almost believed it true.

I've known Hampton a very long time and he was most in earnest in proclaiming your innocence, even to me. I told him I had no need to be convinced and then joked that he did a fine job of looking regretful for what he'd done and would be forgiven by the *ton* in no time. He looked dark as thunder over it. I had begun to wonder."

"Surely, if the lord had ever an inclination to speak to me," Cassandra said, "his motive would only have been to assuage his guilty conscience."

"Perhaps," Lord Burke said. "Though, you might put aside that reason if he chooses to speak now or in future, as you no longer have need of rescue."

Cassandra had only nodded at that idea. Lord Burke had gone on to entertain with more stories of his cook. She worked hard to be attentive and amused at the idea that he'd survived a week on chestnuts in all their various forms—one day roasted, another day in a sauce, a third day ground into flour and made into a pancake.

For all her smiles, though, her thoughts kept drifting back to Lord Hampton. Could it be true that he held real feelings for her? Could it be possible that she could ever forgive him enough to return those feelings?

It was ridiculous. Of course she could not. Even if she could, she had no wish to become a duchess. She'd always said so.

CASSANDRA SPENT A rather fretful night, at once willing herself to sleep and getting up and lighting a candle. She would gaze out the window at nothing but the flickering of a nearby streetlamp valiantly doing battle with the darkness. Seeing nothing, she would blow out the candle and attempt sleep again.

After Lady Blakeley had claimed Lord Hampton heartsick and Lord Burke told her of the rumors of his affections, it had been impossible not to think of it. She'd spent the remainder of the dinner with her thoughts in two places at once—both attending to the people around her and considering Lord Hampton.

Alone in her bedchamber, she had no need to attend to anybody and was left to herself. Lord Hampton remained still two gentlemen before her, the one who had nearly ruined her and the handsome and educated man that had existed so pleasantly in her imagination.

Cassandra knew she ought to cease examining her confused feelings, as it would only lead to more confusion. She ought to dismiss him forevermore. Were there not a hundred pleasant gentlemen in town? Might she not meet and marry one who had never caused her harm?

Of course she must. Not this season, but perhaps the next. At the end of this season she would return to Surrey and fire off her guns at her leisure and she would not care who said what about it. She would demand of herself that she stop brooding and wondering. She would compel herself to be happy again. She would take herself back to the time before she'd come to town. Life had been simple and enjoyable before she'd ever heard of the dukes' pact.

At breakfast, Cassandra had felt it her duty to inform the dowager that her grandson had briefly made an appearance at the Blakeley's dinner. She said it, including all she had said to the lord, as quickly as possible and then waited uncomfortably to see how the dowager would react to it. The lady had been so kind to her, but Cassandra's disdain of her grandson must wear thin.

Much to her surprise, the dowager had laughed. "I could have told Lady Blakeley it was too soon," she said.

Amidst Cassandra's consternation over the idea that time alone was to patch it all up, she said, "I must be honest, and I hope I do not offend, but I do not think time will heal this particular wound. In deference to you, I wish I could claim otherwise."

"Time? No, I would not think so," the dowager said. "Rather, it is penance. I cannot claim to know what would be enough to appease your well-earned anger but did not think the prince's footmen gambit would quite suffice. Though, it was most amusing to see. As for my grandson ambushing you in Lady Blakeley's drawing room, that was doomed to fail."

Cassandra did not answer, as she did not have a satisfactory answer. She could not imagine what penance the lord might do that she would deem sufficient. What could he possibly say or do that would wipe clean the anger and hurt that still roiled inside her?

"You are not to worry over it, my dear," the dowager said. "My grandson has dug himself a deep hole and we will just see if he can crawl out of it. You should only think of enjoying yourself while he attempts to scramble up the sides of this ridiculous pit of his own making."

Cassandra could not say that her feelings were any more clear than they had been through a sleepless night, but she could at least be soothed by the dowager's views. The lady was stalwart in her defense of Miss Knightsbridge, though it must cost her dearly to throw down her own blood in such a manner.

After breakfast, they had made their way to the drawing room and settled down to Racine's considerate rounds of service. They were never to be without cakes or biscuits. George was delighted, May was hopeful, and the two dogs divided their time between lurking round the tea tray, lounging on the far sofa, and racing to the windows at the slightest provocation. Should they hear the front doors being opened, they rushed headlong to the drawing room door to greet the unwary arrival.

Sybil was the first of those visitors to arrive, though she was not quite as unwary as anybody else. She had spent so much time in the house that she was quite good friends with George and May and happily allowed them to escort her into the room.

As she entered, Cassandra noted she carried a bouquet of flowers.

After curtsying to the dowager, Sybil said, "These were left on your doorstep, Lady Marksworth. They are addressed to Cassandra."

"Heavens," Lady Marksworth said. "Now we are to be pummeled by posies. I would not be surprised if it contains yet another invitation."

Cassandra colored. She had grown tired of being celebrated and wished the *ton* would turn their faces to another subject. Worse, the flowers were red roses. There really was no need for such strong feelings—she had been lied about, now the truth was known. That was all and that must be sufficient.

"I suppose," Lady Marksworth said, "that as a responsible guardian I ought to read the card. Though, no girl should be more trusted to manage such a thing than Cassandra."

Sybil handed Lady Marksworth the card and crossed the room to sit by Cassandra.

Cassandra pretended indifference while her aunt unfolded the note. She could not, however, maintain her indifference in the face of Lady Marksworth's expression upon reading it.

"I see," she said softly, handing the note to the dowager.

The dowager glanced at it and smiled. "It is from my grandson, and not overly worded. It only says: 'I am sorry.' As he should be, mightily."

Cassandra shrugged, as if she could not care one way or the other. She was in some part relieved that nobody mentioned the color of the roses. Did he really mean to press his suit? Why could not he go away, at least for a while, and allow her feelings to settle?

"Will you walk with me to the window?" Sybil asked her.

Everybody in the room, including Cassandra, knew the request for what it was. A simple escape so that the two young friends might have a private talk together. Lady Marksworth and the dowager pretended ignorance and Cassandra's aunt helpfully began asking the dowager about various investments she had heard spoken of.

Cassandra rose and locked arms with Sybil as they casually made their way to the windows. Only George and May appeared to be the slightest interested in their progress.

Once they had put a distance between themselves and Lady Marksworth and the dowager, Sybil said softly, "I would have you look across the road."

Cassandra pulled back the curtain and peered out.

Aside from the usual comings and goings on the street, there was one remarkable sight—Lord Hampton sat on Lord Dalton's stoop like any street boy might have done when needing a rest.

Cassandra let the curtain drop. "What on earth does he do, just sitting there?"

Sybil suppressed a giggle. "Well," she said, "let us see. He sits across from your house and he's sent red roses and begged your forgiveness. I would say the lord has made his feelings known."

"Does he really wish to cause talk, sitting there like a servant across from my house? Has he not already caused enough talk about me?"

"He is causing a great deal of talk about *himself*," Sybil said. "It was spoken of last evening, before this latest gambit. It is said he is hopelessly in love with Miss Knightsbridge, but she will not have him. It was even said, though I hardly give it credit, that he approached you before Lady Blakeley's dinner and was firmly rebuffed."

Cassandra colored. "That part is true, and I suppose a compliment to the ability of the English to ensure that no news goes unadvertised. I did not wish to encounter him and urged him to go, which he did."

"Goodness," Sybil said, "and now he does watch the house like a soldier on guard duty."

"It hardly matters to me what he does," Cassandra said. "He might guard the Tower of London for all it signifies to me."

Sybil glanced up at her friend. "If he had not been a part of what happened to you, would you look upon him differently?"

"Well, I would say, that is, as you know, I never had a wish to become a duchess. For one thing."

"Putting that aside," Sybil said, "if he had never injured you and was always to be a viscount, what would you think?"

"The idea is so far removed from what is true that I had not thought of what I would think. Why do you ask me, Sybil?"

Sybil bit her lip and said quietly, "We did so wish to marry for love, Cass. For all his faults, I believe he loves you. Truly loves you. While I, myself, could never forgive what those gentlemen have done, it strikes me that you are of a different temperament."

"How can you say so?" Cassandra said, for lack of anything better to say while her thoughts were in such a jumble.

Sybil pulled the curtain back and peeked at Lord Hampton in his vigil on Lord Dalton's stoop. "I say so because of that," she said. "He's making himself a laughingstock and I do not think Lord Hampton is accustomed to making himself the butt of jokes. It seems to me that he no longer cares for humiliation, he has a loftier goal in mind."

"Ridiculous," Cassandra said. Though she said it, she could not deny that something stirred in her. The lord had been forced to dress as a footman, but he was not forced to appear a lunatic sitting in front of her house.

Sybil was right—he was making himself a laughingstock. It would not be an hour before the gossipers got hold of the idea. One person would pass by in a carriage and off the report would fly over the city like a hawk dropping mice from its maw.

"He is entirely ridiculous," Sybil said, "though I wonder if you hold it against him."

"Sybil," Cassandra said, "you have just said yourself that you would not forgive."

"True, but my family has a long history of maintaining feuds until every party involved is dead. For all that, though, I will admit to having struggled against Lord Lockwood's apologies—there have been so many of them! *He* is only a friendly acquaintance; I cannot say what I should do if there was something more there."

"I did not say there was anything more than friendship between me and Lord Hampton," Cassandra corrected.

"No, you did not say it," Sybil said gravely. "And yet, I think it."

Cassandra had no answer to that, so crossed the room to May and gave her a pet. She felt uncomfortably questioned and examined and at least her mastiff had nothing to inquire about.

CHAPTER NINETEEN

As far as Cassandra could tell, Lord Hampton finally decamped from Lord Dalton's steps sometime after sunset. Throughout the day she'd found little opportunities to casually peek out a window, and there he'd sat. She'd even seen Lord Lockwood stop on his horse and been waved away. Lord Dalton had come out of his house and appeared to argue with his friend, before marching back inside and slamming the door.

She supposed she must now believe that he held a real regard for her. The question she could not firmly answer was what her own feelings might be. She was torn between her heart and her head.

Her heart, if she were to finally be honest with herself, was drawn to Lord Hampton. Had always been, really. Her clear heart, that did not give quarter to the stings of insults and the pricks of wrongs, beat faster for him. From that first moment of seeing him on his horse as he approached the Bergrams' ball, to their rather uncomfortable start, to the various dinners in which they better understood each other. He stirred feelings in her that no other gentleman had.

If only those feelings were not intertwined with her feelings over what he and his friends had done to her. Her head appeared to be the master of *those* particular feelings and her head called her heart deranged for even entertaining any idea of Lord Hampton. Her head, while clear in its own way, could not ignore the stings and pricks. Like an old wound, she was healed on the outside but still ached on the inside.

She would be ridiculous to countenance him! Her head railed against looking the fool for giving way to him. In truth, considering him would not confer any favor on either one of them. If she accepted him, convincing herself that she had forgiven him, would not ugly feelings resurface sometime in future? Would she not experience some little irritation and find all those feelings flooding back?

No matter. He'd thoroughly debased himself by sitting outside of her house all the day long and got nothing for his trouble. She suspected she had delivered the message of her intent quite clearly. He would take her at her word and make himself scarce going forward.

If he suffered at all, it would not last. A man like that would never suffer long. There were too many who wished to entertain such a gentleman that he would soon be diverted and wonder why he had ever thought to pursue a lady who wished to have nothing to do with him.

He would likely consider it a lucky escape.

Cassandra could not ignore the sense of disappointment that settled over her upon imagining the lord walking away, never to turn his head back.

She sighed heavily.

Lady Marksworth and the dowager played a quiet game of cards at the table nearby. Cassandra noted the dowager's glance.

She smiled and said, "I am only tired and think that even so I might have trouble sleeping. I wonder if I might take a glass of wine and retire?"

Lady Marksworth nodded. Before the footman had time to fetch it, the dowager said to him, "Make it Canary, and a large one. That is the most soothing, I find."

The footman did as he was bid, and quite a full glass of Canary was brought to her. The dowager nodded her approval and Jimmy blushed up to his ears, always pleased and embarrassed when the dowager acknowledged him.

Cassandra suppressed a smile. Every servant in the house had fallen prey to the dowager's charm and was determined to carry out her instructions to the letter. They were at once in awe of her and fond of her, as she was in the habit of showing her approbation generously.

Cassandra drank the wine rather more quickly than was her usual habit, hoping the effects of it would send her to sleep.

She rose and bid her aunt and the dowager good night.

"Sleep well, my dear," Lady Marksworth said.

After she'd left the room, Lady Marksworth said, "I do not know what is to come of all of this."

"Fear nothing, Lady Marksworth," the dowager said in all confidence. "It is only two people discovering their own hearts. One, my idiot grandson, has discovered it first. Your niece will discover her own in time, though I am very encouraged by how often she looked out the windows this day."

CASSANDRA DID SLEEP through the night, the wine and her own tiredness helping her on her way. She might have woken later than she did, had it not been for the commotion both indoors and out that penetrated the walls of her bedchamber. She could hear May and George barking like mad below her, and noticed that her door was slightly ajar. May had finally discovered how to let herself out.

She slipped out of bed and pulled the curtain aside to discover the reason the dogs so enthusiastically raised the alarm.

It was only ten o'clock, and yet the street was congested with carriages. They were not tradesmen's carriages, nor carriages for hire, but well turned out private carriages.

Though the branches of a tree blocked some of her view, she could see two things clearly.

Lord Hampton was back on Lord Dalton's steps, this time ensconced in a chair as if he never intended to leave, and the various occupants of the carriages were pointing and laughing.

They laughed at Lord Hampton, who appeared entirely unconcerned. But they also laughed and pointed at her own house.

Somewhere far below, she heard Racine shouting, "Move along now! There is nothing to see here!"

Cassandra rang for her maid. She must be dressed in all haste.

PEGGY HAD HELPED her mistress into her clothes with nary a complaint on her choice. Cassandra hurried down the stairs.

She found Racine appearing rather haggard in the front hall. He did not speak to her, but rather, pointed to the drawing room.

Cassandra hurried in and stopped short.

The drawing room was filled with bouquets of red roses. They were in every available vase, bunches were laid on tables, and some even propped up on windowsills. In the middle of it all, the dowager and Lady Marksworth sat at tea.

The dowager, appearing rather gleeful, said, "They are all from my idiot grandson and they all say the same thing—I am sorry. They were left on the doorstep in a pile so high that poor Racine had a time of it getting them all indoors."

"That accounts for the mayhem out of doors," Lady Marksworth said. "Racine tells us that some fellow informed him that Lord Hampton camping out across the road was talked of everywhere last evening. It has become some sort of event to rouse oneself and drive by to view the scene."

"And now half of them have seen all of this on your doorstep!" the dowager said, waving her arm at the roses.

Cassandra sat down, furiously trying to comprehend what she saw, and how she should feel about it. She was both complimented and furious.

"Lady Marksworth," the dowager said, "might I have a moment alone with your niece?"

Lady Marksworth nodded and rose, determinedly avoiding her niece's eye. Cassandra felt a wave of trepidation. What could the dowager wish to say to her that could not be said in front of her aunt?

After the door had closed behind Lady Marksworth, the dowager hopped up in her energetic fashion and sat next to Cassandra, taking her hand.

"It is my understanding from all of this that my idiot grandson is prepared to stay where he is until the end of time if necessary. So I was wondering, will it be necessary? Or could you find some affection in your heart for him?"

"If I could give you an answer," Cassandra said slowly, "I would. I do not care for any pretense between us, and rather think you do not either."

"You are correct in that opinion, my dear," the dowager said.

"Though I would prefer to give you an answer, I really cannot. My feelings are all in a jumble and I cannot say where they will settle."

"Ah well," the Dowager said. "If he is to remain out there until the end of time, I daresay it serves him right. I have a great affection for my grandson, but then I have a great affection for you, too."

Before Cassandra could answer, May and George's ears had suddenly perked up and they leapt off their sofa and raced to the door. The drawing room door being closed might have once been an impediment to their progress, but May reached up and pawed at it until she turned the knob and they were out like a flash.

Cassandra heard Racine shout, "May! George! No! Come back!"

She leapt to her feet and ran to the window just in time to see a carriage bearing down on May. Her heart gripped in terror.

"May! No, May!" she cried.

The carriage wheels were nearly upon the mastiff. May turned, seeming to finally perceive the danger. Lord Hampton suddenly appeared on the other side of the road and threw himself upon her.

A horrifying sound reached her ears, a sound of collision.

Cassandra could not see either May or Lord Hampton. The carriage blocked her view. The driver, no doubt fearing trouble, whipped his horses and sped off with no care for what he'd done.

The carriages behind the accident had halted and an eerie hush descended on the street. May and Lord Hampton lay in a heap together on the cobblestones. Neither stirred.

The dowager joined Cassandra at the window, and they gazed at the lifeless bodies across the road. The dowager clutched Cassandra's arm. "No," she said softly. "It cannot be."

Racine jogged across the silent street. He leaned over the two bodies. Cassandra felt her head swim. She held tight to the dowager's arm.

May gave the smallest wag and raised herself up on her forepaws, looking dazed. George barked to her from the steps and she struggled to her feet. She limped toward the sound.

Racine was bent over Lord Hampton. Cassandra and the dowager stood still as statues, waiting to see what expression the butler would turn to them with. Cassandra saw him lay two fingers along the lord's neck.

Racine suddenly stood and shouted, "He is alive! Ben, fetch a litter. Jimmy, run for the doctor!"

The dowager's grip lessened on Cassandra's hand. "Thanks be to God," she said.

"Yes," Cassandra said softly. "Thank God."

George slinked back into the drawing room, with May limping behind her. Cassandra glared at them and pointed to their sofa. They willingly went to it and began grooming themselves furiously—a sure sign they understood the gravity of the trouble they'd caused.

"I will see to a bedchamber they may carry him to," Cassandra said. She hurried from the room just as Lady Marksworth came into it to see to the dowager.

Cassandra dashed up the stairs to find a suitable room. She suddenly remembered her uncle's room. Though he had long passed, Lady Marksworth had noted that she'd never redone it as it suited her to maintain one masculine chamber.

She threw the door open, refusing to consider the lord laying lifeless in the street. She must only concentrate on what needed to be done. Cassandra raced down the hall to a small closet that held various materials for bandaging and brought them back to the room.

She threw open the curtains so the doctor might have more light just as Racine and Ben came through the door with Lord Hampton on a litter.

His eyes were closed and he was pale. There was a trickle of blood that ran in a steady stream down his forehead and onto his cheek.

He had struck his head. Cassandra well knew the consequences of an injury such as that. He might never regain consciousness. He might simply stop breathing. She had seen Mr. Drescher die in just such a way after being thrown from a horse—he breathed until he did not.

At the thought of the lord's breath fading from him, Cassandra's mind was at once all clarity. Where her thoughts had felt muddled, they now presented themselves as clear as crystal.

She loved him. Of course she did. She had all along. She'd only let her hurt pride hide it from her. Now, he might be taken from her. How stupid she was! To allow embarrassment and stung feelings to overshadow love.

He would die and it would be her fault. *She* had been the reason he'd been on Lord Dalton's steps. It had been *her* dog who'd raced into the street.

They would both be punished terribly for her idiocy—he, not to live the life he had been given, and she to live a joyless one.

Racine and Ben had carefully laid the litter on the bed and shifted the lord out of it. He moaned softly.

Cassandra raced to him and took his hand. It was warm to the touch, it had not yet begun to go cold.

His eyes fluttered open.

"My lord," Cassandra said, chafing his hands.

"Edwin, to you," he rasped.

When she did not answer, he squeezed her hand. "Edwin, say it."

Cassandra looked away and said softly, "Edwin."

He attempted to sit up but did not get far with it and rested his head back on the pillow. "I am sorry," he said hoarsely.

"Oh, do not speak of that now!" Cassandra cried. "You are hurt!"

"Ah," he said, his voice rough, "had I known I must only be run down by a carriage to convince you to speak to me, I would have done it days ago."

"You should not speak," Cassandra said. "You really should not. The doctor has been sent for."

"Of course I must speak. This may be my last opportunity."

Cassandra took in a breath. What did he mean, his last opportunity? Did he feel himself dying? She had sat at enough bedsides to comprehend that the dying often knew when it crept close. He could not die. He simply could not.

"Do not talk of dying, my lord… Edwin," Cassandra said.

Edwin smiled and then winced. "I have no intention of dying just now. I have yet to win the heart of Miss Knightsbridge."

Cassandra looked away. "Oh, that," she said quietly.

"Yes, that. I cannot undo what has been done. I, we, can only go forward, if I can convince you of it."

"I am sure now is not the right—"

"It is exactly the right moment," Edwin said, his voice low and guttural. "I will be miserable all my life if I do not have my heart's desire."

Cassandra had no words. She'd rehearsed no end of words to punish, but none to acquiesce. Her feelings had crystallized only a moment ago and words had not yet attached to them.

Lord Hampton smiled, seeming to comprehend that something in her feelings had shifted. "To convince you of the attractiveness of my offer, I vow that I will buy you an arsenal of guns and you may shoot my estate to pieces if it pleases you."

"Well," Cassandra said softly, "you *did* rescue my dog. I am very fond of her."

"And then there is the little matter that I love you. Entirely. I think someday you might come to love me too."

"Perhaps," Cassandra said slowly, even now resisting a surrender. "I suppose anything is possible."

Edwin struggled to prop himself up on his elbows. "Then you will? You say yes? You must say it! I have asked you to wed and you have said you will."

Cassandra pushed the lord back on his pillow. "I agree to it at great cost to myself and only if you will stay still."

The dowager rushed into the room, "The doctor will be here in moments. Good, he is awake. That is promising."

"We're to be married," Edwin said to his grandmother. "She's said it, let you be a witness. She cannot change her mind now."

The dowager's expression showed worry. "Lord, he's delirious. That is *not* a good sign."

"He is not delirious," Cassandra said quietly, finding herself somewhat embarrassed to have reversed herself so entirely.

"I promised her a lot of guns," Edwin said.

The dowager crossed her arms. "I hope, dear grandson, you also spoke of love."

"Most ardently," Edwin said. "I believe she will come to love me too, over time."

"We shall see," Cassandra said, turning her head away.

"Cassandra Knightsbridge," the Dowager said rather sternly. "Now is not the time to prevaricate."

Cassandra blushed up to her ears. She did not know how the dowager had divined her real feelings, but it appeared that she had. Perhaps she had before Cassandra even knew them herself. "If you imply," she said to the Dowager, "that I love him already, well then I do. Though it is certainly not my fault!"

Edwin squeezed her hand tight in his own. "My darling, darling girl," he whispered.

The dowager turned to Ben, who stood near the door, red in the face. "Do be good and fetch my writing things. There is a gentleman here who needs to pen an appeal to a certain young lady's father before the sun has set."

"Ma'am! He is grievously injured," Cassandra said. "He will not have the ability to write a letter so soon."

The dowager turned back to Cassandra. "My dear, if he has one ounce of strength left in his limbs, he will manage it. We have not come this far to cry off now."

"Just so," Edwin said.

"I will send your maid in to chaperone while we wait for the doctor," the dowager said, "though I warn you, I will be remarkably slow about it."

Cassandra blushed up to her ears. The dowager, seeming pleased that she had arranged things to her satisfaction, bustled from the room.

"You have truly forgiven me?" Edwin asked with some trepidation.

"I have," Cassandra said, playing with the torn cuff of his sleeve.

"I expect when I irritate you on some matter, which I am highly likely to do, you'll wonder to yourself why you ever did forgive me."

"Perhaps," Cassandra said. "But then I will remind myself that I have come out of this experience far different than I went into it.

Goodness, when I first arrived, I was so frightened of the *ton* and doing everything right and not disappointing anybody."

"You? Frightened?" Edwin said. He laughed, and then clutched his head.

"Do be still," Cassandra said in a firm tone. "Yes, I was frightened. And I was terribly affected by other's opinions of me."

"But you are not now?"

"No, I am not now. I hope you meant what you said, for I have every intention of shooting your pheasant out of the sky to my heart's content."

"If your heart is content, then so is mine," Edwin said.

THE DOCTOR HAD seen to Lord Hampton and pronounced him having a slight concussion. He would not be any worse for it, though it would be some days before he could be moved. The doctor had also been prevailed upon to examine May, who had come out of the whole thing with only a few scratches and a strained hindquarter.

The viscount had received Lord Hampton's letter in good time, which had been prefaced with great apologies for not arriving in person due to the accident. Cassandra's father wrote his daughter back that he would be as good as his word. She was to decide for herself who she would marry and she'd have to live with it if she chose wrong. It was perhaps not the most ringing endorsement, but it suited the couple well enough.

Though the lord's concussion may have been slight, the care he received at Marksworth House was not. Racine directed all manner of bone broths made and sent them up to the sickroom on a regular schedule. News of the accident spread like a fire, as was only too predictable. Perhaps it was also predictable that the story grew to Lord Hampton being run over by all four carriage wheels and somehow surviving it on the strength of his love for Miss Knightsbridge.

The dowager stayed on at Marksworth House to assure the rest of the family that Edwin progressed well. That her son, the duke, was delighted to hear that his own son had finally decided to marry, and that he'd chosen Miss Knightsbridge, was a foregone conclusion. The duke admired Miss Knightsbridge's fortitude in the face of difficulty and even went so far as to cease referring to his eldest son as an idiot.

Not many an engaged couple had the opportunity to spend so much time together, almost alone. Peggy sat in a corner pretending to sew but mostly asleep, May and George came in and out as they pleased, and Cassandra and Edwin spent hours talking. Cassandra would invariably bring in a book she planned to read to the patient, but very little was actually read. They had much to discuss.

Theirs was to be an unconventional marriage and they were thoroughly agreed that Cassandra must ride as she pleased and shoot when she felt the inclination. Their children would be raised the same—there would be no drooping violets in the lord and lady's nursery.

As for becoming a duchess, Cassandra had developed a different view, thanks to the dowager. She began to see its convenience—she might do what she liked and nobody would dare breathe a word about it. She might back the next Cassandra when some worthy girl ran into a difficulty. She might quash the bad intentions of those of Lady Montague's ilk. But most of all, she might wake each morning to her beloved's presence beside her. They were thoroughly agreed that wherever the lord went, his lady would go too. *This* duchess was never to be left behind, lonely on a country estate.

Their respective mastiffs, Mayhem and Havoc, were to have the run of Carlisle House, chewed-up valuables be damned. With any luck, Cassandra and Edwin might find themselves overrun with a new generation of pups determined to destroy everything they owned.

When Edwin was not planning his future with his intended, he was busy sending people here and there to organize it. He obtained a special license so there should be no delay to the marriage, and he arranged for a wedding trip to Italy.

He would meet his intended at St. George's, and he fully expected to find the soon to be viscountess and future duchess in a gown sparkling with diamonds. She would not care who said what about it, and neither would he.

When he was finally permitted to rise and leave the sickroom, Edwin sent word to the gentlemen of the pact to meet at Dalton's house at a proscribed hour.

He found them there, sitting around the table in the library, while the ever-decrepit Bellamy shuffled round with brandy. It was as if nothing at all had changed, but of course everything had changed.

"There he is," Lord Dalton said, as Edwin entered the room. "Rumors of broken bones were obviously exaggerated."

"Let us hope some other things have been exaggerated," Lord Cabot said.

"It was in the newspaper," Lord Lockwood said to Lord Cabot. "I cannot fathom how you still hold out hope that there is no engagement."

"Still," Lord Ashworth said, "it seems a rum sort of game. The man was injured and helpless, they had him a veritable captive in that house. Who knows what a man might agree to while suffering a concussion?"

"Undue influence," Lord Grayson said, nodding knowingly. "Course, if he was to try to wrangle his way out now, he might be slapped with a breach of promise."

The men around the table fairly shuddered at the mention of breach of promise.

"*She* might call it off, though," Cabot said hopefully. "She already shoots bird, I don't suppose she'd mind becoming a jilt."

"The fact is," Dalton said to Edwin, "if you carry through with the marriage, it will only encourage our fathers in this ridiculous pact of theirs."

Edwin had listened to his friends' outrageous statements with equanimity. Nothing they'd said had surprised him in the least. How could it, when he had himself been in a similar frame of mind so recently?

He waited patiently as his friends flailed this way and that, grasping at even the slimmest hope that might present itself. Lockwood speculated that Miss Knightsbridge might suddenly realize that Hampton was not such a good catch after all. Cabot wondered if Miss Knightsbridge had even yet noticed Hampton's sad lack of humor and wit. Grayson concurred and postulated that it would dawn on her soon enough that he was a dead bore. Finally running out of ways to abuse him, they fell into silence.

Edwin had remained standing, his arms clasped behind his back. He smiled and said, "Get married, you idiots."

With that, he turned and strode from the room.

The End

About the Author

By the time I was eleven, my Irish Nana and I had formed a book club of sorts. On a timetable only known to herself, Nana would grab her blackthorn walking stick and steam down to the local Woolworth's. There, she would buy the latest Barbara Cartland romance, hurry home to read it accompanied by viciously strong wine, (Wild Irish Rose, if you're wondering) and then pass the book on to me. Though I was not particularly interested in real boys yet, I was *very* interested in the gentlemen in those stories—daring, bold, and often enraging and unaccountable. After my Barbara Cartland phase, I went on to Georgette Heyer, Jane Austen and so many other gifted authors blessed with the ability to bring the Georgian and Regency eras to life.

I would like nothing more than to time travel back to the Regency (and time travel back to my twenties as long as we're going somewhere) to take my chances at a ball. Who would take the first? Who would escort me into supper? What sort of meaningful looks would be exchanged? I would hope, having made the trip, to encounter a gentleman who would give me a very hard time. He ought to be vexatious in the extreme, and *worth* every vexation, to make the journey worthwhile.

I most likely won't be able to work out the time travel gambit, so I will content myself with writing stories of adventure and romance in my beloved time period. There are lives to be created, marvelous gowns to wear, jewels to don, instant attractions that inevitably come with a difficulty, and hearts to break before putting them back together again. In traditional Regency fashion, my stories are clean—the action happens in a drawing room, rather than a bedroom.

As I muse over what will happen next to my H and h, and wish I were there with them, I will occasionally remind myself that it's also nice to have a microwave, Netflix, cheese popcorn, and steaming hot showers.

Come see me on Facebook! @KateArcherAuthor

Made in the USA
Monee, IL
18 October 2021